SNAKE EYES

John Denson, the Seattle private eye with his partner, Willie Prettybird — a shaman of the Cowlitz tribe — face their deadliest case: an engineered outbreak of anthrax in the Pacific Northwest. A ballooning list of suspects includes a rodeo cowboy; a barkeep with a roving eye; an ancient teacher at a high-school reunion — and the chief of police. Then there's the fund-raising televangelist Hamm Bonnerton. One of them is playing liar's dice, and coming up snake eyes. And killing people . . .

D1076686

RICHARD HOYT

◆

SNAKE EYES

Complete and Unabridged

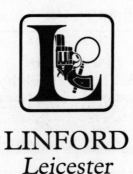

LINFORD
Leicester

First published in Great Britain

First Linford Edition
published 2012

This is a work of fiction. All the characters and events potrayed in this novel are either fictitious or are used fictitiously.

British Library CIP Data

Hoyt, Richard, *1941 –*
    Snake eyes. - - (Linford mystery library)
    1. Denson, John (Fictitious character)- -
    Fiction. 2. Private investigators- -United
    States- -Fiction. 3. Indians of North America
    - -Fiction. 4. Detective and mystery stories.
    5. Large type books.
    I. Title II. Series
    813.5′4–dc23

ISBN 978–1–4448–1184–1

Published by
F. A. Thorpe (Publishing)
Anstey, Leicestershire

Set by Words & Graphics Ltd.
Anstey, Leicestershire
Printed and bound in Great Britain by
T. J. International Ltd., Padstow, Cornwall

This book is printed on acid-free paper

This book is for my brother, Robert C. Hoyt, of Hermiston, Oregon, and our father, Clyde L. Hoyt, a bronco-busting, whiskey-making man.

1

This is the story about a lethal outbreak of infectious anthrax in the beautiful high country of Wallowa County, Oregon. It is also the story of the Great Hoop of life. We join the hoop and continue along it, but the hoop itself is without end.

First things first. To understand the Great Hoop, which is a Native American belief, I should first tell you about my partner, a full-blooded Cowlitz named Willie Prettybird.

There were times when it was exasperating as hell to have a partner who was a sorcerer, or Coyote, or whoever or whatever Willie Prettybird was supposed to be. I called him a redskin or Tonto, Spanish for idiot; he called me white-eyes or Chief Dumsht, for dumb shit. Fair enough.

In fact, Willie's calling me Dumsht was his way of expressing affection and respect. If he'd been polite to me, as though I were a necktie-wearing banker, he would have been expressing total scorn. But I was his partner, the white-eyed Dumsht, who had played Little League baseball with Umatillas as a kid. He was, as Sam Spade said of Miles Archer, my partner. In both our cultures, that simple statement carried a lot of weight. We understood each other. We wanted to know the truth, no matter where it led. We were private detectives. It was our job to find things out.

Anthropologists classified Coyote as a mythological trickster, what with his ability to impersonate human beings if he wanted. If Willie was Coyote, that was hip. How many private dicks had a coyote for a partner? Willie never took offense at my 'No shit, Sherlock' or 'Mon Dieu, Maigret' rejoinders to a conclusion he had arrived at by his curious form of intuition.

If the claims of Willie's Indian friends in the Northwest were true, he was capable of descending to the realm of the animal people, who, if the Native American version of the prime mover was correct, were the creators of the present world. We were made in the image of our creators, that is, animals. Even though I was skeptical of Willie's animal people hoo-hoo, I always listened.

Readers of the anthropologist Carlos Castaneda would recognize Willie as a sorcerer. For years I had called him a medicine man, but had lately settled on Castaneda's term. 'Sorcerer' had a certain lunatic quality about it that I liked.

In an attempt to better understand Willie's imagination, I had read several of Carlos Castaneda's accounts of his relationship with the Yaqui Indian sorcerer Don Juan, but couldn't make up my mind whether I was reading fiction or nonfiction — although, in truth, it really didn't matter.

But I was certainly no Castaneda, whose alleged apprenticeship to Don Juan was rather that of a befuddled but determined novice to a Zen master. In Castaneda's accounts, Don Juan was always laughing at Castaneda's earnest questions and attempts to 'see,' as though Don Juan was onto some great secret beyond the abilities of a blockhead like Castaneda to understand.

I was more like a curious, amenable skeptic, or blockhead, happy to let my Cowlitz friend do his thing as a shaman or sorcerer or whatever, but in the end insisting on a logical explanation for everything. That way Willie and I always had two ways of looking at a particular question.

Willie's was the way of hallucinogenic mushrooms and the world of the animal people; in a pinch, he could talk to elk, deer, squirrel, or whomever. They were personal friends of his. It was said that the reason he was able to communicate thus was because he was one of them. Willie never made this claim himself, but his many Indian friends in the Northwest routinely did. He never denied it, but then again he never confirmed it, either. If nothing else, his was an entertaining conceit, and I gave it the same credence that I gave all religions and hocus-pocus forays into the metaphysical.

I proceeded in the manner of Aristotle, put labels on everything according to their logical classification, and followed doggedly the trail of cause and effect. But still . . . it behooved me to keep an open mind. I believed that a variety of imaginations was useful in the complexities of the universal hunt. In the end, the rewards of our partnership were nearly always there, and I often learned something whether I wanted to or not.

Once, on behalf of the animal people, Willie got me hooked into running down the murderer of a spotted owl. It turned out that the owl had indeed been murdered — had its neck wrung before it was thrown onto a highway to be flattened by log trucks. Willie and I ran the son of a bitch to ground, so what can I say? A lawyer later told me that a spotted owl can be killed but not murdered. Animals are killed, she said; humans are murdered. I said tell that to Willie Prettybird.

I had always been struck by the similarities between Don Juan's beliefs and the notions of Zen Buddhists, although the Buddhists didn't have invisible allies roaming around or mysterious powers emanating from their navel. I assumed the similarity in beliefs I had noted among Hindus, Taoists, Buddhists, and Don Juan was based on the fact that the Yaquis were transplanted Asians, and their beliefs went back further than most people imagined.

The Zen Buddhists ask: What is the sound of one hand clapping?

The best answer, if I understand the philosophy correctly, is another question: What is the significance of anything?

Once, in the good old days of Isaac Newton, we had a universe that made logical sense and followed laws we could confidently chart in textbooks. Then the wild-haired Einstein came along to inform us that time speeded up or slowed down, depending on gravity, and there were curves in space, and two parallel lines need not necessarily remain forever parallel. So, who knows, maybe the Zen masters and Willie Prettybird were onto something long before writers of *Star Trek* episodes happened along.

In the case of Snake Eyes, Willie and I tumbled onto an extraordinary curve or kink in the human imagination that led to vomitous results. It was as incomprehensible to me as the business about parallel lines converging at the far end of the cosmos. But keep in mind, Einstein said there are no parallel lines. Curves, yes. Parallel lines, no. Willie Prettybird, I have to admit, understood this intuitively.

For us, the story began one night when we were drinking elderberry wine and waiting for the boxing matches to begin on television. An American Indian heavyweight named Joe Hipp, out of Yakima, Washington, a southpaw with a flaccid-looking belly, the most unboxerly-looking boxer I had ever seen, had risen to number five in the world against Latin American macho men and African-American giants with muscles like slabs of chiseled marble and necks like cast-iron fire plugs.

Willie contended that the animal people were watching Hipp's progress closely, with much enthusiasm. Unable to accept the idea that the roundish Hipp was a boxer of skill, much less of power, I put the question directly to Willie: Was Joe Hipp really a brown bear or grizzly masquerading as a boxer?

Willie was amused at the idea, but, as was his practice with such questions, refused to say yes or no. Better that I should think it over and wonder. 'Joe Hipp? Bear?' He gave me an impish smile. 'Oh, calm down, Dumsht. Have another glass of wine and watch the news.'

The main drama of the day took place in Alberta Province, Canada, and was, of course, televised for the amusement of the masses. There on the television screen, in this age where we get to see everything and then some, a man with a high-powered rifle was crouching in a thin stand of timber.

Then a bison, with his great, shaggy head and massive shoulders, was seen grazing quietly by a fallen log.

'Another half hour before Joe Hipp. You want me to change channels or turn it off?' I said.

Willie Prettybird clenched his jaw and shook his head. He poured himself some more elderberry wine, and ripped off another chunk of peppery smoked salmon with his teeth. 'Leave it on. I can take it,' he said.

The rifle bucked against the man's shoulder.

The bison dropped to its knees, mouth open, eyes wide. The camera zoomed in on the stricken animal as a stain of blood spread from the lethal wound just behind its front shoulder.

The camera returned to the rifleman, a Canadian wildlife official who looked as if he was about to weep. He bit his lip. He cranked another round in the bolt-action rifle. He took aim at another buffalo.

Another animal fell to its knees and toppled over.

The cameraman cut to the man with the high-powered rifle.

The man grimaced and shook his head. He lifted the rifle slowly to his shoulder and took aim through a telescopic sight that was hardly needed; the animal was no more than fifty yards away. He put the rifle down. He didn't like this chore. He put the rifle butt back to his shoulder, his cheek against the stock. He had to do it.

The bison in Alberta Province had contracted anthrax, a scourge that normally afflicts cattle and sheep. When anthrax breaks out in a herd, the only way to stop it is to eliminate every animal in sight and burn their bodies. The slaughter of infected animals was evidently an entertaining spectacle, because both Canadian and American television crews had arrived in force to tape the grisly action.

The gruesome images of grim-faced Canadian officials dropping infected bison with high-powered rifles and burning their corpses had become nightly fare in the news, distracting popular attention, momentarily, from the more lovable whales and dolphins, who could be trained to jump through hoops and toss plastic balls for the amusement of tourists in Florida and Hawaii. More recently, cases of anthrax had popped up among cattle and sheep grazing in northern and western Montana, and there were fears that, unless it was stopped, the disease would spread farther south.

This was what the poor Canadians had been forced to do. Nobody wanted to shoot the bison, but it had to be done to prevent the spread of the disease.

The buffalo was a grand, even splendid beast, and I always thought it was bullpucky that it had been yanked from the American nickel, to be replaced by Thomas Jefferson. I didn't have a bitch against Jefferson — I was an admirer, in fact — but the American bison were special, and if I had my druthers, I'd bring back the buffalo nickel. In fact, I was all for Willie Prettybird's idea to replace the politicians on all our coins with animals. In that respect Canadian currency was clearly superior.

Willie was visibly affected by the sight of the slaughter. He sat there in his tattered Reeboks, faded and patched blue jeans, and Creepy Bill's Awful Tavern T-shirt, biting his lower lip. Willie, with his rich, copper skin and lined face, looked a bit like the movie actor Charles Bronson.

'Really, I don't think I want to watch any more of this,' I said.

Willie took a deep breath and released it slowly with puffed cheeks. 'I agree,' he said, then added, 'Why? That's what I don't understand.'

'Why what?'

'They execute criminals in private, don't they? Why do we have to watch

11

them shoot buffalo on television like it's some kind of spectator sport? At least boxing is man-to-man stuff. If you want violence, why not watch Joe Hipp?'

'Beats hell out of me,' I said.

'What if we went around slaughtering people with HIV positive to prevent the spread of AIDS?'

I shrugged.

'Then why this?'

'We're special, made in God's image,' I said.

'And bison are not?'

'They're animals.'

Willie's face turned hard.

'That's the pitch. It's in the Bible, the Christians say. We've got souls, Willie. Animals don't.'

'No?'

'Bison are just big dumb things who stand around waiting for us to shoot them. We've got to shoot bison to protect Herefords and Angus.'

'Some kind of God.'

'The Bible is God's word, they say.'

Willie snorted. 'The animal people are the gods, Dumsht. We're made in *their* image, not in the image of some amorphous god out there somewhere.' Looking up at the ceiling, he gestured to the presumed heavens.

I said, 'It's a matter of faith, Willie. I'm not going to argue with them.' As a Canadian official prepared to shoot another buffalo, I punched off the set.

Outside the window of Willie's one-room cabin, Oregon's coast range was lit by a large yellow moon partly hidden by the shaggy tops of Douglas fir. There was no subliminal hum of city noise outside. No honking of horns, revving of engines, squealing of brakes, or any of that machine-substituting-for-brains horse-pucky.

There was silence. What was Willie thinking about, I wondered. The diseased buffalo?

I tapped the jug of elderberry wine for another round. The tiny, dark blue elderberries were easy to come by in the coast range, and they made exquisite wine. One thing about having Willie as a partner, the food was nearly always wild, delicious, and rarely loaded with awful cholesterol, which I was now having to watch in keeping with the hard facts of middle age.

After watching the slaughter of bison, a second round of elderberry wine was called for, if not a third and fourth.

I speared another pickled thistle shoot, watching Willie out of the corner of my eye. In addition to pedestrian sugar and salt, Willie's pickling brine included juniper berries, pine needles, and a vinegar made of cactus juice.

Willie got out his little Bull Durham bag with the drawstrings. His frayed, threadbare little bag looked like it must have been twenty or thirty years old; I didn't know whether Bull Durham still marketed tobacco in these neat little bags. But Willie didn't keep tobacco in his bag. Nicotine was a stupid white-eye drug whose addictive qualities were profitable to tobacco companies in Virginia and North Carolina, but did smokers little good.

Willie took off his tattered Reeboks and threw them into a corner. He wiggled his toes.

He fell into a solemn mood.

On the occasions of his mushroom-inspired trances, I functioned as Willie Prettybird's window on the outside world. I was his human correspondent, chosen, I had long suspected, because I was a skeptic and not a wide-eyed believer. Willie was put off by white-eyes too eager to believe anything they were told by a Native American pretending knowledge of the ancient world. Willie said most of them had the IQs of fence posts, if not worse.

Now I asked Willie what was wrong.

'I'm hearing a moaning,' he said.

'A moaning?'

'Among the animal people,' he said. 'Barking, yapping, screaming, cawing, croaking, hissing, you name it. Concern. Discontent.'

'What?'

'It follows the wind among the willows and alders and firs. It's out there in the pine and juniper, and manzanita, and buck brush.'

I said, 'A moaning that expresses concern and discontent. Follows the wind? Whaaaaaaat? Say it again in straightforward English?'

'A kind of fear, actually.'

'Oh, shit, Willie!'

'Moaning sort of covers it, but not quite. There's no adequate English translation.'

'No fucking wonder,' I said. 'Concern and discontent?' I rested my forehead in the palm of my hand to register my dismay.

'Does your wonderful English have a word for that moment when you wake up with a full bladder? You don't want to get up and break the cozy warmth of your sleep, yet your bladder will almost, but not quite, let you go back to sleep? You're torn.'

'Well, no . . . ' I knew I'd been had.

Willie rested his case by making a farting sound with his tongue. Translation: Shut the fuck up, Dumsht.

Later on, I knew, Willie would be talking to the animal people. He was working up to it. He never just hollered, 'Hey, mountain lion, I want to talk,' or 'Listen up, crow.' He brooded and thought about the animal people. Then, with the animal people on his mind, he ate his little mushrooms.

16

I suspected these were Liberty Bells, tiny hallucinogenic mushrooms that grew in abundance in the Pacific Northwest. In October, wherever there was a pasture with cow pies on it, the grayish-tan Liberty Bells, no more than an inch and a half to two inches high, were to be found in abundance, a form of fungal fur mixed in with the grass. If the cops were as uptight with Liberty Bells as they were with pot, they'd have to send in the Marines to police everybody from adolescents to jazz musicians.

The mushrooms sent Willie's imagination traveling the tangled highways and byways of his brain, presumably from the cortex to the limbic and back again, although I doubted all the way to the R-complex or the brain stem. Solidly in this loop, Willie and the animal people talked.

I had been through many of these sessions with him over the years, and could only take his word for the identity of his mysterious correspondents, if there were any. I never blinked at Willie's mushroom-induced conceit, if that was what it was. I

17

was stuck with the elderberry wine.

Willie said he, like the animal people, had more respect for me than for white-eyes who gulped mushrooms and pretended to talk to the animal people. He said the animal people regarded these pretenders as a real howl. Rattlesnake, especially, just curled up with laughter at the idea.

The idea of Rattlesnake curling up with laughter I found amusing too, I have to admit.

I poured myself another glass of wine.

Through the cabin window we could see the ridge of Douglas fir highlighted by a yellow moon. This was the coast range of Oregon, nothing to compare with the Cascade Mountains at the eastern edge of Willamette Valley farther inland, but mountains still.

Willie flipped off the light. It was time.

*　*　*

By the light of the moon I watched Willie dig into the Bull Durham bag. He didn't offer me any. Sitting squat-legged in the shadows, he consumed a large pinch of mushrooms.

I gave him a few minutes for the mushrooms to take effect.

'You want to tell me about it, Tonto?' I said.

'Not much to tell.'

'Well, tell me anyway. Might as well get on with it.'

He sat, silent.

'You in touch with the animal people? That's what this is all about, isn't it?'

He said nothing, which meant yes, he was.

'Which ones?'

'Elk, for one.'

'Roosevelt?' Roosevelt elk were found west of the Cascade Mountains.

'No,' he said. This meant the smaller Rocky Mountain elk found east of the Cascades.

'Mmmmmmmm,' I said. This was like a game of twenty questions; the territory had to be systematically narrowed. 'Who else?'

'Deer.'

'Whitetail or mule?' Whitetails were

found in the thick forests of Douglas fir west of the Cascades; the larger mule deer, with their distinctive outsized, floppy ears, were found in the thinner stands of ponderosa and white pine to the east.

'Mule,' he said.

Okay, that narrowed it to eastern Oregon or Washington. Or maybe Idaho or Montana. 'I see. Who else?'

'Jackrabbit.'

That pretty much nailed the territory. 'Coyote?' I asked, hoping to clinch it.

Willie made a snorting sound which was beyond interpretation. He glanced at me. Was he smiling one of those canine-like smiles of his? I couldn't tell.

I said, 'Well, out with it. What are they saying?'

Willie thought about it a moment. 'They first heard it up at Deadman's Creek, then over at Bummers Flat and Sarcee.'

I knew those places. Deadman's Creek was an Indian reservation near Kamloops in British Columbia, Canada; Bummers Flat was also in B.C., in the mountains in the eastern part of the province; Sarcee was a reservation near Calgary in Alberta. Willie had friends on most of the reservations in the Pacific Northwest and western Canada and on more than one occasion had dragged me there to get drunk and powwow with his friends.

Willie and his Indian friends regarded the border between the United States and Canada as an artifice of the white-eye newcomers and did their best to ignore it. We might consider ourselves two peoples with one government based in Ottawa and one in Washington, D.C.; Indians like Willie did not.

Now Willie said, 'Then the Bloods in Lethbridge and the Blackfeet and Flat-heads in Montana heard it, and the Nez Percé.'

'Heard what?'

'The Lummis and Swinomish and Tulalips all heard it,' he added quickly. The Lummis, Swinomish, and Tulalips were Indian tribes along Puget Sound, between Seattle and the Canadian border.

'Oh, for Christ's sake, Willie.' I stopped short of saying 'Here we go again,' in imitation of Ronald Reagan.

Willie said, 'We've been through this before, Dumsht.'

I said, 'Chief Dumbshit to you, pal, and don't you forget it.'

Willie grinned in the moonlight. 'Chief Dumsht, then.' From the outback of mushroom land, the sorcerer Willie Prettybird said:

> In the slumbering hours of night
> When petals are folded
> And elk sleeps standing,
> Between the shadows and the light,
> 'Twixt the resting and the fight,
> The animal people stirred,
> Calling their reckoning, beckoning call.

So what else is new? I thought. Willie's enigmatic routine called for patience on my part. I snagged another chunk of squaw's tit — the smoked salmon — and started gnawing on it. I was ready for whatever animal people horseshit Willie was about to lay on me. It was fun, in a way, to hear what woodpeckers and worms had on their mind.

'It's not good,' he said.

'The squaw's tit?' I gnawed on some more salmon. 'I thought it was one of your better efforts. Flavorful sucking. Takes a person back, back, back . . . '

Willie gave me a shut-the-fuck-up-Dumsht look in the darkness.

'What's it about?' I waited ten minutes, maybe twenty. I had been through this drill many times before with Willie.

Finally he said, 'It's about the bison we saw on television.'

'You really do need to lay off reading the *Oregonian*, Willie.'

'There's a moaning, Denson. They're all afraid. Scared shitless. Elk. Deer. Rabbit. Mouse. It's not good, Dumsht. It's truly not.'

I saw him peering at me through the darkness. Then, with that way of his that said the session was over, he looked back through the window at the ridge in the moonlight.

I went to bed with him sitting there looking like he was about to weep.

Later, when I got up to take a leak, he was gone. Most people, being diurnal, liked to sleep at night. Not Willie. He was the most nocturnal human being I had ever met. Willie liked to roam around under the moon or stars or whatever. I don't know what went on out there that gave him such a kick, but he was into it.

In the early morning hours I awoke again, startled by a coyote yipping and yelping in the moonlight. Could it be? On the other hand, any moron can imitate a coyote. A coyote call has to be one of the most easily mimicked sounds in the animal kingdom.

Thinking *Aw, Willie, give me a break with the coyote hocus-pocus*, I fell back to sleep.

2

The next thing I knew, I woke up to the smell of frying bacon and fresh coffee as Willie Prettybird bustled about his tiny kitchen making breakfast. He seemed chipper enough despite all his nighttime prowling.

He watched me rub the sleep out of my eyes. 'Get a good night's sleep, did you, Dumsht?'

I said, 'After all that business about the buffalo, we forgot to watch Joe Hipp last night.'

'We should have watched, you're right. Joe knocked him out in the second round, got him with a left uppercut. Pow! Cold-cocked the poor son of a bitch.'

'How do you know that?'

Willie grinned. 'I went down to Creepy Bill's last night after you went to bed. Wilma had it on tape for me.'

Creepy Bill's Awful Tavern in Vernonia was our hangout. Creepy Bill's had a

VCR, and it was true that Wilma, the bartender, taped all Joe Hipp fights for Willie to savor. Willie was one of her favorite customers.

'At Creepy Bill's?' I was clearly skeptical.

'Ask Wilma if you don't believe me.'

He knew I wouldn't do that. Wilma didn't start her shift until four o'clock. 'Are we still going crabbing today?'

'No, we're going to Enterprise.'

'We've been through that, Willie.' For months, for some obscure, mystery reason, Willie had been trying to get me to Enterprise with him, but it was a long drive, and I was lazy.

'This time we've got a job, so you're trapped. You can't say no.' He gave me a cup of coffee. 'Drink this. You need to get your blood circulating.'

I sat up in bed and accepted the coffee. 'A job in Enterprise? Really?'

'A maybe job. A definite maybe.'

'Right,' I said. 'Maybe yes. Maybe no. Is that it?'

'A well-placed insider with maximum pull has recommended us highly. Whether the potential client hires us remains to be seen.'

'I see.' I eyed him over the coffee cup. 'What kind of job? Who is this might-be client?'

'It's an extremely interesting case, believe me. If I told you who the client will be, you wouldn't believe me. Better to wait and see if we get the work.'

'And when will we find out?'

'Tomorrow afternoon, probably. But the way I see it, there's no use sitting on our ass today. It's a long drive to Enterprise. We'll want to be fresh tomorrow.'

'When we're on the job and everything.'

'Correct. But we should take the big plunge today. We have confidence that we'll get the job. Tomorrow we'll go to work. No question, the way I see it. More coffee?'

I held out my cup for more. 'Okay to ask who recommended us? Maybe that will help instill some confidence.'

Willie smirked. 'Why, the animal people, Dumsht. Who else?'

'The animal people. Sure, sure,' I said. 'Will this maybe-yes, maybe-no job be through Olden or somebody else?' Olden Dewlapp was the Portland lawyer who ordinarily hired us for jobs in the sticks, a category for which Enterprise surely qualified.

Willie turned the bacon with a fork. It smelled knockout good. He said, 'Through Olden, probably. But he won't know until tomorrow either. The final decision hasn't been made.'

'But we've got the animal people in there working on our behalf.'

'There you have it.'

'The animal people. Shit, knowing that makes me feel a whole lot better, Willie, you just don't know.'

Willie pretended to be exasperated. 'You're my partner, Dumsht. I try to do things on your behalf. Ever think of that? Why do I want you to go to Enterprise, you ask? Why, why, why? Did it ever occur to you that there are times when it's better to be surprised? You always want to weigh everything like you were a research scientist or a grocer selling potatoes. If we don't get the job, we'll have a good time anyway, guaranteed.'

'God, that bacon smells good.' Having said that, I surrendered. I was going with the flow.

Willie was pleased. He grinned. 'That's better. Sometimes you're a real pain in the ass, do you know that, Dumsht? I try to help you out, but all you can do is ask questions. Move your buns now.'

I started putting on my pants. 'You got those potatoes nice and crisp. All right!'

Frying pan in hand, Willie started filling our plates with eggs, bacon, and fried potatoes. Ordinarily we didn't eat breakfast; we only drank coffee. But when Willie had a long drive ahead of him, he liked to load up with the works. He said, 'Have another cup of coffee, Dumsht.'

★ ★ ★

Willie and I threw our gear into my VW microbus and crawled up on the high seats in our usual action outfits: running shoes, cotton shirts, photographers' multi-pocketed vests, and blue jeans. We threw in our fly rods. We were two months late

29

for the morel mushrooms that were abundant in late May, but this time of year there would likely be trout fishing action on the Grande Ronde. Few experiences were lovelier or more thrilling than to watch a honking big old rainbow shoot, twisting, out of the water in pursuit of an artfully placed dry fly.

Willie Prettybird had a hunk of red ribbon tied on the end of his neatly braided pigtail and wore a Portland Beavers baseball cap. A faithful fan of the Beaves was Willie.

I resolved to play this trip Willie's way. I was determined not to ask why he was so anxious for me to go to Enterprise. Also, although I was curious as hell, I was determined not to ask him anything more about the identity of our mystery client-to-be. In due time I would learn the answer to his nagging. And if we got the job, fine; if we didn't get it, no big deal. We'd had jobs fall through before.

Ahead of us we had a 140-mile trip up the Oregon shore of the Columbia River to Boardman, where Interstate 84 angled to the southeast for the run to the Idaho border. At La Grande, another hundred miles, we would turn north for a forty-mile drive to Elgin, then east for another fifty-mile run to Enterprise.

The place where Willie and I were headed was about forty miles west of Hells Canyon on the Snake River. Eight thousand feet deep in places, the narrow Hells Canyon was the deepest in North America. Beside Hells Canyon, the Grand Canyon, while far broader, was a cute little ditch, good for day trips from Las Vegas, but if you wanted to see a real canyon, you went to the border between Oregon and Idaho.

We listened to some country and western music for a while; then it was time for the news. The controversy of the day was the continuing quarrel over medical care. Bored with the whining of AMA pooh-bahs and insurance executives, I switched stations, and there, as clearly as anybody could want — and no doubt then some — the Reverend Thaddeus Hamm Bonnerton was holding forth with his profitable country drawl. The Reverend Bonnerton, Ham Bone to

Willie and me, preached that the earth was the Bosom of Christ, capital *B*, and in treating it like a toilet we were all committing a terrible form of sacrilege.

The responsible remedy for this sacrilege, it appeared, was for Christians to yield part of their purse to Ham Bone so he could take direct action. To fund his legion of Christian cleanup squads, Bonnerton's Institute for the Restoration of Christ's Bosom was selling T-shirts for $29.95, plus $4.95 shipping and handling. The front of these T-shirts featured a fallen crucifix fashioned from a dead, charred tree, plus bottles, cans, litter, debris, and the words 'God Squad,' with 'Cleaning the Bosom of Christ' on the back.

For $19.95 plus $4.95 for shipping and handling, a follower could buy a God Squad plastic trash bag, with handles for Christ's fervent helpers, to use while cleaning empty lots, the sides of roads, and beaches.

For a mere $49.95 plus $4.95 shipping and handling, one could buy the Reverend Bonnerton's slender little book,

Heavenly Scrubbing, published by the Institute for the Restoration of Christ's Bosom in Tulsa, Oklahoma. *Heavenly Scrubbing* was filled with biblical citations, according to Bonnerton, that told of the duty of God's followers to take care of the earth.

Whenever there was an oil spill, a leaking of hazardous chemicals, or almost any conceivable environmental fouling, the Reverend Bonnerton was there the next day, raising funds to finance the Christian cleanup. Whether whales ran aground or there was a forest fire or somebody ate a tainted hamburger, all environmental causes appeared identical and critical to Ham Bone, who preached eternal damnation if the sinners did not mend their slothful, earth-befouling ways.

When the bison in Canada had become infected with anthrax, Bonnerton, predictably, made an appearance in Calgary and Edmonton — where the most potential suckers were to be found — preaching disaster if man did not alter his sinful ways. On these occasions, I was sympathetic to Canadians who were skeptical of the benefits of having to live so close to such a behemoth, oddball neighbor. The U.S. seemed a natural breeding ground for righteousness of nearly every description.

Bonnerton's usual MO was to work one disaster until the public began to get bored and until fresh and presumably more profitable bad news popped up in the media. I could remember only one cause that Bonnerton had cut short, presumably because even he recognized that he had somehow blundered into quicksand; that was the occasion on which he lashed out at growers of swine and cattle as polluting the ozone layer with the methane released by the digestive systems of their animals. So many unnecessary farts! — although, in an attempt to be high-minded, he had referred to 'digestive gases' and 'flatulence.'

Well, the digestive systems of human beings also gave off gas. The Queen of England. Donald Trump. Michael Jordan. Billary Clinton. Nobody was spared. I wondered: Did Bonnerton, in a lurch to the logical extreme, propose nuking India or China to prevent all that methane from reaching the ozone? The Indians ate a lot of beans and lentils to pump up the vegetable protein. Were we, in the name of holy ozone, going to tell them to knock it off?

But Bonnerton regarded picky reservations as un-Christian annoyances. When he was asked whether he proposed drying up the Everglades because swamps too produce methane, he wisely went on to a fresh emergency as if nothing at all had happened. Now, on the radio, Bonnerton was holding forth on the bison.

As most Oregonians knew, the Reverend Thaddeus Hamm Bonnerton was a graduate of Enterprise High School, his Oklahoma-raised father having served a five-year tenure preaching in a Baptist church there.

Before he was able to make his pitch for *Heavenly Scrubbing* or God Squad trash bags, I switched stations and found some music. I said, 'Old Ham Bone gonna save the buffaloes, Willie. Man like that can't be all bad.'

Willie gave me a look. He hated the

Reverend Thaddeus Hamm Bonnerton with a passion. He felt it was bad enough that any number of half-baked idiots and adolescents were giving an honorable concern for the land a bad name. Currently some morons who obviously relished being interviewed by television reporters were trying to keep people off the beaches in the name of preserving obscure — even, one suspected, imaginary — shore birds.

Willie assured me that the animal people had no objections to regular people enjoying the beach as long as they cleaned up after themselves. That religious nuts like Bonnerton had jumped on the environmental bandwagon as a profitable endeavor was just too much for Willie. He was afraid that nobody with any brains or common sense would want to be identified with the same cause as a religious hustler.

I had to take Willie's word for the opinions and feelings of the animal people, having no communication with them myself.

His animal people weren't stick-in-the-mud, always-serious biblical types. No, no, no. They had personalities. Some were greedy. Some were smart. Some, like Bear, had a perverse sense of humor.

Willie said — and I have only his word for this — that Bear in particular had some decidedly un-Christian, in fact downright painful, ideas about what he would like to do with *Heavenly Scrubbing*. Bear's notion of the best use of Bonnerton's book had to do with the good preacher's lower orifice; while Bear's claws were obviously more suited for digging up edible roots or snagging fish, he was convinced that if he tried hard, he could get a good enough grip on Bonnerton's book to do the job.

If parrots could ride unicycles, Bear reasoned, why couldn't he, with practice, teach Bonnerton a painful lesson with a book?

I told Willie I was one hundred percent on Bear's side; Willie, laughing, said he'd pass along the word.

★　★　★

As we drove up the Columbia River Gorge, enjoying the wonderful scenery,

Willie said, 'This all has to do with the Great Hoop, Denson. You're aware of that, I take it.'

'You mean that things have a tendency to loop back and repeat themselves?'

'Right.'

'We can't straighten out the untidy kinks to achieve some grand notion of the perfect, however wonderful in the abstract.'

'Right again,' Willie said. 'It's a lesson the animal people teach us, if we would only listen.'

'Mmmmm,' I said.

Willie raised an eyebrow. 'You don't believe in the Great Hoop?'

'Well, I don't know,' I said. 'I suppose it's always possible that the notion of history as a linear progression, an onward and upward march toward perfection, is a delusion, an unattainable snare.'

Willie approved. 'Well, you may not be hopeless after all, Denson. I was beginning to wonder. Maybe you have a chance. A guy like you, with at least marginal intelligence, can make all kinds of sense if you put your mind to it.'

I said, 'They say the idea of attainable

perfection is a conceit that's essential to us Americans. That's why our president is always lecturing people frying under the tropical sun about why they're not more successful.'

'It's an invention of people in temperate climates who have never known dirt between their toes.'

'I'm afraid we may be stuck with it,' I said.

We lapsed into silence as great tan bluffs rose on either side of us like majestic earth butts. A couple of miles later, I said, 'There is a Great Hoop of sorts that scientists have found, Willie. Actually, we're told it's a double helix, a three-dimensional spiral.'

'Oh? And what would that be?'

'DNA, the genetic code that carries our biological inheritance from one generation to another. They say we're only twenty percent more evolved than fish and just a couple of genes different from chimpanzees. All plants and animals are ultimately composed of just four substances, blah-blah, blah-blah, blah-blah, and blah-blah. These blah-blahs, as they're called, are the stuff of the genetic code that determines the qualities of all living things. But I'm sure the animal people didn't know about DNA.'

Willie looked triumphant. 'The effect is the same, isn't it? A repetition of behavior both by plants and animals? In the case of animals, males competing for females. Females competing for males. The predictable appearance of shits and assholes, all clones of their ancestors. True both of the animal people and you humans.'

'*You* humans?'

'Well, we humans,' he amended. 'But you see what I mean. And you always give me that amused look of yours when I talk about the animal people.'

'Yes, I guess you could look at it that way,' I said.

'The Great Hoop at work. And you white-eyes think you know more than the animal people.' Willie shook his head at my pathetic stupidity. 'The animal people know all about you because they created you. You just said so yourself. Think about it, Dumsht.'

'Mmmmmmm.' Arlington was coming

up; a drive-in there with superior french fries was one of our favorite refueling stops. Arlington was a small town that had been moved slightly inland up a small canyon to make way for the reservoir behind the John Day Dam. 'What do you say, Tonto? Cheeseburgers?'

'I'm game. Tell me, Dumsht — how many of our cases have we ultimately cracked because we traced somebody's personal hoop until we found the solution? People don't hurtle blindly out of an obscure past to commit crimes; they rise in an arc of cause and effect, a path that loops back on itself.'

I geared down for the Arlington exit. 'As detectives, we study the hoop.'

'There you've got it, Chief.'

After lunch, Willie took the wheel and we kept on rolling, lulled by the wonderful hum of the VW's air-cooled engine. It was a blessing of driving east up the gorge that one ordinarily had a tail wind; if you were in a VW bus, the return west was the hard part.

Just east of Pendleton we passed through the Umatilla Indian Reservation, where the Indians had lucked out and ended up on some prime wheat land. This area produced hard durum wheat that was first-class noodle wheat.

Still in the Umatilla reservation, Willie geared the bus down for the six-mile-long, seven-percent grade at Cabbage Hill, which, in the bad old days before the interstate highway, had been a real killer. I was down to second gear, mouth dry, the VW's air-cooled engine laboring hard, when we finally made it to the top. Then we were into the Blue Mountains for the run to La Grande.

At La Grande, an hour later, we turned north for the run to Elgin at the confluence of the Wallowa River and the Grande Ronde; we followed the Wallowa east through the hamlets of Minam and Wallowa. It was because of these distances that westerners resented the gasoline taxes that seemed so sensible to people on the East Coast.

The road followed the Wallowa River, a lovely river of cold mountain water — clear as forever — that rippled and danced over rounded basalt stones as smooth as a baby's butt. To the north of the river, on our left as we drove to Enterprise, were rolling hills, cattle country reminiscent of the Alan Ladd movie *Shane*. To the south, behind the river, rose the Eagle Cap mountains, the northern face of the Eagle Cap Wilderness Area. The Eagle Caps were nothing less than alplike; they shot straight up from the landscape, towering above the cattle country, jagged and snow-capped even in July. They were mountains out of Henry Fonda's *The Oxbow Incident* or Joel McCrea and Randolph Scott's *Ride the High Country*. I had been to this corner of Oregon many times over the years, and every time, without exception, I had to suppress the urge to moan out loud over the sheer, rapturous beauty of the landscape. In the wintertime, I supposed, one moaned over the occasional blizzards that whipped down out of Canada.

At five o'clock, eight hours after we had left Willie Prettybird's cabin outside of Vernonia, we pulled into Enterprise near the base of the Eagle Caps.

A couple of miles beyond Enterprise was the hamlet of Joseph. Joseph, on the western shore of Lake Wallowa at the base of Eagle Cap Mountain, was named for Chief Joseph, the Nez Percé chief who, in 1877, led his people on the ill-fated run for the border of Montana.

In words as elegant and immortal as Lincoln's at Gettysburg, it was the defeated and sorrowful Chief Joseph, later buried in the Colville Indian Reservation in northern Washington State, who told the world, 'From where the sun now stands I will fight no more forever.'

A quarter of a mile before the Enterprise city limits, in one of the many bends of the state highway that flanked the Wallowa River, we pulled into a place called the Wallowa River Inn, which advertised kitchenettes.

3

The Wallowa River Inn was one of those old-fashioned, locally owned motels that were still to be found on American byways — the Highway 101s and Route 66s — in this case State Highway 82, locally called the Wallowa Lake Highway. The more profitable interstate highways had been saturated with Best Westerns, Holiday Inns, Motel 6s, and the rest of the chain-owned rest stops for those who wanted to 'make time' as opposed to seeing anything of the world.

I had once read that Albert Einstein had noticed that the buildings in Vienna were larger and contained more details when he walked; when he whipped by them on the tram, they became smaller, and he was able to see less of them. The faster he went, the smaller they became. Thus travelers on the interstate highway system, in their rush to arrive at their destination as quickly as possible, opted to see and, I might add, to learn, as little as possible; it was like hurrying to one's death without having bothered to experience anything of life.

Judging from the number of cars parked in front of the units, the Wallowa River Inn was nearly full, which wasn't surprising in late July. Chief Joseph Days, the annual rodeo and celebration in nearby Joseph, was only a few days away. The early arrivals might be trout fishermen, here to try their luck on the Grande Ronde or on their way to backpack into the high lakes of the Wallowas. Still, the neon NO was turned off on the NO VACANCY sign, and unless the manager had goofed, we still had a chance.

The motel was laid out in the traditional U-shape facing the highway. It struck me that this layout had the perverse effect of catching and trapping as much highway noise as possible; logically, the U should have faced away from the highway.

The manager's office was located at one end of the U, with red Coke machines on the sidewalk circling the interior of the motel; the sidewalk was protected by the overhang of the asphalt composition roof. The glass window in the office door was plastered with VISA, MasterCard, and American Express decals; a small sign beneath the window said SOUND THE BUZZER FOR SERVICE.

Through the window I could see through an open door into the manager's apartment at the back of the office. The manager, or someone, was watching a game show on television. The volume was turned up perhaps a tad too loud.

I rang the buzzer button.

I could hear the MC's voice on the tube. He was listing all the many wonderful prizes to be given away. The audience applauded.

I buzzed again.

The audience, as though responding to me and not the bonanza of the day, applauded again.

I tried a third time.

A small lady with frizzy gray hair, a hearing aid, and thick-lensed eyeglasses appeared in the open doorway between the apartment and the office. She was closing fast on seventy years old or thereabouts. She unlocked the door, and looked at me with alert, pale blue eyes. 'Eh?'

I said, 'My friend and I would like to rent a unit with a kitchenette, if you have one vacant.'

Looking at Willie, her eyes magnified by her glasses, she bunched up her face. It was impossible to tell if this was because Willie was an Indian, but I didn't think so. It wasn't a disapproving bunching of the face; it was more likely because she had a hard time seeing. She fiddled with her hearing aid. She said, 'You boys're lucky today. One unit left. Half an hour ago, I was filled up.'

'Ah, good,' I said. 'What've you got, fishermen out to try their luck? Or are these folks here early for Chief Joseph Days?'

She looked mildly at the vehicles in the parking lot in the interior of the U. 'I've had these customers for better than a week now. They're advance men here to lay cables and get ready for the Reverend Thaddeus Hamm Bonnerton to give one of his Christian environmental revivals. Tells people to use the trash can and put out campfires.'

'Well,' I said, 'the Chamber of Commerce must be pleased. Money in your pockets, at least. Good for you.'

She said, 'Can't guarantee you'll find much in the way of cooking gear in your unit. Just don't understand why anybody'd want to steal a bunch of dented aluminum. It's not like it was fancy enameled cast iron.'

'Makes you wonder how some people are raised,' I said.

'I'll need a credit card or payment in advance.' She looked apologetic. 'A person learns over time.'

Glancing at the prices listed on a sign behind the desk, I dug out the Denson & Prettybird company VISA. A framed certificate with the woman's picture on it identified the small lady as Leiat Podebski, a member in good standing of the Enterprise Chamber of Commerce.

Behind Ms. Podebski, the television audience moaned in disappointment. She glanced back at the set, looking concerned. 'Aw, that sweet little thing from Sacramento didn't make it. A brand new Chrysler minivan.' She shook her head.

She squinted at the credit card and put it in her machine, stamping a billing form with the heel of her hand. She grabbed a key from a rack of hooks. 'That'll be unit six. I can't guarantee you'll get a lot of sleep. They're real partyers in unit eight on the end there just around the corner from you. I guess Christians have a right to have a good time like anybody else. You know about the Reverend Bonnerton, I take it.'

'Only what we read in the newspapers,' I said. That was more than enough, I might have added but didn't.

She said, 'I knew Thad Bonnerton when he was a love-struck kid at Enterprise High School.'

'You did?'

'He spent all his time mooning after a cheerleader who wouldn't have anything to do with him. He was a big, awkward know-it-all with a terrible case of pimples. Whatever made him think the best-looking cheerleader would have anything to do with him was beyond me. Always had his nose stuck in the Bible when he wasn't working as a box boy at Food City. All the girl could think about was a rancher's son who knew how to throw a football and shoot a jump shot.'

Willie and I both laughed.

'She was a pretty thing, it's true; if I'm not mistaken the boys all looked forward to those days when she wore a sweater to school.' Podebski grinned wickedly. 'Thad looks a lot better as an adult, judging from pictures of him in magazines and the newspapers. Time passes. I suppose he feels everybody has forgotten that awful business of — '

Podebski stopped. She had obviously thought better of telling us whatever it was she was about to say. Then she said, 'At least his zits went away. But he's still got that assured, self-righteous way about him.'

Willie said, 'I suppose any preacher worth his salt has gotta believe in himself.'

The awful business of . . . of what? I wondered what it was that Podebski had almost told us. The really good stuff, I bet. I said, 'How did you know all that? Did you work at the high school?'

She grinned ruefully. 'Why, I used to be an English teacher. Old English teachers never die, you know, they just manage motels and watch stupid television with the sound turned up too high.' She tapped her hearing aid with her forefinger. 'Can't see to read anymore. Gives me a headache. And there's nothing on the tube worth watching in the daytime, I'll tell you that. Soap operas and game shows all day.' She paused, looking thoughtful, then said, 'I wonder if Thad Bonnerton's real reason for showing up in Enterprise might not be the big do on Thursday night.'

'Big do?'

'Why, they're holding an all-Enterprise High School class reunion.'

'On a Thursday night?'

'Oh, sure. This is Chief Joseph Days, remember? People will want to relive old times in old places on Friday and Saturday night. Most of the graduates will be here on vacation from out of town, and precious few locals will be working on Friday. That's when they hold the prelims over at the rodeo grounds.'

She was right. The Friday of Chief Joseph Days was the same as a legal holiday in Joseph and Enterprise. This was a three-day bash. 'Big affair!' I said.

'They'll be having three parties at once, grouped by decade: forties and fifties combined, sixties and seventies together, and eighties and nineties, everybody from hoary old dodderers to fuzz-cheeked kids, with music to please every generation. Motels are already booked from here to La Grande and then some.'

'Well, that's a real undertaking,' I said.

'All-school reunion at Enterprise and the Chief Joseph Days in Joseph all in one weekend? You're talking one heck of a hot time. Have you heard about those folks up in Spokane, Tom and Linda Beaumont and Memory Lane?'

'I'm not sure I have. You, Willie?'

'I don't think so,' Willie said.

'Tom and Linda are singing mimics. They imitate famous singers from the past. Tom's supposed to do everybody from Elvis Presley to Bruce Springsteen. Linda can do Peggy Lee, Madonna, you name it. They make their living traveling around to school reunions.'

'Name the year, and they'll take you down memory lane, I bet. Is that the idea?' I said.

She grinned. 'That's it. They'll be at the big dance over in Joseph on Saturday night.'

'Good for them. The pimple-faced kid come back to strut his stuff, you think?'

'The Reverend Thaddeus Hamm Bonnerton? Harboring such un-Christian thoughts as that?' Leiat Podebski grinned and raised an eyebrow. 'Now, you wicked, wicked boy! Shame on you!' Laughing, she waggled a finger at me.

'Can you recommend a place where we could get something to eat? Nothing fancy, but real food, if possible.'

'The best bet would be the Pheasant Café on the main drag going into town. You can't miss it.'

I said, 'You'll be going to the reunion, I take it?'

'Oh, sure, I'll be one of the honored

guests. All I have to do now is rustle myself up a date. It isn't easy at my age.' She laughed. Behind her, the television audience applauded. 'Now, you boys don't hesitate to let me know if you need anything.'

One of the first things we needed was to stock our refrigerator. 'Where's the best grocery store?' I asked.

'That'd be the Enterprise Food City, just down the highway on your left. You can't miss it.'

Willie and I moved our gear into unit six, and pushed off for Food City.

4

I had no sooner parked my VW bus in the asphalt parking lot in front of Enterprise Food City when a caravan of maximum-fancy travel buses of the sort used by well-heeled rock musicians wheeled grandly in behind us. Only these buses were not owned by entertainers, unless the term 'entertainer' is used in a larger sense.

The buses, six of them in all, had REV. THADDEUS HAMM BONNERTON written on the sides in a huge, fancy green scroll. Under this, in rather more modest lettering, was INSTITUTE FOR THE RESTORATION OF CHRIST'S BOSOM, TULSA, OKLAHOMA overlaying photographic images of Bonnerton's famous high five for Christ. The high five for Christ was Bonnerton's signature ending to his big-tent revivals; in this ritual — over which the credits rolled in his televised performances — the sweating Bonnerton waded joyfully into the assembled faithful, slapping upraised palms while they sang the amen chorus. This rip-off of athletes celebrating triumphant victory was enough to make the jocks drop the practice, in my opinion.

Finally two ten-wheeler trucks pulled into the lot. The sides of the first truck featured reproductions of the dust jacket of Bonnerton's book, *Heavenly Scrubbing*, plus depictions of God Squad trash bags, T-shirts, and baseball caps. The second truck was adorned with a depiction of Bonnerton's Institute for the Restoration of Christ's Bosom revival tent, flanked on each side by Bonnerton's green God Squad trash bags — to be purchased, in support of Christ and the environment, for a mere $19.95 plus $4.95 shipping and handling.

The revival tent was necessary because Ham Bone, a practical man, didn't want his preaching restricted by the availability of basketball arenas and football stadiums, and besides, I suspected his brand of religious sucker was ordinarily found in the sticks, not the cities.

This, then, was the money-churning caravan of the fast-talking Ham Bone;

God's chief greenie had arrived in Enterprise, Oregon, to do battle with the evil forces of filth and waste. Unless Bonnerton was mortgaged up to his elbows, money was no object for the righteous legion of clean. I wondered if Leiat Podebski's suspicion might not be right: his real motive was to show the local folks — most especially a former cheerleader and onetime high school quarterback — what the pimpled Bible nut had accomplished over the years.

I thought of the lines from a poem by Percy Bysshe Shelley:

> *My name is Ozymandias, king of kings:*
> *Look on my works, ye Mighty, and*
> *   despair!*

Did Thaddeus Hamm Bonnerton ever read poetry? Probably not, I thought. And if he did, he probably didn't pay any attention to what was being said.

Willie and I were in no hurry to go inside the store. More fun to wait and see if the Great Man himself was in one of the vehicles.

We waited, watching eager, well-scrubbed young men and women pile out of the buses. They were wearing Cleaning the Bosom of Christ T-shirts and God Squad baseball caps. If they saw anything amusing or outrageous about their costumes or their enterprise, their faces did not reveal it. They were all business. But Ham Bone himself did not make an appearance, which was disappointing to Willie and me; he was no doubt remaining inside one of the buses so as not to dilute the drama of his arrival. Timing, most show biz folks will tell you, is everything.

Willie and I were about to give up the wait and go inside to buy our groceries when a sleek, jet-black Cadillac stretch limousine pulled in the lot. A vehicle of this sort was ordinarily reserved for the hottest of hot-damn big shots. *This* had to be the mighty Ham Bone himself. We stayed put.

The eager young followers gathered around the limousine as the doors opened; one by one, Bonnerton's yes-men — armed, no doubt, with a biblical quotation for every question — piled out, wearing splendid suits and ties. Bonnerton himself, wearing a double-breasted, blue, pin-striped power suit — far grander than the rest — was the last to emerge, with solicitous aides-de-camp hovering at his elbow.

It was as though the ostentatious tour vehicles were a fleet of ancient Greek vessels, and Bonnerton was Ulysses, arriving home from years of travel and adventures. He had survived the dangerous call of the beautiful sirens of fame, and tricked the one-eyed giant, the IRS, which would have kept him prisoner in a cave of poverty. He had even married once, but his wife had died of cancer, leaving him to care for their four adopted children, apple-cheeked towheads he liked to display on his television specials; they were passionate lovers of the environment, just like Dad, and flashed wholesome grins and said cute things about Jesus.

Now Thad Bonnerton, decked out like a Wall Street investment banker, was prepared to rout the rascals who had surrounded his beautiful lady — no doubt the cheerleader Leiat Poedebski had mentioned — and lay claim to what was rightfully his.

Mighty Ulysses, having returned from his many battles, would kick butt and take names.

He would begin, one presumed from the drama of his arrival, with Food City.

The commander of Christian troops, looking slightly distracted if not outright bored, murmured to one of his yes-men and gestured to Food City with a languid flip of his left hand. Responding to the gesture as though the Maximum Leader had fired a starting gun, the assembled troupe was off, like a gaggle of determined geese, headed for the entrance of the grocery store.

With such fanfare and ceremony the former box boy returneth.

Willie and I piled out of our microbus to watch the fun.

The sidewalk in front of Food City was loaded with bags of fertilizer, that is, dried cow manure.

Bonnerton reached down and slapped

a bag of fertilizer with the palm of his hand and several of his followers, like solemn-faced babies or determined monkeys, did the same thing.

Willie and I, wanting to eavesdrop, moved closer. We missed Bonnerton's comment on the paper sacks of cow dung, but it was apparently good, because there was a murmuring of agreement by his followers; several of them squatted down to study the labels on the bags, bunching their lips in approval. Did they expect the labels to contain a treatise on the digestive process of a Hereford or polled Angus?

Then Bonnerton strode through the automatic door. Willie and I trotted quickly on the heels of his followers, noting that the bags of dung were made of recycled paper. No plastic. So far, Food City's buyers had scored high marks.

Bonnerton went immediately to the vegetables, displayed in the rear of the store, where he was met by the store manager, a bespectacled, middle-aged man wearing a green apron.

This time Willie and I got close enough to listen in.

Why the manager should give a damn what Bonnerton thought of his store — or anything else, for that matter — was beyond us, but he was obviously gripped by the syndrome Famousmanitis. The Famousman was constantly to be seen lecturing people on television; therefore his opinions mattered.

The manager said, 'All our vegetables are free of measurable pesticides, Reverend Bonnerton. We do our best to buy only organically grown produce.'

'Mmmmmm,' Bonnerton said, displaying interest but withholding outright approval. The Famous One did not wish to dilute his authority by being too easy on the manager.

The manager bit his lip. Did he expect God to clip him with a bolt of lightning if he did not kowtow to Thaddeus Hamm Bonnerton? He said, 'The vegetables come from Arizona and Texas in the winter. It's not easy assuring quality for our customers.'

'And from Mexico,' Bonnerton said.

'Uh, yes, from Mexico.' The manager blinked.

'And fruit from Chile.' Bonnerton gave the manager a look of reproof.

The manager, by way of accepting the reprimand, looked chagrined; indeed, his face said, he sold produce grown by Roman Catholic beaners south of the border. A terrible admission. He said quickly, 'But in the summer, we get most of our vegetables from Yakima Valley, and we know the growers there.' He licked his lips. The Yakima Valley in Washington State was surely safe territory.

'And California,' Bonnerton said. It was obvious from his tone that he did not approve of California vegetables any more than he did produce grown by Mexicans and Chileans. Even in Yakima, the produce was harvested by Mexicans and Mexican-Americans, people who believed in the Pope and had brown skin.

'We do the best we can,' the manager said. 'We demand clean vegetables, I assure you.'

I wondered: Did Ralph Nader behave like this? I hoped not. I didn't believe in everything Nader did, but I was convinced he was essentially civilized.

The manager said, 'But we have an easier job of it with beef. This is cattle country, and we're able to buy locally grown meat. We're able to guarantee our customers quality meat free of steroid growth chemicals.'

'Do you buy meat from a rancher named Hook?' Bonnerton asked.

Was I right? Was Bonnerton a modern Ulysses, taking names and kicking butt?

The manager looked trapped, wondering what had been wrong with his answer. His licked his lips. 'Monty Hook? Ah, well, yes, we do on occasion.'

Willie glanced at me. This Hook was apparently on Ham Bone's shit list.

Just then a reporter and a photographer from the *Wallowa County Chieftain* and a camera crew from a television station in La Grande arrived nearly simultaneously; the Reverend Thaddeus Hamm Bonnerton, having demonstrated his power to the poor manager of the store where he had once worked, went to one of the checkout stands, where he donned a green apron. Then, relaxing a little, but only a little, he allowed himself to have his picture taken loading a grocery bag for a little old lady of Leiat Podebski's generation. The high school alumni arriving for the reunion would be greeted that night by Bonnerton spouting his opinions on television, and there would likely be a photograph of the Great Man on the front page of tomorrow's *Wallowa County Chieftain*.

The woman — to her credit, in my opinion — seemed unimpressed by the fuss given her overdressed and self-important bagger. She just wanted her groceries packed so she could be on her way.

Ham Bone, all smiles for the reporter and photographer, appeared unaware of her indifference, but Willie and I both noted that he put her tomatoes in the bottom of the bag, where they were sure to get smashed.

Did Bonnerton go so far as to give the tomatoes a little push just to make sure he received proper respect the next time around? It was hard to tell; I thought he had, and Willie later claimed there was no question that he had. Bonnerton was an experienced competitor, after all, and knew how to work his way to the fresh air at the top of the bag.

If the tin cans of life were going to weigh anything down, it most assuredly wasn't going to be the Reverend Thaddeus Hamm Bonnerton.

5

The Pheasant Café, identified by a colorful brace of flying cock pheasants painted on the glass front, turned out to be exactly what Willie and I had in mind. It was what Ernest Hemingway might have called a clean, well-lighted place, and it was clearly a local favorite.

The entrance faced the cash register at the end of the counter; to our right was a rack for newspapers and news magazines and the mandatory jukebox, a huge, colorful Wurlitzer. The Formica-topped counter featured a glass case of generous pies; the stainless-steel bases of the twelve stools were bolted to the floor, their swivel tops covered with red plastic cushions.

The seats and tabletops of the five booths opposite the counter were also respectively covered with plastic and Formica. Each booth had a stainless-steel control for the jukebox, with listings of the songs that diners could flip through while they waited for their orders. Framed color photographs above each booth honored the game birds found in the area: a cock and hen pheasant, a group of scurrying quail, a pair of Hungarian partridges, a pair of doves, and a brace of handsome chukar partridge.

Only the chukar partridge booth was vacant, which meant Leiat Podebski's recommendation was likely sound. Amid the clicking and clacking of forks and knives and ceramic plates and cups and the murmur of diners, we took our seats beneath the chukar partridges. We knew without looking at the menu which would likely be the best bets in a place like the Pheasant: a hamburger or cheeseburger, a BLT or club sandwich, chili topped with cheese and onions, a chicken-fried steak, a T-bone or rib steak, or liver and onions. The steaks and liver and onions would come with tossed green salad and choice of potato, baked, mashed, or fried.

We both went for a chicken-fried steak with mashed potatoes and a cup of coffee. While we waited for our order, we read the framed description of the chukar partridge, indigenous to Asia, which was introduced in 1952 and 1953, when ten thousand birds a year were raised at a game farm in Hermiston, Oregon. The description claimed that chukars, average weight twenty ounces, were the most delicious of all game birds, pheasant included, and I didn't think that was hyperbole.

When it arrived, we were not disappointed with the food except, predictably, with the salad dressing. Rather than make genuine French dressing, which is a simple enough matter — a clove of garlic steeped in olive oil, vinegar, salt and pepper, and a touch of dried mustard — the cook used a bottled commercial goo, an orangish-yellow, sweet concoction thickened by an unpronounceable chemical.

As I ate my salad, topped with French dressing that would have made a Frenchman vomit, I thought about Thad Bonnerton's trials as a pimple-faced know-it-all at Enterprise High School. High school was not without its trials for many young people; for some, memories of that period in their life, both good and bad, lingered with a virulence beyond all logic. Some were forever scarred. Others moved on, putting the memories behind them.

I said, 'I once played a high school football game up here in Joseph. Did I tell you that, Willie?'

'You?'

'One of the memories of my life, I have to admit. It was in November, the quarterfinals of the state Class B football championship.' Class B, since renamed Class A, was the class of the smallest Oregon high schools allowed to play football with eleven players.

'The Cayuse Broncos?'

I chewed on a forkful of lettuce that was overwhelmed by the orange goo. 'The Thundering Broncos, Willie.' Cayuse, where I grew up, was located on the banks of the Columbia River about twenty miles west of Umatilla.

'I didn't know you were an athlete.'

'I was a natural assholete. Everybody said so.'

Willie grinned. 'That's more like it.'

'Everybody in the school was on the team in one form or other. I was a little

71

squirt. I didn't start growing until I was eighteen years old, so I sat on the bench in football, basketball, and baseball in that order. Every year.'

Willie shook his head in sympathy.

'I was small, but slow,' I said.

'Good combination, I have to give it to you, Dumsht.'

'Got regularly flattened in football. Couldn't shoot a basketball. Couldn't hit a baseball. I never stopped trying, though. Never quit. If I had been the same size I am now, I would have been a hero and gotten laid whenever I wanted. As it was I had to dance with my face in the girl's chest.'

'Hey! Lucky guy.'

'The girls all wanted stupid hulks.'

'Of course they did. That's not surprising. They wanted power and manliness, not a squeaky-voiced runt with his face buried in their chest like a rutting squirrel.'

'Or a pimple-faced creep like Bonnerton,' I said.

'What happened in the Joseph game?'

'I was an end. My only starting spot in four years of trying. We played the Eagles in a snowstorm. A blizzard, actually. It was balls-ass cold with a hard wind blowing. The field was packed with snow, and people in bright jackets stood on the sidelines so we could locate the out-of-bounds.'

'Who won?'

'We did, nineteen to thirteen, with a dramatic touchdown on a fourth-and-eight play with two minutes left.'

'Ahh, see! Good for you.'

'I remember the play clearly, a double-reverse out of a single wing. I remember going down the line of scrimmage and hooking back to throw my block, and it was a dandy. I remember looking up from the frozen ground and watching the wing-back being escorted into the end zone by a phalanx of blockers. He went untouched. *Untouched!* It was a splendid sight. And I still dream about the coach, Mungo was his name, a tall man with a face like a morose hound. Why is that, do you suppose, Willie? Why do I dream about Coach Mungo?'

Willie said, 'You remember it for a reason, Denson. Your balls were just getting the juice at that age. The memories of battle linger with us. They are the most provocative memories a man can have.'

I grinned, even then remembering the moment. 'I pulled a muscle in my groin and had to ride a yellow schoolbus a hundred and fifty miles in a snowstorm with my balls packed with ice. Whenever the ice melted, Coach Mungo had the driver stop the bus so he could get fresh snow for the plastic bag on my crotch. Everybody on the bus was making jokes about how my balls would be the size of BBs when we got back to Cayuse. We had done it; we had pulled off an upset in a blizzard.'

'See. Wounded even.'

'Some wound.'

'How big were your balls when you got back to Cayuse?'

I grinned foolishly. 'The size of BBs.'

Willie laughed. 'See? You were a warrior. When you went out onto the field in that snowstorm, you were being a warrior and you were proud of it. The Cayuse Mustangs were a war party dispatched to do battle against the Joseph Eagles on their turf.'

'Broncos. Thundering Broncos.'

'More dramatic because it took place in a blizzard. You were told it was a football game, but there was more to it than that.'

'Is this all like your Great Hoop, a repetition of the same drama over and over? Is that why we have class reunions?'

Willie paused, then said, 'You might be onto something there, Dumsht. That football game was a memorable point on your personal hoop. For most of us, the hoop was most dramatic when we were young, and we remember it with clarity. The songs. The first loves. With you, it was the attempt to be a warrior.'

'To be a man in spite of having a late start growing.'

'Yes, to overcome all obstacles. But the larger camp recognizes the foolishness of that part of the hoop. That's why we correctly respect age. As we get farther and farther around the hoop, we can see decades of the arc. Only when we are very old can we see the full sweep, but by then we are feeble and infirm, and the youth have taken over. They are young and new, different from us, they think.' Willie laughed softly.

* * *

Later I lay back on one of the two beds in unit six and stretched out, bone-tired from the long day. The bed smelled vaguely of mildew and sagged in the middle, which wasn't unusual for the places Willie and I stayed when we were working a case in the sticks. We weren't exactly what you would call big spenders.

Thinking about our conversation in the Pheasant, I said, 'Say, Willie, if you mention high school kids and warriors in the same breath to most people, they'd burst out laughing.'

'That's because they haven't thought about the nature of the hoop. What do you think urban gangs are? The kids don't have anything to do, so they do what's natural to them. They form gangs and go fighting. Over the millennia that's what young men their age do. When you threw that block against Joseph, you were doing

76

warrior's work without being aware of it. That's what we are now, the two of us.'

'Say again.'

'We're warriors.'

'We are?'

'That's the problem with most white men, Denson. There's no opportunity for you to be warriors. You never test your nerve. You sit on your fat asses and watch warriors on television or in the movies or read about them in novels. You sit under the skirts of your women, and they despise you for it without knowing why. They despise you, and you resent them. You white-eyes!'

'We have our problems, it's true.'

'Your women say they want men like that famous television actor, what's his name?'

I furrowed my brows. 'I'm not sure who you're talking about.'

'The thoughtful, charming doctor in Korea. The eternal joker.'

'Ahh!' I grinned. 'That would be Alan Alda of *M*A*S*H*. Hawkeye was the character's name.'

'That's the one. When Hawkeye fought

death in the operating room, he was a warrior. When he played the clown to impress the women, he was pathetic. Slope-chested clowns don't make a woman's pussy wet.'

'No?'

'Women may admire wit, but they value courage more. You take an actor like Sean Connery or Clint Eastwood now. Men of courage and presence. We'll remember Eastwood's serape and evil-looking little cigars in *A Fistful of Dollars* long after we forget Alda's one-liners. Alda was ha-ha-ha. Eastwood was serious business.'

This was Willie Prettybird's sorcerer's talk, which I always found interesting even if I didn't agree with everything he said. I said, 'Women want, uh, let me guess. You're going to tell me they really want warriors.'

'Yes, they do. They want Gary Cooper, not Jerry Lewis. They can't help them-selves. Cops are warriors. Detectives are warriors.'

'Making war on . . . ?'

'Why, whoever threatens the cleanliness and safety of the camp. Who on earth do you think? That's why we drove all this way from Portland.'

'To protect the camp. The communal grounds.'

'That's right. To keep the camp from being fouled. It's the eternal struggle of the Great Hoop.' Willie frowned and shook his head, pretending to be disgusted with me for not recognizing the obvious.

6

We were still asleep Tuesday morning when the phone rang. Willie Prettybird's bed was closest to it, so he answered. He listened for a moment, still half asleep, then said, 'Hey, hey, how're you doing?' he said. To me, he mouthed 'Olden Dewlapp.'

'The job?' I mouthed back.

Listening to Olden, Willie nodded yes, mouthing 'Got it!'

'Asshole,' I said, but I was pleased and Willie knew it. We had to work to eat.

Willie gave me an aw-it-ain't-nothin' look. He mouthed, 'Didn't I tell you?'

Olden Dewlapp, in Portland, was Willie's chief contact; mine was brother Boogie Dewlapp in Seattle. The Dewlapps crassly advertised their services on television and so had few respectable — that is, well-heeled, urban, necktie-wearing — clients. Mostly they represented rural people caught in the jaws of modern life.

These people suspected that high-powered slicko lawyers secretly ridiculed people who grew up saying 'I seen' and 'It don't.' When they got in trouble, they called the only lawyers they knew: the just-folks Boogie, who appeared in the ads on *Beverly Hillbillies* and *I Dream of Jeannie* reruns, sitting in a plastic-upholstered easy chair with a cocker spaniel in his lap and a baby tugging at his leg, and the down-home Olden, in a goofy chefs hat and with an apron tied around his substantial girth, delivering his pitch as he tried, unsuccessfully, to light charcoal for a barbecue.

Boogie and Olden knew we didn't mind driving to some far corner of Oregon and Washington to have a cup of coffee in the tiny house of somebody caught up in the coils of the law. That's why we were regular investigators for the firm of Dewlapp and Dewlapp, of Seattle and Portland.

'Little birdie told us,' Willie said. He listened, then laughed. He said to Olden, 'One of his hands is a friend of mine, a Nez Percé. I had a feeling we'd get it, so I conned Denson into coming on up. I've been trying to get him to come up to this part of the country for months, but he's so lazy it's unreal.'

'Whose hand?' I mouthed.

Willie, listening, nodding, put his hand over the phone. 'Monty Hook.'

I didn't have to be told who Monty Hook was. He was a colorful figure frequently quoted in the mass media because he was the outspoken president of the Oregon Cattlemen's Association, and was said to carry a Texas Buntline pistol in the cab of his pickup to protect himself from environmentalists. Hook owned a cattle spread north of Enterprise, and a few days earlier he had popped into the news again when a state policeman was found dead on his property.

Willie said to Olden, 'Is his money good?' He listened, still grinning.

'Says Hook's money spends, eh?' I said.

'That's what Olden claims,' Willie whispered to me. 'He says Hook's no counterfeiter, as far as he knows.' Without hesitating or asking my opinion, which was out of form for him, he said to Olden, 'Aw hell, yes, we'll take the case. Denson's just digging at his nuts in anticipation. He wants to wear a cowboy hat and jeans with dried shit on them. Claims his old man was a cowboy. We'll see what he's made of.' He winked at me.

'We're going to work for Monty Hook? You've gotta be off your nut,' I said.

Willie, still grinning, listening to Olden Dewlapp, nodded yes.

'Aw shit, Willie,' I said.

Willie motioned with his hand for me to be cool.

Willie's quick agreement surprised me somewhat because Monty Hook had become public enemy number one in the minds of the many environmentalists in our neck of the woods. At issue was grazing rights to federal land administered by the Bureau of Land Management. The environmentalists claimed the BLM was selling grazing rights at a third of what they cost on the private market. One result of this give-away, besides the casual screwing of the taxpayer, was that public land was being overgrazed — or so the environmentalists claimed, and I suspected they were right on this one. Besides chewing up food that would have gone to deer and elk, the practice of overgrazing destroyed the ground cover, causing the erosion of topsoil in the foothills.

The ranchers argued that grazing cattle on BLM land meant cheaper beef at the supermarket and money in the federal treasury. They said that state management of fish and game had actually increased the numbers not only of mule deer and elk, but also of bighorn sheep and, in southern Oregon, Idaho, and Nevada, of pronghorn antelope. When there was a hard winter, and the state game managers in those states pulled back on the hunting licenses, the states had to resort to lotteries.

Now the evil Monty Hook, who earned part of his living running cattle on federal land, wanted to hire Willie and me, who were well known for our record of digging up sordid and sorry facts on the uncivilized trashing of the common ground. We had accepted assignments from all manner of greenies, including the Sierra Club and

Ducks Unlimited. Some of these well-intentioned greenies were self-righteous, out-of-control loonies, we had to admit, but the more sober-minded and responsible of them had a long-term point that was hard to argue. Few longtime residents wanted to see the Pacific Northwest Californicated by lovers of shopping malls, cars, and fast-food outlets.

When Willie finished jabbering on the phone with Olden Dewlapp, he hung up and told me that besides the dead state cop on his range, Monty Hook had some infected cattle on his hands.

'Infected by what?' I asked.

Willie clenched his jaw. This meant it wasn't good.

'Anthrax?'

He grimaced. This meant yes.

I said, 'Does it have anything to do with the dead cop found on his spread?'

'Could be, Hook says. But he doesn't know what.'

'Ay! He doesn't need to hire himself some detectives, does he?'

Willie Prettybird said, 'Didn't I tell you this was a hot one, Dumsht? Next time you'll shut your mouth and listen to your old pal Tonto for a change.'

★ ★ ★

We decided the smart move was for Willie to borrow his friend Al's pickup and move in with Bobcat Bill so he could investigate the site where the cop had been killed. I would stay in Enterprise, sissy white-eyes that I was, and work out of the Wallowa River Inn.

Bobcat didn't have a telephone, but Willie could take our cellular phone with him, and we could communicate that way.

As Willie got up to set the coffee going, he suddenly said, 'Say, Dumsht, after you take me over to Al's for the pickup, why don't you walk over to the desk and ask that old lady if you can go to that all-school reunion with her. In a place like this people like to talk. If you're up-front with her, maybe she'll say yes.'

'What?'

Willie closed his eyes, then opened them. He was being patient with me. 'This old lady really knows this place,

Dumsht. And an all-school reunion? You have to remember, in gossip lie the details of the Great Hoop.'

'Jesus!'

'Humor me. A reunion is the act of returning to a memorable place on the hoop. You said so yourself. It is coming full circle, only later, with bellies and sagging boobs. But the same passions still apply. If the hoop did not exist, there would be no reunions.'

'Even if we know history, we're likely to repeat it.'

Willie grinned. 'People do grow and change, of course, but that's pretty much it. That old lady is educated, experienced, and smart as hell. She knows the hoop because she's been there herself. She would laugh if you called her a sorceress, which she has been taught is a primitive concept. But she is, believe me. I bet you'll have a good time in spite of yourself. There's no telling what you'll learn about the local hoop.'

Willie was partly right, of course; I did need to learn more about the local hoop. But I wouldn't go so far as to consider

Leiat Podebski a sorceress.

Willie drew me a map with a ballpoint pen showing me how to get to Bobcat Bill's house. 'I'll go on ahead and talk things over with Bobcat. After you talk to the manager, you come on out, and we'll see what we have to do. Bobcat's a first-rate guy. You'll like him.'

I studied the map. 'Looks complicated.'

He said, 'I bet the old lady has some freebie tourist maps in the office for her guest. Grab one of those if it'll make you feel better.'

★ ★ ★

After I had delivered Willie Prettybird to Al's house to borrow a pickup for his drive to Bobcat Bill Kemiah's house, I drove back to the Wallowa River Inn and went straight to the manager's office.

I could see through the window that Leiat Podebski was reading what seemed to be a large-print book for people with bad eyes. I punched the buzzer button, and a moment later she was at the door saying, 'Yes?'

I said, 'Say, Ms. Podebski, when my

88

partner and I checked in yesterday afternoon, you said you were looking for a date for the big reunion. I was wondering if you might consider me. I thought it might be fun, and I truly am trustworthy.'

She looked surprised. 'You?'

'Why not? I'm not into date rape or anything like that, truly.'

She looked puzzled, but not concerned in any way. 'A boring old lady like me?'

'I just bet you're anything but boring. But I do have an ulterior motive, I'll admit. My partner and I are private investigators representing a cattleman named Monty Hook, and we're interested in any speculation that might help him out.'

'Monty Hook?' It was obvious she knew Hook.

'He was one of your students, I bet.'

'Why, he sure was.'

'As you know, a state cop was killed on Mr. Hook's land last week, and, of course, he wants to know who did it and why.' So I was embroidering a little. Well, why not?

Leiat Podebski looked concerned. She thought about my proposal for a moment.

I added quickly, 'I should tell you my redskin partner believes in something called the Great Hoop. In his way of looking at the world, all histories are circular, whether they're personal, a high-school class, or something larger. In the hoop lies the truth, he says.'

Podebski had a curious look on her face. 'You do have an unusual partner, Mr. Denson.'

'John, please. Yes, Willie is unusual, but if you think about it, he's probably right about the hoop business.'

'Has your friend Mr. Prettybird been reading Oswald Spengler, by any chance?'

I shook my head. 'Willie gets all his dope straight from the animal people.'

'The animal people?'

'He says the animal people created us, so we're made in their image. Sometimes, he says, I remind him of Turtle. I plod along, he says, and when there's danger, I pull my head in and assess the situation. When it's safe, I proceed with caution.'

'And Mr. Prettybird is what animal?'

'His friends all say he's Coyote, but if you ask him he won't confirm or deny it.

I've called him Toad, Carp, Skunk, and worse, and he never gets sore. Mr. Enigmatic. Right now he's on his way out to his pal's house, a Nez Percé who happens to be one of Monty Hook's top hands. That's how we got the job.'

Podebski laughed. 'Okay, you've got a deal, Mr. Denson. And I tell you what, if you can find a lady more your age, you go ahead and bring her on along. At my age, three is not a crowd I guarantee, but you never know. Maybe I can help you out.'

'You never know, indeed!'

'I'd be pleased to do anything for Monty. I know darn well he didn't kill any state cop.'

'What's a good time to pick you up?'

'Eight o'clock, say. We've got a lot of generations to cover.'

'Okay, how about seven o'clock Thursday? I'll spring for steaks at the Pheasant.'

'Done.'

'We'll have a good time,' I said, and we shook on it.

As Willie had suggested, I grabbed a tourist map for my drive to Bobcat Bill Kemiah's house.

7

It was the practice of large ranchers like
Monty Hook to lease or own one or more
spreads. Willie said Hook owned two
adjoining fenced ranges east of the lower
Imnaha River and south of the Snake
River; these were called the north spread
and the south spread. The cop's body had
been found on the north; Bobcat Bill
lived on the south. Hook's private range
was flanked on the east by Hells Canyon
National Recreation Area, and on the
west by BLM land he rented from
the government.

Following Willie Prettybird's crude
map to Bobcat Bill's place on Monty
Hook's south spread, I took State
Highway 350 east from Joseph; about
seven miles out, the highway intersected
Little Sheep Creek and angled northeast,
along the creek, for a twenty-mile run to
Imnaha.

It was a gorgeous day and a downhill

run, so the VW's air-cooled engine whirred with that delicious, purring sound that is impossible to describe but so dear to the hearts of VW lovers everywhere.

A cold VW engine sounds like bolts tumbling in a clothes drier; but when it's warmed up and on the open road — ahhhhhh! This low-tech, nonconsumerist's hum would have been appreciated by Henry David Thoreau; the classic Volkswagen repair book featured classic hippie drawings in the manner of R. Crumb. Any moron with simple tools could study the drawings and do everything from adjusting the dwell of the distributor to tuning the carburetor, and now there were VW graveyards at the edge of most cities where determined VW lovers scrounged for everything from doorknobs to dipsticks to rehab their beloved vehicles.

In fact, as I drove, I passed the time by imagining an entry in Thoreau's log — if the neighbors in his time had had automobiles mixed into the stew of earthly competition:

★ ★ ★

Walden Pond, July 12 . . . I adjusted the valves of my VW this morning. This has to be done when the engine is cold. When I finished, it ran so sweet it made me smile. As I was putting my tools away, the first of the Sunday drivers — escaped from the debilitating suburbs — circled the pond, the mothers and fathers showing their children that curious body of water, circled by cattails and yucky mud, of a sort they had previously seen only at a sanitary remove in movies or on television. They were driving a new Honda Accord, painted a currently fashionable metallic blue, cool and passionless. Thus encapsuled in comforting high tech, theirs is the soul of a new machine, which they are convinced they cannot do without, but which they cannot tune themselves, being always dependent on the expertise of others.

★ ★ ★

A couple of miles short of Imnaha, itself a hamlet of less than a thousand population,

I turned left on the road that followed Camp Creek, which flowed west to east, eventually emptying into the Imnaha River. Camp Creek Road, said Willie's crude map, led to Bobcat Bill's house on Monty Hook's south spread.

Imnaha, according to my tourist map, was on the edge of the Hells Canyon National Recreation Area, about twelve miles at its widest, which followed the Snake River from Payette, Idaho, to the Washington border, close to eighty miles to the north. Immediately east of this was the narrower Hells Canyon Wilderness, about four miles wide, ending at Doug Bar Camp, a couple of miles south of the spot where the Imnaha emptied into the Snake.

At Imnaha, I could have taken an all-day drive to Hat Point, 6,982 feet above the Snake. The East Rim of the canyon was 8,043 feet above the river; the best the Grand Canyon could muster was a sissy 6,000 feet above the Colorado River.

The private road to Hook's north spread, where Officer McAllister had been murdered, was north of Imnaha. There, an eight-mile-long rectangular stretch of private land lay on the west side of the Imnaha River and formed part of the western border of the Hells Canyon National Recreation Area.

Stopping several times to check my bearings, I eventually entered a meadow maybe a half mile long and a quarter of a mile wide and cut in half by a slow, meandering creek about ten feet wide.

Then I spotted the house in a stand of sugar pine on a small rise at the edge of the meadow. It was more than a line cabin now; thanks to the remodeling efforts of Bobcat Bill and his friends, it had been transformed into a small, elegantly simple house with a large chimney on one end, made from local stone, from which smoke now drifted. A shed on the opposite end was filled with firewood, tools, and a gas generator — this area being far beyond the ken of electrical hookups.

Two pickup trucks were parked in front of the cabin: the one Willie had borrowed in Enterprise and an old Dodge, once blue but now mottled with patches of rust-colored primer. This proletarian vehicle presumably belonged to Bobcat Bill.

The house itself was made of rough-hewn, weathered lumber, but it looked well insulated and cozy. Behind the house, two spotted Indian ponies, Appaloosas, roamed in a corral made of lodge-pole pine. I didn't know a whole lot about horses, but I could tell these animals were real beauties.

I thumped on the front door, and it was opened by a young Indian woman who had to have been less than five feet tall and probably no more than ninety pounds, soaking wet. She had huge brown eyes and a wonderful smile, showing dazzling white teeth. She was beautiful.

I inadvertently made a noise and licked my lips, feeling foolish as I did. 'I'm John Denson,' I said. 'I'm looking for my friend Willie Prettybird and Bobcat Bill Kemiah.'

She opened the door to let me in. 'You've come to the right place. We've been expecting you. I'm Lenora Kemiah,

Bobcat's daughter.'

I cleared my throat, hesitating. 'Beautiful horses out back.'

'Thank you,' she said.

From inside, Willie said, 'Well, don't just stand there, Dumsht. I bet you've seen a good-looking woman before.' He was grinning so wide I thought he was going to break his face.

So this was the reason Willie had been nagging me to come to Enterprise. I gave him a shut-the-fuck-up look.

Willie, amused, would have none of it. He had seen the look on my face, and he wasn't about to be denied his fun. He said, 'The lady won't bite. Come on in.'

I stepped inside, doing my best not to stare at Lenora Kemiah. What a little beauty!

Willie said, 'A person would think you just got out of prison.'

Lenora blushed and said, 'Oh, that's enough, Willie. You be quiet.'

'Tonto,' I said.

Willie said, 'And this is my good friend Bobcat Bill, Lenora's father, so watch your mouth.'

I shook the hand of an Indian in his late fifties who wasn't much larger than his daughter. He had a substantial beak and deep-set black eyes. His copper-colored skin was wrinkled and much tanned by the sun. He wore jeans, moccasins, and a blue cotton shirt. His long black hair was braided into a single pigtail, tied at the end with a scrap of red cloth.

Of course Willie Prettybird would have told Bobcat all about me, so Bobcat knew that I had sat in many times on Willie's mushroom-induced talks with the animal people. I was Willie's friend and partner, not a wide-eyed, brainless sap eager to believe anything because it seemed cool or fashionable. He seemed pleased that I had admired his daughter.

The small, cozy living room — furnished with well-used but comfortable furniture — was dominated by the large stone fireplace. Above it on a mantel of varnished knotty pine, was a clutter of trophies with golden figures atop golden ponies. Somebody was a horseman. Bobcat Bill, I wondered? Or daughter Lenora?

'Would you like a cup of coffee, Mr.

Denson?' she said.

'John,' I said.

'Oh, John, is it?' Willie said. He was pleased whenever I was attracted to an Indian woman, and couldn't stop himself from giving me the razz.

Now I gave Willie an aw-come-on-asshole frown, finding it hard to avoid looking into Lenora's large brown eyes as she removed a large, enameled percolator from the top of a cast-iron, wood-burning kitchen stove and poured me a large mug of coffee, which was strong and good. This wasn't just an old-fashioned stove, it was flat-out nineteenth century. My friend Thoreau would have approved.

Behind the stove was a tank that, I knew, contained hot water, which was produced by copper coils that lined the firebox of the stove. Lenora obviously cooked food on the stove, which also heated water and the kitchen.

Then I felt something pawing at my leg. I looked down at a baby, perhaps ten months old, on her hands and knees. She had dark brown hair that formed natural tubes of curls in the manner of Shirley

Temple. She grinned a huge grin, showing two diminutive teeth on top and two on the bottom.

I said, 'And this would be?'

'Jessica,' Lenora said.

I wondered where Jessica's father was.

Bobcat Bill, as though reading my mind, said, 'Jessica's father ran a log truck into the river over by Baker City while Lenora was still pregnant.'

'Oh, I'm sorry.'

Lenora said, 'Jessica and I will get out of your way so you can talk.' With that, she scooped up her daughter and disappeared into another room, a bedroom presumably, with a curtain for a door.

Bobcat Bill said, 'It's a terrible thing to say, I know, but the truth is that Lenora and little Jessica are better off the way things turned out. To my way of thinking, it's not much of a man who gets drunk and knocks women around.'

I was aware of Lenora watching from behind the curtain in the doorway. I said to Bobcat, 'You have a chance to poke around a little?'

Bobcat said, 'I took a quick look shortly after it happened. The sheriff and the state police were in there muddying things up, so Willie and I've got a lot of work ahead of us before we get 'em sorted out. You should have seen those cops — tromp, tromp, tromp. It's a wonder they ever learn anything.'

'What'd you find so far?'

Bobcat said, 'Well, I identified McAllister's prints. That was easy.'

'Where was this, exactly? You need to help me get my bearings before you tell me the rest of it.'

Bobcat said, 'We're talking about Monty's range north of here, closer to the Snake. We call that the north spread, and this the south. It's separated from this one by BLM land, where Monty also runs cattle.'

'Is the north spread also fenced?'

'Yes, it is. The way Monty sees it, what's his is his, and what's theirs is theirs. The south is the larger of the two spreads. The north's open country, with just two roads in and out, Monty's private one from the east, up the canyon wall overlooking the Imnaha, and Zumwalt Road that runs to the northeast from Enterprise and Joseph. The south's better for casual rustlers because there's more cattle here and more connecting roads. The more roads out, the less the risk of running into a cop. That's why I live here instead of the north spread.'

'How about poachers?'

Bobcat said, 'The best poaching territory is to the east of here in the Blues. Mulies in the foothills. Elk further back in the deep canyons. We're talking cattle country out here, not a lot in the way of cover, although you can occasionally spook a mulie sleeping it off in a draw. First-rate hunting for Huns and chukars, though.' By Huns, Willie meant Hungarian partridges; chukars too were partridges.

'Okay,' I said to Willie. 'Now I've got that straight, have you had a chance to take a look around this morning?'

Willie said, 'Bobcat and I took a quick look. McAllister was wearing state cop boots, which helped.'

'Mmmmmm,' I said.

Bobcat said, 'He was killed about a

quarter of a mile from where we spotted the first of Monty's sick cattle, which I found interesting.'

'Really?' I said.

Bobcat said, 'We found some mystery hoofprints from two horses near the infected cattle and the dead cop.'

'Two horses!' I looked at Willie. 'What now?'

'Now comes a little hard work,' Willie said. 'The state police and the communicable-disease people are just as curious about the hoofprints as we are. But they don't have the tracking skills, and they've got sense enough to know it.'

'Couldn't tell their ass from a hole in the ground,' Bobcat said.

Willie said, 'They might be able to bring in some hounds, but that would take time. They gave Bobcat and me anti-anthrax injections this morning.'

I said, 'Doesn't that stuff ordinarily take time to build up an immunity? Jesus! What if you still catch the disease?'

Willie said, 'Then they'll stab us with antianthrax serum. Somebody's got to do it, Dumsht.'

'They've got a serum, then?'

Bobcat said, 'They've got it, and they say it works well. You should ask Monty. They've given him a crash course on this shit.'

'When are they going to burn the diseased animals?'

Willie shrugged. 'Maybe as early as tomorrow. They haven't made up their minds. They've got the gates locked on both the east and west entrances, and we're supposed to keep this all to ourselves.'

Bobcat said, 'The disease people're supposed to tell Monty later today. What the dead cop has to do with this is still not clear.'

I said, 'If the prints near the body don't belong to rustlers or poachers, who, then?'

Bobcat shook his head. 'Fishermen, maybe. There's a nice creek on the north spread, and some guys use horses to visit isolated stretches of water.'

'But you don't think so.'

Bobcat said, 'The hoofprints were well away from the creek. What would a fisherman be doing that far from the creek?'

Willie said, 'But like I said, there's a lot of work to be done. If Bobcat and I really work at it, we might be able to find out what the riders were doing out there. Incidentally, there's a lot of traffic across the north spread — people wanting to look down on Hells Canyon, which is farther north. Monty has cattle guards at the entrances. He has gates, too, but he keeps them unlocked as a courtesy to fishermen and sightseers.'

Suddenly little Jessica, with Lenora close behind, made a break from the curtains, heading my way on her hands and knees with her huge grin, showing her new teeth. A person would have thought a grin that big would hurt her face. What a little sweetie!

I glanced up at her mother, who watched her daughter with pride and amusement.

Willie said, 'Say, Dumsht, speaking of working the town end of it, did you ask Leiat Podebski for a date to the Enterprise high school reunion?'

'Yes, I did. Monty Hook was a former student, and she said yes, of course.'

'Do you suppose she'd kick if you brought along Lenora?'

'I . . .'

'An old lady like that, what would she care?'

It had been Willie's idea for me to ask Leiat Podebski to the reunion. Had he been setting me up all along? Yes, of course, he had. He hadn't said a thing about Lenora, just sprung her on me. A woman with a child is not always the greatest attraction, but Willie had sense enough to know baby Jessica would hold up her end.

Lenora looked embarrassed. It had been a long time since I had met a woman capable of being embarrassed. I said, 'As a matter of fact, Leiat said at her age three's not a crowd, and if I could find someone closer to my age, I should bring her on along.'

Willie beamed. 'Well, then, why don't you ask Lenora?'

Lenora, still looking flushed, said, 'I graduated from a high school on the Nez

Percé reservation, Willie.'

Willie said, 'Aw, hell, that don't matter none. The two of you'd be escorting Leiat.'

Baby Jessica, still grinning her grin as though she agreed with Willie, tugged at my pant leg.

Willie said, 'You don't always have to be a dumsht, you know. You ought to try using your brains once in a while, wouldn't hurt.'

He was right. I sighed. My mouth was dry. I felt like a stupid high school kid. 'Willie has been my partner so long he can read my mind.'

'Mind?' Willie looked surprised.

I ignored him. 'The Leiat Podebski we're talking about is a retired English teacher at Enterprise. She's the manager of the Wallowa River Inn, where we're staying. I was wondering, uh, if you would like to go with us? I'm good for steaks at the Pheasant before the reunion stuff.'

Lenora gave Willie a look of remonstration. 'Oh, you, Willie Prettybird.'

I said, 'I bet Leiat would put you up so we wouldn't have to drive all the way back here in the middle of the night. She's a widow with the manager's apartment all to herself.'

Bobcat said quickly, 'Lenora doesn't have a damn thing to do, guaranteed. She spends all her time home here with Jessica. She cooks and cleans up after me and rides her horses and reads books. That's it. Do her good to get out, have some fun. Life goes on.'

Lenora said nothing. But I noted she didn't flat say no.

Bobcat said, 'Your sister Ellie will be pleased to take care of Jessica for you. If Jessica could say something more than 'Mama' and 'Bobcat,' she'd tell you to go have fun. Jessica likes Ellie. It'd be a break for her too. She'll have a good time with Ellie's dog.'

I said, 'Looks like Willie and your father aren't going to let us off the hook. Would you like to go to the reunion with Leiat and me? I can't imagine we won't have a good time.'

Lenora, still embarrassed, said, 'Sure. I'd love to go.'

Willie said, 'See? It was easy. All you

had to do was open your mouth. No problem.'

'Quiet, Tonto,' I said.

Willie said, 'You'd have been a fool if you hadn't opened your mouth. What do you say to your dependable old partner now?'

I momentarily closed my eyes. 'Thank you, Tonto.'

'What else?' He looked triumphant.

'I should have listened to you months ago.'

'There you go. And I was right not to tell you everything in advance, wasn't I? Better to let you be surprised.'

I sighed, but didn't say anything.

'Come on now.'

I said, 'All right. Okay. You were probably right about that as well.'

'Hah!' Willie looked pleased.

Glancing at the trophies on the mantel above the fireplace, I said to Lenora, 'I noticed the two Appaloosas in the corral out back. These aren't your trophies, by any chance? Are you the rider?'

Bobcat Bill burst out, 'You can't see 'em here, but she's got her own barrels and stakes set up out back so she can practice. Practice, practice, practice. Those ponies of hers earn their keep, believe me.'

Lenora bounced Jessica on her knee. 'Not much practicing lately on account of having to take care of Miss Smiley here.'

I walked to the mantel and examined the trophies — there were ten or twelve in all. Lenora Kemiah's name was engraved on the base of every one. She had won at Chief Joseph Days and at rodeos in Ukiah and the one held annually by the Umatilla Sage Riders.

Bobcat said, 'She keeps the second- and third-place trophies in boxes under her bed and in the closet. Pretty soon there won't be any room for us.'

I picked up one of the trophies, 'You once won at Pendleton?' The Round-Up was one of the traditional rodeo biggies long before television turned indoor sports arenas into rodeo grounds.

Pleased, Lenora nodded yes, she had won at Pendleton.

'You going to ride this year?'

She shook her head. 'When Jessica gets older, I'll get back to it. But it's fun riding out here, plus there's a good fishing stream. You want to go riding?'

'With somebody who won these?' I burst out laughing. 'I think I'll pass. Say, there's one more thing I need to know before I talk to Monty. I need to learn something about anthrax, how it spreads and so on. Does Monty have a vet or somebody who could help me out?'

Bobcat said, 'That'd be Doc Walsh, Monty's regular vet. When we found our first sick cows, we called Doc right off. He knew immediately what was ailing them and called the people at the state. He's been told to expect you, and he'll do anything he can to help.'

'How do I find Doc Walsh?'

'A couple of miles before you get to Joseph on your way back to Enterprise, keep your eyes peeled on the right-hand side of the road for a large green house and another building that serves as Doc's clinic. You can't miss 'em. He's got an orchard between the highway and his house and clinic. Just pull in and introduce yourself. If Doc's out on a call, his wife will beep him. There's no confusing Doc Walsh; he's bald and has a big, black beard. You can find Monty at the High Country Saloon tonight.'

8

Bobcat Bill had been right. It was impossible to miss Doc Walsh's place. There was the orchard between the highway and his large green house and his clinic. There was a trailer parked by the clinic. As I turned into the driveway, flanked by fruit trees on either side, I could hear the pathetic bawling of a cow. As I drew close to the clinic, I could see there were figures in the trailer struggling with an animal.

I parked my VW and walked around behind the trailer to see what was going on. Three cowboys in Levi's and denim jackets were subduing a stricken cow, while a bald, bearded figure in a Portland Trail Blazers T-shirt was poking a hose down its gullet. He made a final, vigorous jab and withdrew the hose. The cow, having had something knocked from her throat into her stomach, looked relieved and ceased her bawling.

Doc Walsh straightened, laughing. 'Those goddamn crab apples are the worst, I swear. Lucky you found me home, Ted, or you'd've had a dead cow on your hands.'

Ted, the oldest-looking of the three cowboys, was apparently the animal's owner. 'She was gettin' a little air, we could see that, so we just shoved her in the trailer and drove over here as fast as we could.'

The youngest cowboy, whose leg was wet with fresh cow manure, said, 'Goddamn it, would you look at this! She shit all over my leg.'

Ted burst out laughing. 'Aw, come on, son, what's a little cow shit among friends.'

The third cowboy, whom I took to be a hired hand, said, 'You can bet gettin' a crab apple poked out of its neck ain't no damn fun for a cow. I think I'd probably drop a load too.'

Doc Walsh said, 'If you don't get that stuff off before it dries, Bobby, it'll be like having your leg in a cast.'

'Yuch,' Bobby said. Bobby looked like a clone of Doc Walsh. Had to be his son. He jumped cheerfully off the back of the trailer and began scraping manure from his leg with a stick.

Ted said, 'Maybe next time she'll stay away from those damn crab apples. I'd cut that damn tree down, but Mary likes to make crab apple jelly. Bobby here can't get enough of it.'

Bobby, still scraping goo from his leg, said, 'It's good. Nothing like it.'

Walsh, seeing me, said, 'Be with you in a minute. Soon as I get these folks taken care of.'

'I'm in no hurry,' I said.

Walsh charged ten dollars for removing the apple; he wrote Ted a receipt, and then the cowboys were on their way with their relieved cow placidly chewing her cud as though nothing had happened. So she had almost choked on a crab apple. She could breathe now. Why all the fuss?

I said. 'My name's John Denson. Bobcat Bill Kemiah said you were the one to talk to about the anthrax infection on Monty Hook's land.'

Walsh sighed. 'The private detective. Monty and Bobcat said to expect you. Follow me up to the faucet so I can wash my hands, and I'll tell you what I can.'

'Sure,' I said. I followed Doc Walsh up to his clinic, and he squatted at a faucet poking out the end of the building. As he lathered his hands, he said, 'What is it you want to know, Mr. Denson?'

'It's hard to know where to start with something like this. Anthrax! Jesus!' I thought a moment, then said, 'I guess I need to know the answers to three basic, biggie questions: What is anthrax? How is it spread? What does it do to its victims?'

'You ask what anthrax is?' Walsh washed the soap from his hands, then stood and flipped the excess water off before he dried them on the thighs of his jeans. 'Anthrax is caused by *Bacillus anthracis*, which, under certain conditions, forms virulent, highly infectious spores that can contaminate soil or other materials for years, but it's ordinarily a disease of grass eaters. It's most commonly found in cattle, horses, sheep, goats, and mules. Deer and elk can catch it, also bison, as the Canadians found out. But other animals can catch it too, including humans. When pigs get it, or dogs and cats, it's ordinarily because they were fed contaminated meat. You see the danger here. A mule deer catches the disease. He dies. A coyote eats the mule deer. The coyote gets the disease. The coyote dies and its carcass is eaten by other eager eaters. They get the disease. So it goes, working its way through the food chain. What was the second question?'

I followed him to a hose reel by the corner of the building. I said, 'How does it spread? You might begin by telling me how animals other than cattle catch it?'

Walsh squatted by the reel and began winding in the hose. 'Sure. Humans can become infected by handling the hides, the hair, the wool, the meat, or the bones of a sick animal. People have caught anthrax by wearing spore-bearing fur and by using shaving brushes made from infected hair. You lather up and shave, and the next thing you know you got a face full of boils.' He smiled grimly.

'I take it cattle ordinarily catch it from grazing on infected soil.'

'That's right,' he said, winding the hose in with his right hand.

'Do you think that's how Monty Hook's cattle become infected? How did that happen?'

He stopped reeling momentarily. 'That's a puzzle I just can't figure, Mr. Denson. Monty bred the stock himself from the time they were calves. He didn't bring any cattle in from the outside, so it couldn't have been brought in that way. His animals are range fed. In the winter, he fed them alfalfa grown here in Wallowa County, and he was fattening them up for market on grain he bought from farmers in Umatilla County and southeastern Washington. An infection of anthrax was the last thing he had on his mind, believe me. I don't think it would have occurred to him in his wildest dreams.'

I said, 'Could the animals have caught it from infected alfalfa or grain?'

He continued reeling. 'They could have. But the state checked both sources and couldn't find a hint of anthrax spores.'

'Okay. Now for the fun part. Exactly what happens when you catch it?'

Walsh thought a moment, then said,

'The answer depends on the kind of anthrax involved. There are four varieties: extremely acute anthrax; acute anthrax; subacute, an internal form; and external anthrax, which is a chronic, local variety. If an animal gets the extremely acute or acute forms, it comes down with a high fever, followed by muscle spasms and problems with breathing and its heart. It trembles and staggers, various parts of its body can swell up with fluids, and it might bleed from the mouth or rectum, followed by convulsions which come just before it dies.'

'Whoa! How long does that all take?'

The hose was wound. Walsh secured the end in a metal clamp and rose, rubbing the small of his back. 'A day or two. The subacute form shows the same symptoms but takes three to five days to be lethal. Pigs and dogs ordinarily get chronic anthrax. Their mouths froth up with a bloody foam. Their throats swell up, and they have a hard time breathing. They usually die of suffocation. Say, do you like a good sour apple? I've got a tree of yellow transparents that's loaded right now. It's a cooking apple, but I just love to eat 'em.'

I said, 'Sure,' and followed him toward his orchard. 'What can you veterinarians do?'

'We quarantine the infected animals. That's been done with Monty's herd.' Walsh licked his lips. 'Thank God they weren't on BLM land. Monty and the ranchers renting federal land would have hell to pay then, what with all the pissing and moaning about private animals grazing on public property at cheapie rates. We'll have to kill the sick animals, of course, then burn their corpses and bury the ashes.'

We stopped at an older tree that was loaded with yellowish-green apples. Walsh picked himself one and so did I.

I bit *crr-accck* into my apple. It was so sour it made my mouth pucker, but it was good at the same time. I said, 'What happens to humans who become infected?'

Walsh cocked his head, looking concerned. 'No damn fun, I guarantee, Mr. Denson. It attacks your skin, your lungs, or your insides, depending on the variety you get. If you catch anthrax by handling something that's infected, you get pimples on your hands, arms, or neck. The pimples turn into carbuncles or pustules that have a black center of dead skin. The boils are followed by blood poisoning. If you don't get the proper antibiotics, you'll start looking like the guy in those Friday the thirteenth movies.'

'Shit, oh dear!'

Munching his apple, Walsh said, 'Woolsorter's anthrax comes from inhaling spores. It infects the lungs and is usually lethal. If you eat infected meat, you get intestinal anthrax, in which case the symptoms start with vomiting and severe diarrhea and go rapidly downhill from there.'

'Wonderful,' I said. I took another bite of apple.

'It's no damned fun, that's for sure. They say anthrax spread like the plague over southern Europe in the eighteenth and nineteenth centuries. But now if you're infected and act fast enough, we have antianthrax serums and antibiotics that will stop it cold. That's thanks to

Louis Pasteur, who developed the first vaccine in 1881.' Walsh, who had finished his apple, gave the core a toss, and picked himself another.

'That's a comfort.'

'By the way, this is one of the diseases the Pentagon used to have in its biological warfare stockpile, also the Soviet Union. Some of the American stockpile escaped from the Dugway Proving Ground in Utah and eliminated several hundred head of sheep. Can you imagine popping a bomb loaded with anthrax spores over an urban area? Sweet Jesus!'

'I thought they were supposed to have gotten rid of that crap.' I'd finished my apple and went for a second one too.

'They were, but who the hell knows for sure? Former KGB officers claim Russia still has it. And one of the people from Atlanta said a radical magazine was advertising anthrax spores a year ago, but when the feds moved in to bust them, they didn't find anything.'

'Well, what happened?'

Walsh, chewing, said, 'Nothing. The radicals said they were just funning, a right they say is guaranteed by the First Amendment.'

'I thought freedom of speech stopped at crying fire in a crowded theater.'

Walsh laughed. 'You're an old-fashioned man, Mr. Denson. Now, you know better than that.'

'I suppose so,' I said.

'Also, anthrax pops up once in a while like it did in Canada, but it usually goes away. You see a story in the newspapers every once in a while, an outbreak among squirrels or kangaroo mice. All you'd have to do is get your hands on a sick animal and grow your own culture. The buffalo in Canada are an example. Anyway, the state and federal people say we're supposed to keep the untidy news under our collective Stetson until they announce the quarantine and countywide vaccinations.'

'The taxpayers' dollars at work.'

Walsh said, 'They have the idea they're going to post quarantine signs and fly around with helicopters and still keep it secret.'

I said, 'They're always hopeful, I suppose. They have to try.'

Walsh said, 'These apples sometimes give people the green-apple quicksteps, but they never affect me.'

'What?' I said.

He grinned. 'I was just kidding. If you're lucky, nothing will happen.'

'Such a sense of humor.'

'You have to have a sense of humor to be a veterinarian. Have you talked to Monty yet?'

'I'm going to talk to him in the High Country Saloon tonight.'

Walsh clenched his jaw. 'Monty Hook is a good cattleman, but I guarantee, Mr. Denson, anthrax is deep, serious shit. If you need my help again, anytime, day or night, you just give me a call.'

9

The High Country Saloon had a wooden façade in the manner of nineteenth-century western saloons, or at least movie versions of Old West saloons. This facade featured a colorfully painted plywood cutout of a determined cowboy lassoing a steer.

The sidewalk in front of the High Country was cement, not board as in western movies, but the town fathers of Enterprise had not yet seen fit to install mechanical bandits; parking was not yet at such a premium in Enterprise as to require meters. In a town of 1,900, life was measured at a leisurely pace, not according to the dictates of a ticking parking meter. In more bustling towns, it was

> *tick, tick, tick . . .*
> *at my back, I always hear*
> *time's scootered metermaid hurrying*
>   *near*

In Enterprise residents turned off the key and enjoyed, plenty of time to admire the dresses in the window of Muldoon's or to have a beer in the High Country, confident there would be no surprises left under the windshield wiper in their absence.

The door to the High Country was not the swinging variety which cowboys from Tex Ritter to John Wayne had pushed open on their way to confront the villain, but it had class nevertheless. The heavy glass door had a proper knob of cut glass that had an antique look about it.

I stepped inside.

The bar was to the right of the entrance. Drinkers on the high wooden stools faced a handsome mirror etched on the corners with curls and loops and flowers. Above and on both sides of the old-fashioned mirror were stuffed heads of locally indigenous animals: an elk, a bear, a bobcat, a mountain lion, a mountain goat, and a mule deer with an incredible rack of horns. Tucked in among the antlers, glaring eyes, and snarling teeth were the inevitable signs prescribing proper behavior:

IN GOD WE TRUST, EVERYBODY
ELSE PAYS CASH.
WHOEVER ORDERS THE BEER, PAYS.
NO SHOES, NO SHIRTS, NO SERVICE.
WE RESERVE THE RIGHT TO REFUSE
SERVICE FOR ANY REASON THAT
MIGHT STRIKE OUR FANCY.
NO GUNFIGHTS, PREACHING THE
GOSPEL, OR PISSING ON THE FLOOR.
NO LADIES IN THE MEN'S ROOM
AND VICE VERSA.
TWENTY-FIVE-DOLLAR FINE FOR
EATING THE URINAL CRYSTAL.
GO AHEAD AND HIT ME, I NEED
THE MONEY.
THERE IS NO BEER IN HEAVEN, THAT'S
WHY WE DRINK IT HERE.
TWENTY-FIVE-CENT FINE FOR USING
THE F WORD AT THE BAR,
PROCEEDS TO THE ANNUAL PICNIC.

On one sign, a caricature Chinese in a coolie hat said:

I GIVE CLEDIT, YOU NO PAY, I GET SORE;
I DON'T GIVE CLEDIT,
YOU GET SORE; BETTAH YOU GET SORE.

The counter beneath the gorgeous mirror featured a clutter of jars of jerky, dill pickles, pickled eggs, bags of potato chips, and bags of beer nuts — that is, sugar-coated peanuts. The top of the bar, made of a rich red cherrywood, was pitted and scarred from years of use. At the base of the bar, a brass foot rail was provided for cowboys who liked to stand while they consumed their poison of choice; and for those gentlemen who carried a wad of tobacco between their cheek and gum, brass spittoons were scattered randomly by the foot rail.

A large bell hung from the ceiling; a rope from the bell nearly challenged visitors to pull it. A sign on the bell rope said RING THE BELL, BUY A ROUND FOR EVERYBODY AT THE BAR.

On the stool nearest the door, a fat man with bib overalls appeared to be sleeping as he sat staring at the bar, or perhaps he was just contemplating his Budweiser. Next to him a skinny man with moles on his face and a dirty blond ponytail shared a joke with his large-nosed, equally skinny girlfriend, who looked like Ichabod Crane in drag.

Two stools away from the skinny pair, two men in outsized cowboy hats were rolling dice from a leather dice cup and bull-shitting with the bartender, a good-looking redhead in her forties with an outsized but still shapely rump and breasts that poked out like the outlandish chromium bumpers of a 1950s Cadillac. Her black slacks were molded around her admirable rear end, and her white blouse was undone one button too low.

A large glass popcorn popper at the far end of the bar was flanked by a stack of wooden bowls; a sign above the machine said the popcorn was free and customers were to help themselves.

After the popcorn popper came a gap for the bartender to serve the tables, and beyond that, the High Country's kitchen.

The house toilets — marked by silhouettes of a snorting bull with big horns and a smiling cow, if that's an accurate adjective — came after the kitchen. A cow that had just relieved herself might smile; this cow had a goony, sated look about her, eyes rolled upward, that was meant to suggest, I think, that she had just been serviced by a snorting bull and was delighted by the experience. It was my guess that there was no shortage of Wallowa County gentlemen — some with shit on their jeans, others who had their mouths packed with odious tobacco — who regarded themselves as snorting bulls of skill and perseverance.

Opposite the snorting bull and smiling cow at the rear of the High Country, four cowboys played blackjack with a house dealer at one of two semicircular, felt-covered tables that were partitioned from the front of the saloon to give players a measure of privacy from the hurly-burly of drunks and glad-handers at the bar.

On the near side of the partition, opposite the bar, three young men in baseball caps played cricket at one of the two dart boards. I was relieved to see that in Enterprise the young men had the independence, if not common sense enough, to wear their caps with the bills pointed forward to keep the sun out of their eyes and the ultraviolet rays off their faces.

The wall between the dart players and the jukebox in the corner to the left of the entrance featured glass-covered photographs of cowboys herding, lassoing, and branding cattle, cowboys riding bucking broncs and Brahma bulls, and cowboys wrestling steers. These, I took it, were from the annual rodeo at Chief Joseph Days.

Between the wall and the bar was a confusion of round tables and chairs with old-fashioned, curved backs. If they weren't antiques, they were close to it.

From the jukebox in the corner, a singer lamented the departure of his wife, a lady named Lucille. The odious Lucille, it appeared, had left the poor bastard with four hungry kids to take care of, plus, as he groaned most pitiably, crops in the field. He sang with a deep-voiced moan or groan that bordered on pathos. Country opera was the music of choice in places like the High Country, where the songs nearly all emanated from passions, largely thwarted or gone awry, of the crotch.

The singer's complaint was that Lucille had picked a fine time to leave him. If

132

he sang like that all the time, it struck me that Lucille was not entirely to blame.

Halfway between the jukebox and the dart boards, beneath a photograph of a cowboy branding a calf — a large-bellied man in a cowboy hat and pale-green western togs — sat a slender man with a narrow face and high cheekbones. He was dressed in jeans, faded denim jacket, and tattered cowboy hat. A brass spittoon sat beside his left boot. When he saw me step through the door, he perked up, raised an eyebrow, and drooled a rope of brownish yuck into the container. The bottoms of his jeans were caked with dried manure. He said, 'John Denson?'

I hesitated. 'Mr. Hook?'

'That's me,' he said. He rose and extended a callused right hand. 'Well, you made it after all. Pleased to meetcha.' He waved at the sexy bartender. 'A round here, Lil.' To me he said, 'Where's your partner? Willie Prettybird, is it? I expected two of you.'

I sat down. 'Willie's staying with Bobcat Bill to help him sort out the prints of the cop who was killed and anybody else who might have been out there doing God knows what. He'll work your spread while I work town.'

'Bobcat said you two could cover all the bases.'

'Olden Dewlapp said your problems had to do with cows in addition to the dead cop.'

'Yep. I've got a little problem with my cows, that's a fact.'

In an effort to loosen him up, I said, 'For what it's worth, Willie claims he can talk to bear or squirrel if he wants, or crow, or woodpecker. Doesn't matter. Don't know if he can talk to cows, though. That's a fact.'

Hook laughed. 'Well, at least maybe I'll get my money's worth. The cop was found murdered damn near within spitting distance of where we found the first infected cattle.'

'Olden said the murder was giving you cause for concern. I take it you didn't kill him.'

'Oh, hell no, but the state police and the Wallowa County sheriff have been asking me questions all week. Same old questions, over and over.'

I waited for him to say something more, but he didn't. He just sat there looking thoughtful. He was worried. He would tell me what I needed to know in his own time and own way. No rush. Best for me to wait for the Big Worry like a hunter at a blind.

Then the bartender arrived with two sweating bottles of Henry Weinhard beer on a tray. She was sexy in an earthy, natural sort of way. While she no longer made men inadvertently lick their lips, it was obvious the snorting bulls liked watching her move. Whether it was bending over to retrieve a beer from the cooler or stretching up to pull a bag of peanuts from the rack, she must have been a whole lot of fun to have behind the bar, a form of spectator sport for the customers.

She popped the caps off the sweaty bottles of Henry Weinhard.

Hook, grinning as I watched her return to the bar, said, 'Scoop yourself up some popcorn if you like, Mr. Denson, and we'll talk. How many places you been in lately gave out free popcorn?'

I grinned. 'Not a whole lot. Popcorn sounds good.'

After I settled in with my bowl of popcorn, Hook said, 'Long drive up from Portland yesterday?'

'Willie and I both had TB by the time we got here, but we rubbed it out.' TB in the local lingo meant Tired Butt; I leaned to my left and gave my right cheek a squeeze by way of demonstration.

'What was it, about seven hours coming up?' One 'went down' to Portland, which was both downstream and downhill.

'Five hours to La Grande and another couple from there.'

Hook said, 'I bet you're wondering what an evil rancher like me would be doing calling on a couple of guys like you, champions of the environment and all that.'

'Olden Dewlapp claims your money spends too,' I said, still wondering why Hook was being questioned about the murder of the cop.

Hook looked amused.

I said, 'We brought along our fly roads. Besides, Willie claims he's got a couple of cousins who live up in these parts. He's got cousins all over the place, near as I can tell.'

Hook grinned. 'I bet he does.' He sighed. 'I've got a little problem that requires, uh . . . '

He was working up to it. I waited. I was in no hurry.

Hook glanced at the bar. He leaned over and released another stream of brownish goo into the spittoon, which was at least a third full. 'But then, I don't suppose it'd be smart to go into the details in a place like this. Lil's got a pair of ears on her that'd put a jackrabbit to shame. Got nothing better to do than to listen to gossip all day.'

'Lil?'

'The bartender with the big uh-huhs and good-looking oh-ho.'

'Some bartender!'

'She's got all the necessary gear.'

'She does indeed,' I said. 'Both quantity and quality, it appears.'

Hook scooped up a handful of popcorn and munched, his face serious. 'There are times, if a man's got a particular problem that could become a public issue, which I suspect is the case here, when it's better to have things checked out by someone with an independent imagination. Helps calm down the assholes. Do you see what I'm getting at?'

'I think so,' I said.

'Also, you had Bobcat Bill Kemiah pressing your case.' He took a swig of Henry Weinhard. 'I got to have your word that this conversation stops here. Olden Dewlapp and Bobcat Bill both assured me that you two can be trusted to keep your mouths shut. I'm counting on that.'

I said, 'A client's business is his own. The courts in the state of Oregon will back us on that one. If Willie and I can't keep our mouths shut, we're out of business.'

'A man's got a right to look into a problem without reporters on hand to record every fart.'

When the good-looking Lil brought us another round, she said, 'You been telling

your friend about all your teepee creepin',
Monty?' 'Teepee creepin' ' was the local
slang for going to bed with an Indian
woman.

Hook grinned, but didn't deny it.

Lil said dryly, 'He's one-quarter Cherokee, which accounts for his cheekbones,
and he's got a Nez Percé cowboy and his
daughter living in one of his line shacks,
so he thinks he's obliged to chase after
every squaw from here to Canada.'

Hook drooled another glob in the
spittoon. 'Sheee-it, Lil, when're you ever
gonna learn to hold that mouth of yours?
Flaps like a shutter banging in the wind.'

Lil rolled her eyes.

'Don't forget all the squaws I laid in
Idaho and Montana,' Hook said. 'Must've
been hundreds of'em. Thousands even.
Got little Hooks running all over the
place.'

Lil said, 'They're starting to call him
squaw man.'

I laughed. 'My partner's a Cowlitz.
He's done a little teepee-creepin' in his
time. If he were here, he'd say it speaks
well of Monty. Superior taste in women,

begging your pardon.'

Lil grinned. 'I suspect it's all talk, to tell the truth. If Monty actually bedded anyone down it'd be a big deal for him. If he claims he's getting any action other than sheep, I wouldn't believe him.'

'I see.'

When she left, I said, 'Well, Lil seems to know all about your coming and going. In whose teepee have you been creeping?'

'A Umatilla named Rachel, off and on for the last couple of years. She works as a waitress over in Elgin.' Hook took a drink of beer, looking thoughtful. 'Mostly off for the last six months, though, I have to admit. Still annoys hell out of Lil.'

'A woman's a woman, I suppose. Hard for us to understand.'

'The Nez Percé she's talking about is Bobcat Bill.'

'I figured as much,' I said.

Hook said, 'Bobcat wouldn't hear of me hiring anybody other than you and Willie Prettybird. Willie did this. Willie did that. Finally, I said, all right, already, and phoned Olden Dewlapp.'

'A good man, Bobcat Bill.'

'He's been working for me going on six years now. I really don't have a foreman in the strictest sense of the word. Bobcat's the closest thing I've got. He's my main man, anyhow.'

'Lil said he lives in a line shack. I was out there with Willie earlier today. It's a hell of a lot more than a line cabin now. Shake roof. Beautiful stone fireplace. And a wonderful old cast-iron wood stove that has to be a working antique.'

'Bobcat and his friends fixed it up right, didn't they? No electricity or phone, but Bobcat claims not to care. I wanted someone out there to keep an eye out for rustlers.'

'Rustlers?'

'When you've got isolation like I do in some parts of my spread, it's no big chore for a guy with a four-wheeler and a high-powered rifle to knock down a six- or eight-hundred-dollar steer and make off in the middle of the night with nobody the wiser. You met Bobcat's daughter, Lenora, I take it.'

'Oh, yes. I met her.' I refrained from licking my lips.

Hook laughed, as though he'd read my mind. 'Now, there's someone whose teepee I'd most definitely like to creep.'

'She takes your breath away, I have to admit.'

Hook said, 'If you'll excuse me, I gotta recirculate some of this beer in the urinal, or Lil will come over complaining she's run out.' He got up and headed for the room with the snorting bull. As he did, he swung by the bar and yanked the bell rope several times, ringing the bell loudly. 'For the cardplayers in the back too,' he told Lil.

Lil looked amazed. Looking at our table, she said loudly, 'The last time Monty Hook rang that bell was two years ago, when that little blonde in the tight jeans was over from La Grande. Remember her? Oooh la la. Twitch, twitch, twitch.'

'Bull too,' Hook said, and strode to the back of the High Country.

On the way back from the toilet, Hook gave Lil a look of approbation, and gave the bell rope another hard yank.

After he had sat down, Monty Hook said, 'To answer the question you haven't asked yet, Mr. Denson, the reason I'm being questioned by the police about the murder of the cop is that Lil and I have had a thing going since high school, and everybody and his dog knows it. As it turns out, the cop who was murdered was her current boyfriend.'

'He was?'

'I'm afraid so. That comes under the classification of motive, I suppose, plus he was killed on my property. Olden Dewlapp says at the least it doesn't look good.'

'You've had a crush on her since high school?'

'Yep!' Hook took a swig of beer.

'You want to tell me about that?'

'Oh, it's one of those adolescent infatuations that won't go away, I suppose. But it doesn't look like we're ever going to settle in together and live happily ever after. Lil and I have come to terms with that. We've been able to eyeball and razz one another over the years without having the edge dulled by the reality of actually living together. You know how that works. A fuck now and then is a real thrill, but after a few hundred times it somehow loses its edge. Maybe we even like it better this way, who knows? More exciting.' Hook took a deep breath and let it out with puffed cheeks. He cleared his throat.

'If your relationship with her is the way you say it is, why would you want to murder her boyfriend?'

Hook bit his lower lip. 'I still didn't like that damned cop. Lil was married and divorced, same as me. Hell, we still had a thing going when we were both married. After her divorce she had boyfriends off and on, but none of them ever bothered me. But there was something about that son of a bitch that just plain pissed me off, and everybody knew it. I can't tell you what it was I found so annoying, exactly.'

'Worse, I suppose you made no secret of it.'

Hook frowned. 'Oh, hell no. I used to come here and make fun of the silly asshole. A cop. I guess it was just too much to have Lil hanging around with a cop. But I was also just teasing Lil. I bet there's not a regular customer in here who didn't give her the razz about having

144

a cop boyfriend one time or another.'

'Does Lil think you killed him?'

'Lil knows me better than that. She always gives me a ration when I come in here. It's her way of expressing affection. If she didn't give me hell, I'd know she was truly pissed. When she gives me the old silent treatment is when I start looking for cover.'

'Did she truly love the cop, do you think?'

'Love?' Hook raised an eyebrow. 'I don't suppose it was like in the movies or pop music. No mooning or moping around. None of us are kids anymore, face it.'

'You know what I mean.'

Hook closed his eyes, then opened them. 'Oh, hell, I suppose she liked the guy well enough. Maybe that was what I found so annoying. She was shacked up with him and she obviously liked him. Lil's never been one to jump in bed with a guy just because he's got a functional dick. But cops lead dangerous lives sometimes, and somebody killed him, and they buried him. Life goes on. We're both adult enough to know that.'

'Did you kill him?' I watched his eyes.

Hook looked indignant. 'No, sir, I did not. It's true that I'm not overly remorseful that he's not hanging around Lil any longer, but I didn't murder him.'

I believed him. If he was a liar he was a good one, as Lil had said. 'And you want Willie and me to find out who did kill him?

Hook gave me a wry grin. 'I'd be much obliged, Mr. Denson, and that's a fact. Also, there's the matter of my infected cattle. I have a strong suspicion the two are somehow connected.'

I didn't think it took Sherlock Holmes to have a strong suspicion about that. I said nothing.

Hook, glancing at the bar, lowered his voice. 'Looks like I'll have to eliminate every animal on my Imnaha spread.'

'Really? When will that be?'

Still looking at the bar, a vague, faraway look in his eyes, he said, 'Tomorrow afternoon, looks like.' Monty Hook looked grim. He drooled a brown rope into the spittoon.

10

Reporting an infection of anthrax among the cattle of a rancher in northeastern Oregon was the equivalent of announcing the arrival of the black death in medieval Europe. How to address the subject with the man who owned the cattle? I said, 'I talked to Doc Walsh on my way back from Bobcat Bill's this afternoon. Asked him about anthrax and what it does. Infection down from Canada, do you think? On the news the other day, Willie and I saw them shooting bison in Alberta Province.'

Hook shook his head. 'That's the strange part.'

'Oh?'

'As Doc Walsh probably told you, nobody can figure out how they came to be infected. These cattle were grazing on private, fenced range. I didn't bring them in from the outside.' He grimaced. 'They tell me I can't use the range where my

147

cattle were infected until state inspectors say it's okay. That's not weeks or months. Years.'

'In effect putting you out of business.'

'Not out of business entirely, but I'll have to run a reduced operation until I can use that range again. Thank God I had a fence splitting the north end from the south. I also run stock on leased private range and on rented BLM land. If the environmentalists push me off the BLM land, and half the range I own can't be used because it's still infected with anthrax, it'll be tough. I just don't have the money to run around buying rangeland like used cars.' He looped a drool of tobacco into the spittoon. 'No more cattle king of Wallowa County for me.'

'Working your way back will give you something to look forward to.'

'A wonderful challenge. Right. Incidentally, they can vaccinate animals so anthrax won't spread, which is what they'll be doing here in Wallowa County. I'm going to have Doc Walsh vaccinate all the good cattle I have left, as well as my horses.'

I said, 'Mule deer and elk can simply

jump over a barbed-wire fence. That must be worrisome to the infectious-disease people.'

Hook raised an eyebrow. 'They can for a fact, although the north end isn't the best for game. But the possibility is still worrisome.'

'Doc Walsh said you have to kill them and burn their bodies. When is that wonderful sport going to take place?'

'Tomorrow afternoon.'

'Tomorrow?'

'That's right. A pyre of prime beef. I had to buy the entire load of one of those trucks that delivers gasoline to service stations. We'll soak 'em down with that, then I'll set it off with a flare gun.'

'Shit!'

Hook smiled grimly. 'We'll have to be careful, but we'll do it the right way. There's an established drill we're supposed to go through, with mandatory safety checkpoints all along the way. But if any of us become infected, we'll have to move quickly. We can't let the symptoms go too far or they'll get out of hand. The state people are moving serum into the local hospitals just in case. All this will be on the news tomorrow when they hold a press conference.'

I said, 'Let the games begin!' I whistled the familiar opening bars of the circus classic 'Entrance of the Gladiators,' used ordinarily to accompany the entrance of elephants, clowns, fat ladies, and two-headed men.

Hook looked disgusted. 'In addition to a detective, you're a comic. Wonderful.'

'Which again leads to a question Doc Walsh couldn't answer this afternoon. How did your cattle come to be infected on a fenced range close to four hundred miles south of the outbreak in Canada? There haven't been any reports of anthrax in eastern Washington or northern Idaho, that I know of. Or western Montana. Do you think your cattle were deliberately infected?'

'The thought has occurred to me,' he said.

'How?'

Hook poured more Henry Weinhard into his mug and signaled to Lil for two more. 'Doc Walsh tells me an undergraduate science student with access to elementary lab equipment could do it.' His jaw tightened, then he added, 'But judging from what the state people and Doc Walsh told me, they'd better be pretty damned careful.'

'Do those hoofprints near the dead cop have anything to do with it, do you think?'

'Bobcat and your friend Willie are going to run them down. We'll see.'

'I don't know about Bobcat, but Willie can follow spoor like nobody's business. He's real, real good.'

'By the way, the idea of the press conference tomorrow morning is so state vets and the disease people from Atlanta can dispel rumor by giving the facts and answering questions. They're setting up numbers where people can call for information and all that shit. They're gonna keep people calm about an outbreak of anthrax. Sure, sure.' Monty Hook looked like he was about to explode with suppressed rage.

Just then a lean, good-looking cowboy in his midtwenties, who must have been six foot five if he was an inch, stepped through the door accompanied by a pneumatic-appearing woman who, judging by her too-tight jeans, needed to buy larger clothes. Just like in the old cowboy song, the cowboy's spurs went jingle, jangle, jingle, and as they passed our table; the woman — who had a well-used look about her and was maybe a couple of years older than her swaggering boyfriend — displayed a remarkable ass. Restrained as it was by her jeans, her butt hopped like a bag full of coked-up squirrels.

Watching them, Hook muttered, 'Well, I'll be goddamned if this isn't my day. I'll tell you.'

Lil turned on the television set above the bar, at the same time calling, 'Is it true what they're saying on the radio, Monty?'

Hook clenched his jaw. 'What is it they're saying on the radio, Lil?'

'Roy and Opal say they heard on the news coming over that you've got quarantine signs posted on your north spread and helicopters flying around. There's speculation you got a bunch of

152

your cattle down with some kind of disease.'

Opal and Roy, apparently the newcomers, had settled in at the bar.

Hook took a deep breath.

'Is it true, Monty?' Lil had real concern on her face.

Hook grimaced, his look telling her yes, it was true. He said, 'You want to turn that shit off so a person can think, Lil. Ain't no ball game or fights on that I can see. This is a bar, for Christ's sake. A man likes to drink in peace once in a while.'

Opal, her hip at an angle the better to display her outsized rump, said, 'You might as well tell the truth, Monty. Can't hide that many sick animals forever.' She had a triumphant look on her face.

The tall cowboy, Roy, sucked air between his teeth as though he found the entire subject boring in the extreme. Ho hum. 'Quarantine? Helicopters? You got a little anthrax on your hands, Monty?'

Hook's face turned hard. He unloaded a wad into the spittoon. He said, 'I gotta couple of cows down with something, that's a fact. On my north spread, not the south. More cows on the south.'

Roy said, 'You got plenty of cows on the north. How many sick?'

'A few.'

'Anthrax? If it's anthrax, they'll have to take your whole herd under.'

'We're having them checked out. If it's anthrax, the state will vaccinate everybody's animals, don't worry.'

'What the hell else your cows got if it ain't anthrax?' Roy said. 'Mumps?' He looked amused. 'Or maybe they got the chicken pox or measles.'

'A few sick cows could mean anything, now, couldn't it? A lot of things can happen to a man's cows if he doesn't keep his eye on them. Isn't that right? Guy like you oughta know better than to ask a question like that.'

Roy's face tightened. 'If it's anthrax, you can't just rub 'em down with bag balm or run a tube down their gullets to knock out a stuck apple. Gonna have to take all them high-priced beeves down, Monty. Won't that be something?' He leaned his elbow on the bar, his long body at a rakish angle.

Hook looked at him mildly. 'There's a hell of a lot more beeves on the Flying J that're doing just fine, thank you.'

I bit my lower lip, remembering the Canadians burning the corpses of infected bison. This was a total disaster for Monty Hook. For the moment, there was nothing he could do but play dumb and do what the state Department of Public Health told him to do.

'Just like the buffalo up in Canada,' Roy said. 'Did you see that shit on TV? The Canadians having to shoot all those animals like that. Jesus!'

Hook, with an edge to his voice, said, 'I told you we don't know what's wrong with 'em yet.'

'Anthrax. Jesus!' Roy said. 'You and all your hotshot rancher pals. Down the toilet.'

'It's fenced range. I told you, we don't know what's wrong with them yet. If I thought it'd help, I'd fly Jesus Christ himself in this afternoon.'

Roy said, 'Maybe you ought to have the Reverend Bonnerton say a prayer for you at his big Christian environmental revival.

155

Maybe that'd make 'em all well again.'

'Shit, too,' Hook said.

'Say, I bet Thad Bonnerton'll be coming to the high school reunion to do a little showing off. Maybe you can ask him then.'

'More likely you need help from the Lord, Roy.' Hook let fly into the spittoon.

Lowering his voice, Monty Hook said to me, 'I wonder if Bonnerton will try to talk Lil into opening one of those stupid love letters.'

'Love letters? What love letters?'

'He's been writing her sophomoric poems since high school.'

'Who has? The Reverend Thaddeus Hamm Bonnerton? Old Ham Bone?'

Hook nodded. 'I suppose he thinks they're romantic, but that's not how they come off to me.' He looked disgusted. 'It's beyond me how a man could be so pathetic as to actually put shit like that on paper.'

I found that amazing. Bonnerton writing love letters to Lil. 'Did he sign them?'

'No.'

I wanted to know more about those letters. I was trying to unsnarl a tangle of murder and anthrax; under those circumstances, it was a foolish detective indeed who ignored love letters from an evangelical preacher to the dead cop's girlfriend. 'If the writer didn't sign them, you really don't know who they're from, do you? They could be from anybody.'

'Well, I guess they're from Bonnerton. They're typewritten and unsigned, but they've been mailed from all over the country. Who else but Bonnerton? He travels around giving his jackass revivals.'

'Good question. Has Lil saved them?'

'Oh, yeah. Keeps 'em in a shoebox.'

How many does she have?'

'Oh, hell, I don't know. She's been getting one a year since the midseventies.'

'Were they typed or run through a printer from a computer? Sometimes it's tough to tell the difference between an electric typewriter and a computer printer, but if it's a manual typewriter the letters would likely be uneven.'

'Computer printer, looks like. At least, the letters are all evenly struck.'

'You say they're mailed from various parts of the country. From where, exactly?'

Monty thought about that. 'She said one came from Louisiana, I remember. One was sent from southern Florida. All over. I've got a copy of one from Georgia.'

'Who does she think has been sending them?'

'I asked her that, but she won't say. I get the feeling she knows damn well who sent them, but she's not saying. Won't even give me a hint.'

'No? Not even to you?'

'She says poetry doesn't hurt anything. Her mysterious correspondent has a right to write it if he wants. So what if he's in love with her? He's not doing her any harm with poetry, she says. She's flattered, I think, which is why she showed a couple to me. I wouldn't be telling you except that the body of her boyfriend was found on my north spread. Under the circumstances, I think she'd understand.'

'But you're not going to tell her.'

'What Lil don't know can't piss her off, can it?'

'Have you asked her specifically if it was Bonnerton?'

'I've asked her a couple times, but she won't answer. She's adamant about not giving me a hint. But if it's not Bonnerton, it has to be somebody else, doesn't it?'

I said, 'But it's no secret Bonnerton was stuck on her when you were in high school?'

'You should have seen him, pathetic bastard. The whole town's been razzing Lil ever since Bonnerton became a famous preacher. I got a copy of one of the poems if you want to see it.'

I said, 'Like you say, the dead cop was Lil's boyfriend. You bet I want to see one. Can you photocopy the one you have the first chance you get? You can always have somebody drop it off at the Wallowa River Inn. The old lady at the office knows me. I'm in unit six.'

'That'd be Leiat Podebski.'

'The English teacher,' I said.

Hook smiled. 'Don't ever use the word 'hopefully' around Leiat Podebski unless you know what you're doing.'

At the bar, Roy said, 'Maybe Lil could ask Bonnerton to pray for you, Monty. How about that, Lil? Surely you can help out an old pal. He's going to be holding one of his environmental revivals. That's the perfect time to do a little prayin' for some beeves stricken with anthrax. It'd have to be a pretty low-down preacher who'd turn down a request for something like that. All you'd have to do is bat your eyes, and he'd do anything you asked.'

Lil narrowed her eyes. 'That'll be enough of that, Roy.'

I said, 'Surely she wouldn't have told an asshole like Roy about the poetry?'

'Childress?' Hook laughed derisively. 'Oh, hell no. Like I say, as far as I know, I'm the only one she's showed them to.'

Roy, who was not about to be stopped, said, too loudly, 'I suppose praying is the only thing you can do short of shooting all those high-priced beeves, eh, Monty? Having fun with your trusty Buntline, are you? My, my!'

Hook gave him a look through

narrowed eyes, drooling an odious dollop in the spittoon at the same time. 'More fun than nutting skunks.'

'Someday you're going to break your wrist playing with that thing.'

'Better than wearing it out jerking off,' Hook said.

'Hey!' Lil said.

I said, 'You own a Texas Buntline?'

Hook grinned crookedly. 'Forty-four magnum with an eighteen-inch barrel. Big enough to coldcock a bull elk and then some.'

'An eighteen-inch barrel?'

'Fuckin' thing weighs three and a half pounds.' He grinned wickedly. 'I used to carry it around in a rack in my pickup like guys do rifles.'

Roy said, 'They say a man with a little pecker has to make up for it some way.'

Lil glared at him. 'Hey, hey! None of this is very damned funny. If we do have anthrax in Wallowa County, we're all in trouble.'

Eyeing Roy, Hook took out a packet of Copenhagen and repacked his cheek with a brown-stained forefinger.

Roy said, 'Anthrax might put Monty Hook out of business, that's a fact. Now, wouldn't that be something? What on earth would we all do without Monty Hook, king shit of Wallowa County, strutting around spitting everywhere?'

Hook's chair scraped on the floor. He clenched his teeth.

Lil narrowed her eyes. 'You want to order something, then order it, Roy. Everybody in here earns their living off cattle.'

'Except for good-looking Roy Childress, man who loves to eat other people's steaks,' Hook said.

I asked, 'What do you mean, eating other people's steaks?'

Monty Hook took a swig of Henry Weinhard and raised an eyebrow. 'Childress used to work for me until a couple of years ago. He wasn't a bad hand, I didn't think, until Bobcat Bill and I caught him rustling cattle on my south spread. Turned out the snake-eyed son of a bitch and a partner were cutting them up over in Walla Walla.'

'What did you do?'

Hook said, 'Why, we gave the evidence we'd collected to the Wallowa County sheriff. What else? He was convicted and spent six well-deserved months in jail. If he had any brains, he'd be playing with them. Guys like him are one reason I had Bobcat Bill fix up the line cabin on my south spread so he could move in with his daughter.'

'I guess that answers my question.'

At the bar, Childress, looking at Hook sideways, mumbled something unintelligible.

'Easy, easy, both of you,' Lil said.

Childress sucked air between his two front teeth. 'I reckon you got insurance on them beeves, right, Monty? Something like this happens, you need insurance so it doesn't wipe you out. A man like yourself is always prepared, president of the cattlemen's association and all. Going on TV to defend us all.'

Hook started to get out of his chair.

'Be cool. Be cool,' I said. For Hook to take on Childress minus his Buntline looked like a dubious proposition to me. Childress had to be a full twenty years younger than Hook and looked like he could play tight end in the NFL.

Hook stayed put. He said, too loud, pretending to talk to me, 'You know, a kid down by Imnaha told us he saw a cowboy fuckin' our cows in the butt a few months ago. Tall, good-looking guy with fancy spurs on his boots, he said. At first we didn't think much about it. We thought hell, let the pervert have his fun if he wants, a little goose in the rump won't hurt the cattle any. Now we're speculatin' our animals might have come down with AIDS.'

Childress shifted on the barstool.

Watching him out of the corner of his eye, Hook said, 'Got a guy in checking their blood right now for HIV. That could very well be our problem. A sicko fucking cows in the ass! Can you imagine that?'

Lil said, 'Hey, hey! You guys keep it up and all of you are out of here. I'll call Bubba and have him put the bum's rush on you. I mean it.'

Everybody laughed at that, and Opal squeezed Childress's elbow to get him to behave.

'Cocksucker,' Hook muttered.

Roy said, 'We'll have a couple of Coors and a pair of them cheeseburgers of yours, Lil. And some french fries, lotsa ketchup.'

Hook was seething. 'You'd think he was ordering in the Ritz,' he muttered.

'Who the hell's Bubba?' I said.

'Bubba Tubig. Fatso town cop. He couldn't put the bum's rush on a paraplegic, much less Roy Childress.'

'I see.'

Hook said, 'On second thought, Lil, why don't you turn on the news so I can find out what's supposed to have happened to me. Hell, ain't no reporter talked to me yet. Talked to my help. They're my cattle, dammit; the least they could do is ask me what happened, don't you think?'

Lil turned on the tube, and there was the Reverend Thaddeus Hamm Bonnerton in his ubiquitous fancy suit, allowing as how, yes, he had arrived in Enterprise, Oregon, having just heard there was an infection of anthrax among the cattle in that part of the state. Christ's lovely earth was being polluted and fouled; Enterprise was a good place to have a Christian environmental revival.

'My father was a preacher at the Baptist church here from 1964 through 1969, when he was transferred to a church in Oklahoma. I was a box boy in the Food City store here. It's like a homecoming, in a way.'

'You graduated from Enterprise High School?' The reporter already knew he had. The question was for her dumbo viewers.

Hook said, 'They had this insufferable prick on the tube last night boxing groceries and telling us the same shit. Are we going to have to watch him every damn night of the week?'

On the tube, Bonnerton smiled, 'Yes, I did. Class of '68.'

'Are you going to the all-school reunion tomorrow night?'

'Why, I sure am. See all my former schoolmates. I wouldn't miss it for anything. I've got a little warm-up revival Friday morning to get the kinks worked out for the televised main event on Sunday afternoon after the rodeo finals. In between, I'm going to watch all the action I can. You know, we all appreciate the sport down our way. We hold the national rodeo finals in Oklahoma City. The way I remember it, Chief Joseph draws some pretty fair cowboys.'

'Can you tell us what you know about the report of an outbreak of anthrax in Wallowa County? It hasn't been officially confirmed.'

The righteous Bonnerton, a microphone thrust in front of his face, said, 'As I understand it, this man Monty Hook has got tens of thousands of cattle eating public land to the dirt while the deer and elk starve. Now they're infected with anthrax, threatening all of God's animals. This is a price of sin that we refuse to accept.'

Hook's mouth fell open in astonishment. 'Tens of thousands of head! Jesus Christ, will you listen to that shit? Tens of thousands! He must be watching old John Ford movies. Don't I fucking wish!'

'Mr. Big,' Roy muttered.

'The price of sin,' Hook growled. 'It's

been so damn long since I've done any real sinning, I think I forgot how.'

'Shush now,' Lil said.

Bonnerton said, 'Now, we're told, this same rancher, Monty Hook, wants to run his cattle in a national recreation area.'

Hook said, 'I do? Who the fuck says so? Is this guy allowed to say anything he wants just because he's a goddamn preacher? What the hell's going on, anyway?'

On the tube, Bonnerton said, 'In public parks! Yes! Pretty soon we'll have diseased cattle mingling with the deer and elk in the Eagle Cap Wilderness Area, spreading their sickness as they go, casually destroying the natural cover and relieving themselves in campsites and fishing streams. This is the sweet bosom of Christ, and we're using it for a toilet.'

Monty Hook shouted, 'Why, that lying cocksucker! Bible-quoting motherfucker!' Hook was beside himself with rage.

11

The private road from the highway following the Imnaha River to Monty Hook's Flying J spread was cut out of the left-hand side of the narrow gorge carved by the Imnaha as it wound its way to join the Snake River in lower Hells Canyon.

At this point, the gorge cut by the Imnaha was only a few degrees shy of being a vertical drop. From the plateau to the west of the river — where the slaughter of afflicted cattle was to take place — the river, about four hundred yards below us, looked about the size of a narrow shoelace or fat string.

I couldn't stand on the edge and look down with a flutter in my stomach. I wouldn't do it on my knees, even. On my belly, maybe, except for the embarrassment of it all. The way evolutionary biologists saw it, I knew, was that those of our ancestors who were indifferent to the dangers of height didn't live long enough to beget similarly — might I add stupidly — indifferent offspring; the fear of height, following the same sensible logic as the fear of snakes, was part of our genetic inheritance, with the result that evil snakes and endless falls populated both our dreams and literature. But try to tell that to a he-man cowboy in Wallowa County.

There were too many state and federal people involved for the scheduled slaughter of infected cattle to remain secret. To the telephone inquiries that followed the inevitable leaks, Hook had instructed his housekeeper to reply that the killing would begin at two P.M.

At the same time, Hook told Bobcat Bill Kemiah and Willie Prettybird and his ranch hands to be ready to shoot beeves at eleven o'clock.

There were two ways for the media troup to get to Hook's north spread. The long way was to take Zumwalt Road north from Joseph past Finley Buttes. The short way was to follow the Imnaha north, then cut up the side of the canyon to the top of the plateau.

The radio was filled with excited chatter about the pending slaughter of anthrax-infected cattle. By midmorning the state had released details of what was happening. Now, at eleven o'clock, Bobcat Bill Kamiah was supervising the hunting down and destruction of infected livestock. The animals were being shot from helicopters, which then lifted the corpses and flew them back to the burial pit scooped out by bulldozer. Later in the day, the corpses would be burned and their ashes buried.

Wallowa County ranchers were told by the radio that antianthrax vaccine was available for their cattle, which would be inspected by state veterinarians. They said Hook's infected cattle were on quarantined, fenced range, and there was little chance that the disease would spread. However, in the routine interest of safety, anybody who had recently driven through Hook's property on their way to one of the Hells Canyon overlooks should check into the hospital at Enterprise for a free examination and antianthrax serum if necessary. Anybody who had been through the property and now had a fever and skin lesions should report to the hospital immediately; antianthrax serum was highly effective and would stop an infection cold.

Listening to this on the radio, Hook and I, followed by two Oregon State policemen in a white pickup, drove down the steep road above the Imnaha River to meet the expected media visitors. The people's voyeurs, Hook called them. The top of the road was the most steep, but going down wasn't so bad, because the driver, Hook, was next to the near-vertical drop; the passenger, me, got the side of the gorge.

The road leveled out somewhat near the bottom of the gorge where it came to a spring. There the road crossed a cattle guard with six-inch metal posts on either side sunk into concrete, upon which hung a metal gate. A state cop guarded the padlocked gate. The cop unlocked and opened the gate so we could turn our vehicles around and park them north of the cattle guard, facing uphill; he relocked the gate behind us.

A weathered sign by the gate, put there

by Monty Hook, said PRIVATE PROPERTY, NO TRESPASSING WITHOUT PERMISSION. Another, larger sign, recently posted by the Oregon State Department of Public Health, said in large, bold letters QUARANTINE. Beneath that, in smaller letters: UNTIL FURTHER NOTICE THIS PROPERTY, WHICH STATE INSPECTORS HAVE DETERMINED MAY BE INFECTED BY COMMUNICABLE DISEASE, IS OFF LIMITS TO UNAUTHORIZED PERSONS. Then the fine print in which the Department of Public Health cited the relevant legal statutes and penalties for breaking the state-imposed quarantine.

State cops had been posted at the turn-off from the main highway to turn the curious away. Reporters and photographers were to wait until there were enough to form a caravan, after which they would be allowed to continue — this on the grounds that they might yet be given permission to enter the quarantined area beyond the gate at the spring.

We got out the lunches and thermoses of coffee which Hook's housekeeper had packed for us and for the grateful cops and sat down in the shade. Hook said he ordinarily left the gate open; the cattle guard kept his animals penned, and there was a road through his property to Buckhorn Lookout in the federal Hells Canyon Recreation Area where people could look down on the lower Snake. It was eleven-thirty.

When the cops at the highway reported that five media vehicles had gathered, including one vehicle from the nonjournalist Reverend Thaddeus Hamm Bonnerton, the cops with us said to let them proceed to the spring.

We'd been at the spring on the downhill side of the locked gate for a half hour, bullshitting and eating, when we spotted the caravan coming up the road. Both Hook and the boys had binoculars, so we could see the vehicles below us as they followed the curving road up toward us. A van from television station KBMT in La Grande — the BMT presumably standing for Blue Mountain — led the way. The KBMT van was followed by a van with 'Restoration of Christ's Bosom' printed on its panels, then two four-wheel-drive vehicles, a Plymouth Cherokee and a Toyota LandCruiser; the Cherokee and LandCruiser presumably contained newspaper reporters.

As they grew closer, we stowed our lunches and gear. For the moment I thought it better to conserve the currency of anonymity, and went to sit in Hook's pickup with my shades on. I pulled my Aussie cricket player's hat down over my eyes and slumped down in the seat to watch the action in Hook's generous rearview mirror, which was designed to peer around a horse trailer if necessary.

Hook was suddenly at my side. He said, 'Here, I forgot to give you this.' It was a photocopy of one of the love poems.

'Mailed from where?' I asked.

'I think she said this one was sent from Decatur, Georgia.'

While we waited, I studied the poem, entitled 'Of Love and Kudzoo':

> *I sit here*
> *in the land of a creeping vine called*
> *   kudzoo*
> *that covers everything,*

inch by inch,
year by year.
There's no stopping kudzoo, they say.
It grips. Its roots dig deep.
It is a curse.
In such manner thus gripped
by unrequited passion
I remember ponderosas
and meadowlarks
and the lake beneath Eagle Cap
and you.

A few minutes later, the media vehicles and Bonnerton's rig pulled into the turn-around and parked.

A good-looking blonde dressed in tight black slacks and a light-blue nylon windbreaker popped cheerfully from the lead vehicle with a smile on her face and spirit in her stride.

The Reverend Thaddeus Hamm Bonnerton, dressed in what appeared to be a brand-new pair of Levi's — they had obviously not yet been washed — an equally new pair of Nike running shoes, and a plaid shirt, of a kind worn by lumberjacks in the movies, emerged from the second van, Bible in hand.

A half-dozen reporters and still photographers unpiled from the Cherokee and the Toyota LandCruiser.

'Hello,' the blonde said cheerily, eyeing the Buntline on Hook's hip. 'I'm Janet Hooper from KBMT-TV in La Grande. Beautiful day, isn't it?' She might well have been introducing herself at the start of a picnic or fishing expedition.

'Monty Hook's the handle. Morning, ma'am,' Hook said politely. 'Morning, Thad.' He shook Bonnerton's hand.

'Morning, Monty.' If Bonnerton was annoyed at being called Thad rather than Reverend Bonnerton, he didn't show it.

'We're here to tape the destruction of the diseased cattle,' Hooper said.

Hook said, 'Oh? And you, Thad?'

'The same,' Bonnerton said.

'You got cameras and the necessary gear?'

Bonnerton said, 'Oh, yes, we come prepared. We've got everything we need. Professionals.'

Hook said, 'I'll let one newspaper reporter and one still photographer come along, if they agree to share what they get with the other newspapers and the television. No more.'

Hooper said, 'Huh?'

Bonnerton said, 'What?'

'Anybody here from the Associated Press?' Hook said.

A man in the back, grinning, knowing he was to be the chosen one, said, 'The two of us.' He gestured at the man next to him, who wore a photographer's many-pocketed vest.

'You two, then,' Hook said. 'Pool reporters, isn't that what they call this arrangement?'

Hooper said, 'You can't do that! What about television?'

'Television?' Hook looked amused. 'My cattle are infected with anthrax. Do you know what happens if you catch anthrax? You die. That's what happens, whether you've got four legs or two. I've got people up there right now from the Center for Disease Control in Atlanta, Georgia, who are telling me that it's mandatory that these animals be kept in quarantine until they're destroyed. And by God, that's exactly what I intend to do. There's no law saying I have to kowtow to television reporters.'

Hooper said, 'I don't know where you came by this kind of attitude.'

'No?' Hook looked surprised. 'When you get back to your station you might look at some of the tapes of the horseshit, oversimplified stories you've run on the issue of federal grazing rights. *Then* ask yourself why I'm indifferent to television and television spectacle. You reap as you sow, lady, and this time I'm calling the shots, not you.'

'We have lenses,' Hooper said. 'We can keep our distance.'

'You going to pay my court costs if one of you gets sick and croaks and your family sues me?'

Bonnerton said confidently, 'This is public property. You can't keep us off public land.'

Hook raised an eyebrow. 'Public property? Oh?'

'It's federal land. It belongs to the people. We have as much right on public property as you do.'

Hook managed a tired smile. 'Well, I don't know where you're getting your information, Thaddie boy, but you might try listening to the radio. This is private, fenced range. This is my spread, pal, originally bought by my father in 1931. You can check it out at the county courthouse if you want. You want federal land, then go over about a half mile toward the Snake.' He languidly flipped his left hand in the direction of the Snake River. 'You can have a picnic or do whatever you want.'

Bonnerton furrowed his brows in confusion. 'Everybody knows you're grazing cattle on public land. Are you telling us there aren't any infected cattle on public land?'

'We can't find any,' Hook said. 'All the diseased cattle are on my land, and it's fenced with barbed wire, which kept the infection from spreading. It's true that you have to drive through my land to get to the public overlook above the Snake, but this road remains private nevertheless.'

'That's not what we had been led to

expect.' For a man in the market for environmental disaster on public property, this news was untidy in the extreme; Bonnerton looked concerned.

Hook cocked his head. 'Do you mind telling me, Reverend, just who it was who led you to expect anything else? The people on the radio have got the story straight. The anthrax infection is on private, fenced range. BLM land is not involved. It's difficult to imagine why you find that confusing or disappointing.'

'We're here as witnesses,' Hooper said.

'Witnesses?' Hook blinked.

'Public witnesses,' she amended.

Bonnerton obviously liked the ring of that, and upped her one. 'Public witnesses and God's witnesses. We've got a right.'

Hook said, 'I suppose you do have some rights, but coming onto my property uninvited is not one of them. As for witnesses, I've got all the witnesses I need and then some. I've got both state and federal people who deal with cattle and communicable disease, and I've got officers from the Oregon State Police.

They're all paid to see that this infection is eliminated promptly and completely and isn't allowed to spread. I don't object to them being here. It's their job. So the public is adequately represented, and it's apparently too late for God to help out.'

Hooper looked puzzled. Everybody wanted to be on television, didn't they? Why was this tobacco-chewing rancher being so stubborn? 'Why? What I don't understand is why?'

'Because the slaughter of cattle isn't a spectator sport, that's why. Some things are private. You want me to tape you sitting on the toilet?'

Hooper narrowed her eyes. 'Well, what if we get a helicopter?'

'I'm not about to shoot you down with a thirty-ought-six with the state police as witnesses, so I suppose you're safe enough there.'

'I should hope so,' she said.

'I'm not a lawyer, so I don't know the rules about flying over somebody's private property when you've been told to stay the hell out, but if you try flying over my spread in a helicopter, I swear to

Christ, I'll do everything in my power to relieve you of everything short of your underwear in a court of law.'

'What?'

'Besides, where are you going to get a helicopter on this short of a notice?'

'La Grande,' she said.

'La Grande?' Hook looked amused. 'Well, go for it, lady. Be my guest.' They could no doubt hire a helicopter by phone, but La Grande was seventy miles away as the crow flies. Hook paused, thinking, then said, 'Wait a second. I tell you what, Ms. Hooper: my cattle are insured, but I still stand to lose upwards of a hundred thousand dollars in the next couple of hours. If your television station is willing to cover my losses and your medical bills if you catch anthrax, I'm willing to let you tape the fun.'

'We don't *pay* for news, Mr. Hook.' She looked offended.

'The news is that my cattle have anthrax, and I have to destroy them. You already know that. Watching the gory details isn't news.'

'Oh, come on.'

'To me, it's personal tragedy, and I have a right to privacy on my own property. I'm not committing any crime. I'm obeying both the letter and the spirit of the law. This land is quarantined by order of the State Department of Public Health. You can read the fine print on the sign if you want. It tells you everything you need to know.'

'I'm coming across,' Bonnerton said.

'You'll shit too if you eat regularly,' Hook said. 'What are you going to do, try to break down that gate? Good luck.'

'I'm a minister of the Lord.'

'I don't give a flying fuck if you're Billy Graham or the Pope. Am I within my rights, Officer?' Hook turned to the nearest cop.

The cop, in the presence of a television reporter, did his best to retain his mask of neutrality. 'Yes, sir. You are. This is your property, and those are your cattle. The property has been legally quarantined.'

Bonnerton clutched his Bible to his chest, a pious gesture that I thought was a bit much.

Hook said, 'The Bible won't do you

any good. As far as I'm concerned you're still Thad Bonnerton, pimple-faced asshole. Also, what in the hell are you doing with a camera crew tagging along behind you? Gonna tape the slaughter for Jesus?'

Bonnerton glared at Hook, then the cop.

The cop remained impassive. He had been taught to mind his manners in the presence of reporters, and he was doing just that.

Hook said, 'I suppose you could really pack 'em into your revival tomorrow by showing them the carnage on a big enough screen. Why, folks, would you just look at the awful, sinful Monty Hook, having to slaughter his diseased cattle? Well, Reverend, you can pray for my immortal soul or not as you see fit. The gate stays locked.' Monty Hook splashed a big brown wad in front of Bonnerton's new Nikes.

'We won't be able to see any smoke from down here,' Hooper said.

Hook looked past the locked gate up the steep road that had been carved from the side of the Imnaha River canyon. The infected range was on the plateau high

185

above the river. He furrowed his brows in mock concern. 'By God, I think you're right! You might have some problems there.'

She glanced at her watch. 'We've got two hours to circle around and come in from the west.'

Hook looked confused. He checked his own watch. 'You've got an hour to drive back up the Imnaha and up Camp Creek Road to Zumwalt Road and back again from the other side. Have to drive pretty damn fast.'

'An hour. But you're not scheduled to start until two P.M.'

'Not until two o'clock?' Hook looked puzzled. 'Who in the hell told you that?'

'Your housekeeper when we called this morning.'

Hook bunched his face and slapped his thigh. 'Why, damn that woman. She can't get anything right. Tell her to cook beef, she cooks fish. Tell her to cook steaks, she fixes liver. I told her again and again to pay attention. Can't get anything right. She does everything except starch my shorts.'

Hooper, livid, ran for the van, joined in her exodus by the Reverend Bonnerton and the other reporters, except for the pair from the Associated Press. The grateful AP reporter joined us in our pickup, and the photographer rode with the state police, who were grinning like Mr. Carroll's famous Cheshire cat. Unlike the determined Monty Hook, they were forced to kiss reporters' asses in the interest of public relations, and they had enjoyed his performance.

As we started up the side of the canyon on the steep road, I wondered if Bonnerton always had a camera crew trailing after him. I assumed he did, to document the indecencies of environmental degradation for the big show.

* * *

Monty Hook's cowhands had earlier rounded up such cattle as they could find that had not yet displayed symptoms of the disease and had herded them into a makeshift corral of hastily strung barbed wire beside the burial pit that had been scooped out by bulldozers and which was now loaded with more than three hundred corpses.

Around this pit the two Caterpillar bulldozers contracted by the state had scraped a fire lane to the bare earth. Beyond the fire lane, the meadow was ablaze with the beauty of tiny yellow and white wildflowers. In the distance a meadowlark, the state bird of Oregon, gave its complicated, trilling call.

Above the sight, a hawk, curious, floated in the early afternoon updrafts.

The operators of the bulldozers, who wore yellow protective outfits with special masks to protect them from the infection, waited in the shade of a ponderosa pine at the edge of the meadow. The driver of a Chevron gasoline truck, who had been issued a similar protective outfit, waited with the bulldozer operators.

Monty Hook and I, plus Willie, Bobcat Bill, the AP reporter and photographer, the various state and federal inspectors, and the state police officers — a party of fifteen — waited a hundred yards upwind of the corral.

Some sixty or seventy live cattle, now all in various stages of distress, milled about inside the corral. They bulged with odd swellings. Their noses were frothed with blood. They were racked by fever and looked miserable. They bawled and cried out.

The job of dropping the remaining animals with high-powered rifles had been delegated to two of Monty Hook's ranch hands. At the stroke of one o'clock, they pulled their protective masks into place and calmly walked up to the edge of the corral.

The first cowboy raised his rifle and sighted in on a steer. Then he lowered the muzzle. He looked back at Monty Hook.

A meadowlark called.

'Get it over with, Lou,' Hook called. 'Waiting around isn't going to change anything.'

The cowboy named Lou raised the rifle again and pulled the trigger. The rifle cracked and bucked against his shoulder.

The steer dropped, and lay kicking.

The cowboy delivered a second quick round. The animal stiffened and was dead.

Hook said, 'The sooner we're finished, the sooner we can get the hell out of here.'

The second cowboy raised his rifle. Crack! Another steer dropped.

And another.

And another.

And so went the final hour of killing on the Flying J's Imnaha spread.

Boom. Drop.

Boom. Drop.

Hook, looking pale, biting his lip, watched in silence.

The stricken animals, understanding what was happening, that they were trapped in a deadly vortex, began milling, wild-eyed, scrambling over the bodies of their fallen fellows.

The corral was a horror of dead and dying animals, bawling and kicking in a scarlet slick of piss and shit and blood and saliva.

Lou and his colleague kept shooting, calmly working the bolt-action loading mechanisms of their rifles, pausing only to reload.

Hook yelled, 'Get it over with, goddammit. Get it the fuck over with.

Can't you shoot any faster than that? You fire those things like old ladies.'

This was the grisly spectacle he had withheld from the six o'clock news and the concerned followers of the Reverend Thaddeus Hamm Bonnerton. Then Monty Hook began to weep, quietly at first. Then he began to bawl openly. 'My God! My God!'

Bobcat Bill put his arm around him. 'It had to be done, Monty. There was no other way.'

In a half hour, almost all the animals lay dead. When the last writhing beasts were stilled, the cowboys with the rifles withdrew to the shade of the ponderosas. They took off their masks and mopped the sweat from their foreheads with the backs of their forearms.

The two bulldozer operators looked our way, waiting for the word.

'Well, dammit. No sense standing around picking your asses. Do it!' Hook yelled.

The bulldozer operators pulled on their masks and, *clack, clack, clack*ing on the metal treads, entered the bloody corral. They lowered the blades of their machines before them and began pushing the first of the corpses toward the pit.

We watched in silence as the bulldozers *clack clacked* to and fro, pushing dead Herefords into the bloody pit. This chore took close to an hour. When the last infected animal joined the others in the pit, the bulldozers withdrew to the ponderosa at the edge of the meadow.

Hook waved at the driver of the gas truck, who nodded and pulled up to the edge of the pit. 'Come on, dammit. Nobody likes this shit.'

The driver, face masked, the engine of his truck idling, calmly pumped gasoline onto the dead animals. When his truck was empty and the corpses were thoroughly soaked, he replaced the hose and withdrew the truck to a safe remove.

Now everybody looked at Monty Hook, who, stricken, stood with a flare gun in his hand. 'Sweet Jesus, why this?' he said. 'How did this awful thing happen to me and my cattle? Why me? Why?'

'Want me to do it, Monty?' Bobcat said.

Hook shook his head. 'They're my

cattle. This is my spread. I'm the captain of this ship. It's my job, not yours, Bobcat.'

'I'll do it if you want.'

'No, it's my chore.' Hook calmly aimed the flare gun at the pit and pulled the trigger, and the orange flames exploded skyward in a maelstrom. Soon the pale blue sky was filled with dark smoke billowing high, reaching for the heavens where the hawk had floated earlier.

As the fire roared upward from the pyre of his animals, Monty Hook lowered the flare gun and spit a big wad of tobacco on the ground. Then he said, 'You reckon those television people got around fast enough to catch the smoke?'

A state police radio crackled. A cop spoke briefly on the radio, said, 'Well, they missed the wienie roast, but looks like they're gonna be able to tape some smoke rising up above the trees.'

Hook said, 'You want to meet me at the High Country for a little drinking and talk tonight, Denson? We gotta get to the bottom of this shit.'

I said, 'Sure, I'll meet you at the High

Country. If there ever was an occasion that called for tying one on, this has to be it.'

As the smoke rolled, I listened for the call of the meadowlark, but it was gone.

Monty Hook fought back the tears and Willie Prettybird looked positively stricken. I didn't feel so damned wonderful myself.

A breeze stirred, and there was a mournful lowing in the tops of the ponderosas as the black smoke rolled and billowed skyward.

12

When Monty Hook and I stepped into the High Country Saloon that night, the patrons were staring, transfixed, at the television screen, where the black smoke from Hook's burial pyre billowed above the tops of the ponderosa pines. The blonde reporter, Janet Hooper, of KBMT-TV in La Grande, whom Hook had turned away earlier in the day, was narrating the meaning of the smoke in a voice that was borderline hysterical.

The smoke, taped from the edge of Zumwalt Road adjoining Hook's spread, left to the viewer's imagination the details of the slaughter and the inferno that followed. For that Hooper had to rely on the report by the Associated Press, and she didn't like it. She was clearly pissed at this blocking of what she regarded as a First Amendment right.

Hooper said that the owner of the property, rancher Monty Hook, had, 'at gunpoint, backed by troopers of the Oregon State Police,' blocked the media from taping the disposal of the anthrax-infected cattle. She neglected to add that the property at the time was under quarantine ordered by the Oregon State Department of Health.

When Hooper's report was finished and the station began interviewing alleged experts on the consequences of the infection to the cattle business in Wallowa County, Hook exploded. 'At gunpoint! Gunpoint! What kind of shit is that?' He looked at me.

I shrugged. While it was true that Hook had carried his Buntline on his hip, was that 'at gunpoint'?

Lil turned off the set, and the saloon sank into gloom, except for Roy Childress and his flagrant lady of the big rump who seemed largely unaffected by the smoke rising above the burning cattle on Monty Hook's ranch. Childress and the flagrant lady asked for the bar dice.

Lil delivered us cold bottles of Henry Weinhard without being asked. 'It's all on the house tonight, Monty,' she said. She was clearly stricken by his tragedy.

Hook, who no doubt could still afford his own beer, appreciated the gesture. 'Well, thank you, Lil.'

'It must have been awful.'

Hook bit his lower lip. 'It was.'

'You should have used the gun on the television female.'

'Never took it off my hip, the bitch. Besides, the state cops were standing right there. Am I going to pull a weapon on a television reporter with two officers of the Oregon State Police as witnesses? Give me a fucking break, lady.'

'Is there anything I can do?'

Hook, leaning back, scoped her figure and leered.

'Except that,' she added with a grin. She glanced at me and said, 'Can't keep this man's mind off his fuse. He keeps it lit at all times.'

Hook said, 'Just keep those beers coming. Tonight I got a reason to put away a few.'

'You better believe,' she said.

'On second thought . . . ' Without another word, Hook got up and strode to the bell and rang it with vigor, calling loudly, 'A round on the Flying J, celebrating the biggest goddamn barbecue in the history of Wallowa County.'

When he returned and sat back down, Lil said, 'That's the spirit, Monty.'

'*Non illegitimi carborundum*,' I said.

'And that means?' Lil said.

''Don't let the bastards wear you down.''

Monty Hook and I sat in silence for several minutes, watching Childress and Opal play liar's dice with Lil.

Childress slammed the leather cup on the table and took a peek at the dice. Then, cupping the dice with his hand, he said, 'I've got two sixes, two fives, and a four.'

Opal said, 'You've got shit, too. Jesus, Roy, but you're a worthless son of a bitch. No wonder your wife took off on you. They say she was screwing everybody in the county and you were too dumb to know it.'

'Are you calling me a liar?'

Opal considered the dice behind Childress's hand and shook her head.

Lil said, 'Neither one of you two know how to tell the truth.'

Childress said, 'If you're not going to call me a liar, you want to roll them, then?'

Opal rolled her dice. She took a peek and said, 'I've got three sixes and two fives.'

It was Lil's turn.

Opal said, 'You think I've got three sixes and two fives.'

Lil smiled and rolled her own dice. She studied them and said, 'I've got four sixes and a five.'

Childress said, 'Oh, you do? And I say you're a liar. Let's see what you've got.'

Lil showed her dice. She had two sixes, a five, a four, and a three. If Childress and Opal had two sixes between them, she was okay. If not, she sacrificed a die.

Childress showed his dice: a six, two fives, and two fours. He said, 'By God, I only see one six here. How about you, Opal?'

Opal showed hers: two ones, two threes, and a four. 'Oh my, no sixes here at all.'

Childress said, 'By God, let's see now. I only count three sixes total, Lil. Why, you were just lying like hell, weren't you? Four sixes, you said!' He rolled his eyes.

Lil, having been convicted of lying, set one die aside. The next round she would play with four dice.

Childress said, 'You two women are going to have to practice your lying if you expect to keep up with me.' He rattled his five dice and turned the cup upside down.

As we sat listening to the dice players, Monty Hook, aiming a philosophical drool of tobacco at the spittoon, said, 'The state people said I had to destroy the cattle. There was no other way. So I did it. Not much else I could do.'

I said, 'Jesus, what a sight that was.'

'Like the cop said, at least I screwed the television people out of the big wienie roast. Everybody got to watch the smoke billow. Let them imagine the rest.'

'That was well done, I agree.'

'Imagine that television bitch telling people I stopped her at gunpoint. Jesus H. Christ!' Hook let fly into the spittoon.

'Adds to the drama,' I said.

'Maybe I should sue her. Threatening somebody with a gun is a felony, isn't it? I didn't do squat except tell her I didn't want her on my property, which I was entitled to do, and I have witnesses.'

'There you go, sue her ass.' From a distant spot in my hoop, I dimly recited:

Good name in man and woman, dear my lord
Is the immediate jewel of their souls.
Who steals my purse steals trash; 'tis something, nothing;
'Twas mine, 'tis his, and has been slave to thousands;
But he that filches from me my good name
Robs me of that which not enriches him,
And makes me poor indeed.

Hook looked amazed. 'And that would be?'

'Shakespeare, I think, but I can't remember the play, and I probably fucked it up. Read it in Cayuse High School, and

201

remembered it after all these years. Sort of remembered it.'

He said, 'Leiat Podebski ought to be here. She'd appreciate that.'

We drank in silence for a moment.

Then Hook said, 'I still would like to know how in the hell my cattle managed to come down with that shit. I just can't figure it. Those animals were properly fenced. They were mine from the time they were calves. I don't think a spaceship dropped down and infected them, and that's the truth.'

At the bar, I noticed that the cowboy Roy Childress's attention wasn't entirely on the dice game. He looked at us with a positively malevolent eye, which seemed surprising considering all that Hook had been through that day.

I said, 'Is there anything ailing the big cowboy besides you having pinned him for rustling? He gave you a ration last night, and he still hasn't calmed down.'

Hook took a swig of beer. 'Aw, fuck, what's eating him is he knows that I suspect he's a longtime poacher. This is big country, lot of places to poach.'

'On your land?'

'Naw. He's been steering clear of the south spread because Bobcat's living there, and it's too dangerous trying to smuggle a carcass out of the north spread. I don't care where the hell he's doing it. If I could pin the son of a bitch for poaching, I'd see him behind bars a second time. I'd do it without hesitation or apology, and he knows it.'

'Oops!'

Hook said, 'I suspect he's working the Blues, but I'm not going to follow him over there. If he'd spend more time practicing his riding and roping, he might actually make some legit money.'

'Riding and roping. He's a rodeo cowboy, then?'

Hook nodded. 'A damn good one, I have to admit. He was the all-around cowboy at Chief Joseph a couple years ago, and won the bareback riding at Pendleton once. And that was against national competition. Not bad. He never did win calf roping at Pendleton, but that's his best event.'

I took another look at Childress, seeing

him in a new light.

Hook said, 'He doesn't practice enough at riding bulls or bareback, but he knows how to ride a saddle bronc when he puts his mind to it. And he knows how to rope a calf. He's got a horse named Pinecone that's one of the best I've ever seen.'

'He's got some real talent, then?'

'The horse's got talent.' Hook grinned. 'Childress too, of course. But rodeoing takes hard work and practice, and Childress is always looking for an easy way to make a buck.'

'He's got a nose for trouble.'

'He sure as hell does. Ever since that rustling episode, I've been looking for an excuse to stick the barrel of my Buntline up his ass and empty the cylinder. The world would be a better place for it.'

I said, 'The woman with him doesn't look like your admirer either.'

Hook looked amused. 'You mean old big ass?'

'She's got a rump on her,' I said, eyeing the woman.

'No, she isn't exactly my admirer.'

'She Childress's steady lady?'

'I guess you could say that. Childress'd fuck a stump if he wasn't afraid of the splinters. You're the first person I've ever heard call Opal a lady.' He burst out laughing.

'Opal. A real gem,' I said.

Hook laughed. 'I suppose you could look at it that way. She was once a schoolteacher, if you can believe that. Over at Milton-Freewater. That's until the administration got wind that she was fucking her students.'

'Really? Did they bring sexual harassment charges?'

Hook laughed. 'She probably had her eye on the football team until they put a stop to it. Open Hole is what most of us call her. I think she's actually proud of the name, if you want to know the truth. Suppose she figures anybody can be called Opal. She needs a stoplight on her crotch to control the traffic going in and out.'

'What's Opal got against you?'

'Aw, she claimed one of her damn squallers is mine, the issue of a drunken fuck. She got herself a sleazeball lawyer from over in La Grande and slapped a paternity suit on me, claimed she was going to separate me from my shorts, not to mention half my land and all my cattle.'

'Did she?'

'Naw, hell no. Woman like that? Snake-eyed bitch. Every cowboy between here and Idaho has had a turn with that fat ass of hers.'

'I see.'

Hook said, 'A man's gotta watch he doesn't fall in that pussy of hers and drown. Ain't no jury in Wallowa County gonna make a man turn over half his spread because he got drunk one night and dipped his wick in the wrong hole.'

I pretended to be righteously indignant, but couldn't help but smile. 'Well, I hope to hell not!'

'No way. Not happening.' Monty Hook punctuated this by discharging another wad of noxious brown goo into the spittoon. This was a full-stop wad. Hook was finished expressing his sentiments about Childress and the lady named Opal.

I eyed the approach of Lil, bearing a tray with our bottles of Henry Weinhards. I did my best to keep my eyes off her chest as she set our bottles down. Wanting to avoid the depressing subject of anthrax and Monty Hook's destroyed cattle, I said, 'Say, I was curious about the game you folks're playing at the bar. It's called liar's dice, isn't it?'

Lil adjusted the glasses on her nose. A robust laugh rumbled up from her remarkable chest. She understood that I was trying to cheer up my companion. 'You should have Mr. Hook tell you about liar's dice. Right, Monty?'

Hook blinked.

Lil looked amused.

Hook, looking unconcerned, looped an editorial drool of goo into the spittoon.

I said, 'Tell me, how do you play it?'

She said, 'Each player rolls five dice to start. Ones are wild. You get to look at them once and that's it. You tell him, Monty, you're the expert.'

Hook took a swig of beer. 'You keep your numbers under your Stetson,' Hook said. 'You tell the other players what you have. You base this on what you actually have plus what you think they have, judging from their claims. Now, your score has to be better than the player before you, but you don't have to show what you've got unless somebody calls you a liar.'

'I see.'

'If you get caught lying or you call somebody else a liar and you're wrong, the other players each get to set one die aside, then everybody shakes a new hand with however many dice they have left. The last player with a die or dice buys a round of beer.'

'Well,' I said, 'a game of life, eh? If you're a good enough liar, you drink for free.'

Hook said, 'That's pretty much the way it works out. Some people work at being snake-eyed; some are natural liars.'

Lil said, 'There's a good reason why liar's dice is popular here. You should listen to some of the horsepucky in here come hunting season or when the fish are hitting down on the Grande Ronde or over on the Imnaha. But they all agree that Monty Hook is by far the biggest liar in Wallowa County.'

Hook smirked.

She said, 'Liar's dice is his game. Just ask anybody. They'll say the same thing: Monty Hook's the champ. A snake-eyed liar of the first order. Ain't that right, Monty?'

Hook looked disgusted. 'Aw, for Christ's sake, Lil.'

'That's only opinion, mind. The competition for the title's pretty keen in this neck of the woods.'

Hook grinned. 'Jesus, Lil, this man is all the way up from Portland. The least you could do is ease him into the bullshit.'

Lil looked amazed. 'Just how is that possible? My God!'

Hook pretended to be offended. 'Dammit, woman, where's the respect around here?'

'Respect? In the High Country? What on earth are you talking about? Two beers and most of you guys can't hit the urinal.' With that the redheaded Lil was gone, back to the bar, her backfield in splendid, rolling motion.

13

I had always respected the Oregon State Police. They always looked trim and fit in their blue uniforms, high-topped black boots, and neat little Sam Browne hats. These weren't the kind of folks I ordinarily hung out with, mind; their neatness and commitment to the letter of the law was a trifle oral compulsive for my taste. But they were polite and professional, and, I thought, they made a genuine attempt to serve Oregonians in a responsible manner.

Also, I knew, they were required to have a college education; this didn't make them all perfect by any means, but it was a reasonable start. It struck me that young men and women with an imagination so cockeyed as to want to be a cop would first apply to the state police. Only failing that would they apply at Eugene or Portland, where the city administrations aspired to high standards and had examinations and police academies and the rest of it.

A city, where crooks could easily get lost in the anonymity of the crowd, was a far different place from a hamlet like Enterprise. Here, privacy was scarce, if not nonexistent. In large part owing to sheer boredom — there being little besides the weather to talk about — people whiled away the time speculating about the whims and tics of their neighbors. It followed that the chief requirement of the town cop was that he — or she, in these changing times — could blend in and be one of the folks, that is, be talented at the folksy art of gossip.

Owing to marginal budgets, city fathers in these places ordinarily hired whoever would take the job and were glad of it; in the case of Enterprise, that meant Chief Bubba Tubig. Tubig was, I would have thought, a trifle too big for the job. He was about five seven and close to two hundred pounds. His belly was of dimensions that would have done justice to familiar portrayals of the Buddha — qualifying him to be called Buddha Tubig or Ho Ti Tubig, after the familiar god whose belly the Chinese rubbed for good luck. But Buddha or Ho Ti would no doubt have been too much for the residents of Enterprise. The name Bubba, with its popular association with the south — as in Billy Bob or Joe Don — was bad enough.

The rotund Tubig's face was the same shape as his belly, that is, round; his clean-shaven jowls eliminated any suggestion of a jaw or chin. He had large, fleshy lips that looked like those of the actor Charles Laughton, whom he vaguely resembled. His smallish, plump nose appeared to have been glued onto his face. His ears looked like tiny mushrooms that had popped out of pink flesh. His eyes, resting atop fleshy bags, were pale blue and intelligent. His immensity notwithstanding, he looked friendly enough.

If the Oregon state cops looked like made beds, Tubig was forever unmade. There were people who were so congenitally neat that, it struck me, they spent all their energy and imagination on straightening things up. Unmade beds like Tubig, their minds less occupied with everything being in its place, had more energy for the problem at hand — in this case finding out who had murdered Officer Dave McAllister of the Oregon State Police.

When I stepped into his office, Tubig looked up from a pile of papers heaped on top of his desk. His tiny office, hardly large enough to contain his corpulent frame, was a clutter of magazines, files, and police gear.

Although I saw the ID tag on his chest, *Tubig, B.*, I said, 'Chief Tubig?'

He stood, offering his hand. 'Yes, I am.'

I handed him my private investigator's license issued by the state of Oregon. I said, 'My name is John Denson. My partner, Willie Prettybird, and I have been hired by Monty Hook to see if we can help him find the son of a bitch who murdered a state cop on his property.'

Tubig studied my box tops, then handed them back. He sat down. 'Won't you have a seat, Mr. Denson?'

I sat.

'Were you out there yesterday, by any chance?'

'When Monty put his cattle under?'

He nodded.

'I was there,' I said.

He wanted to know what it was like, but didn't want to ask directly.

I said, 'It was pretty fucking awful is the best way to sum it up.'

'Jesus!'

'I don't think we can blame Christ for this one. The Prince of Darkness maybe.'

'I hope to hell that stopped it.'

'Don't we all,' I said.

'They had the smoke on TV, but the reporter said Monty Hook wouldn't let them watch. At gunpoint, she said. Is that true?'

'Complete horseshit.'

Tubig laughed. 'That's what I thought. If he'd actually pointed a gun at her, how come she didn't sic the state bulls on him?' Tubig thought a moment, then said, 'On the matter of the murder of Officer McAllister, I take it you know he was murdered in Wallowa County, not in the city of Enterprise. That puts it in the jurisdiction of the county sheriff and the state police, not me.'

'But they will have to work with you,

won't they? You being the chief of police here in Enterprise. You'd be the guy who knows who's doing what and why in the only town of consequence.'

Tubig smiled. 'True, nobody out there except a few birds and maybe a mule deer or two.'

I started to mention Willie's animal people, but thought better of it. No sense having Tubig write me off as a nut case right from the start. 'Maybe a porcupine here and there,' I said.

Tubig said, 'You and your partner are regular investigators for Boogie and Olden Dewlapp, as I understand it.'

'Yes, we are. Olden, in this instance.'

'I would have thought Olden Dewlapp would be a curious choice as a lawyer for the president of the Oregon Cattlemen's Association, but never mind. How can I help you?'

'Well, I'm not certain. For starters, I guess, it would be nice to know what Officer McAllister was doing on Mr. Hook's range.'

Tubig pursed his fleshy lips. 'The state police have asked me to keep that information confidential for the moment, Mr. Denson.'

I sighed. 'Chief Tubig, if Officer McAllister was on the range doing his duty, surely the killer is aware of that. I fail to see how keeping it secret would hamper anybody's investigation.'

Tubig frowned.

I said, 'I don't see why I should be forced to have Olden Dewlapp go through the legal drill of righteous indignation and judges and the rest of it. But if I have to, I have to. I'm being paid to do a job.'

Tubig pulled resolutely on one of his tiny mushroom ears.

I said, 'Besides, sooner or later, I'll find out anyway. We both know that. I grew up in Cayuse. I know how these small towns work.'

'Cayuse.' He looked surprised. 'Really?'

'All I have to do is hang out in the High Country Saloon. Sooner or later I'll find out what McAllister was up to.'

Tubig considered that, then said, 'We don't get murders every day in Wallowa County, and I've got a county sheriff to deal with as well as the Oregon State Police. They're all excited and everything. You'd think everybody in the country short of the president has got their eyes glued on this one murder.' He pursed his lips. 'You see my problem.'

'Yes, I do,' I said.

'They're polite and everything, but I suspect they find it hard to regard me as a colleague, if you know what I mean.'

'Oh?'

'They appear to regard me as a fat man who couldn't find his pecker on a cold morning.'

I laughed.

'What was it that lady sang, 'Everybody Wants a Hero'? Well, when a cop gets killed, other cops get maximum exercised and pissed off, me included. Everybody and his cousin wants to solve this case and read about himself in the newspapers.'

'I bet they do.'

'They sure as hell don't want a fat boy showing them up.'

I rolled my eyes. 'Jesus!'

'They all want to pick my brains for

possible motives, but they don't want me poaching on their turf. They all want to be the hero.' Tubig leaned forward across his desk, apparently having made up his mind about me. 'Just between you and me, Mr. Denson, I'd love to show those hotshots a thing or two about fat people and brains.'

I laughed. 'I bet you would. Willie Prettybird and I both know how to scratch backs, guaranteed.'

'Even if the truth leads to Monty Hook?'

I didn't say anything for a moment. Then, 'Monty Hook didn't do squat.'

He bunched his face. 'He's your client and all that, I know. Private dicks and lawyers.' He pursed his lips again, then said, 'The state cops tell me Officer McAllister was looking for poachers when he was killed.'

'Poachers?'

'Correct.'

I said, 'They tell me Monty's north spread is pretty slim pickings for poachers. The real action's farther west.'

'All I know is what I'm told.'

'Any particular poacher?'

'They didn't say.'

'Shiner or salt licks?'

'Either, I assume. They didn't say that either.'

Deer and elk feed both at night and in the day, but they prefer the night. When confronted by a spotlight in darkness, they stop in place, looking directly at the light, their eyes reflecting ruby. Shining deer meant using a spotlight to freeze the deer. Easy matter to drop them with a high-powered rifle and spirit their carcasses off to be butchered.

Other poachers used a salt lick, a large block of salt ordinarily set out by ranchers for their cattle. A salt lick contained other minerals and nutrients needed by cattle in addition to sodium chloride. All a poacher had to do was place a block of salt in an isolated spot where there was traffic in deer or elk and wait for his quarry to show up for a salty treat — ordinarily at dawn or dusk. A salt-lick poacher skilled with a crossbow was one of the hardest poachers to catch.

I said, 'A poacher has to move his

meat, doesn't he? If somebody was poaching on the north spread, surely the state cops could stop him with a simple roadblock. Hear shooting, set up roadblocks on Zumwalt Road and Monty's private road to the highway that follows the Imnaha. Why don't they do that?'

'A person would have thought so, but so far no luck.'

'I see. I would have thought Monty Hook has got all the prime beef he can eat at cost. Why on earth would he be out poaching?'

'You asked what McAllister was doing out there. I said he was looking for poachers. I didn't say that's why he was murdered.'

'Why was he murdered?'

'Boy-girl stuff, they think. Oldest, most predictable motive on the books.'

'You're talking about Hook's relationship with Lil Peters.'

Tubig shrugged.

'Figures. See, I told you I grew up in a town like this.'

He said, 'Yes, well, people do like to talk, that's true, but I didn't have to rely on gossip to know that Monty and Lil have had a thing going since high school.'

'Oh?'

'I was a member of that same class.'

'Really?'

'Yes, I was. The class fat boy. I played right guard on the football team. But I didn't look fat in a football uniform with all those pads and everything, no sir. I looked like a human tank.' Tubig grinned.

'You'll be going to the reunion, then?'

'Oh sure, wouldn't miss it for the world.'

'And Monty didn't like McAllister. Everybody knows that too.'

'That's so,' he said. 'I should add here that knowing Monty since high school gives me more reason to want to be the one to prove him innocent of this thing.'

I said, 'Then there's the mysterious appearance of anthrax on the same spread where the cop was killed. I suppose you're taking all that into account.'

'Oh?' He looked interested.

'Didn't it strike you or the sheriff or the state police that there might be a connection between the two? What if somebody deliberately infected Monty's cattle? It's not beyond the realm of possibility.'

Tubig narrowed his eyes, thinking that over. 'Deliberately infect his cattle with anthrax? What on earth for?'

'Good question. Did the state cops tell you about two sets of hoofprints they can't figure out?'

'Hoofprints? No, they didn't.'

We sat for a moment in silence, me thinking about the hoofprints, Tubig no doubt sore that he hadn't been told all the facts by the uppity state bulls.

His stomach gurgled loudly.

I glanced at my watch. 'Say, it's close to noon, lunchtime. You've got to be getting hungry.'

Tubig seemed pleased that I was so alert.

'It is lunchtime for me, yes. Stomach like mine is unembarrassed when it comes time to eat. I'm a regular down at the Pheasant Café. The cook there puts on a real feed for me. Big old steak. And she just piles those mashed potatoes on the plate. Makes a big hollow and fills it with gravy like it was a barge or something.

Boy, does she know how to make gravy.'
Tubig grinned and patted his Ho Ti belly.

I stood to leave.

'Do we have an understanding, then?'
he said.

'My partner and I are after the truth,
Chief Tubig. We're being paid by Monty
Hook, not the city or the county or the
state, so we're not bound by the city
limits or the county line. If we have any
luck, and we can help you pin the killer,
from right here in Enterprise, we'll do it.
Does that sound like what you have in
mind?'

Tubig grinned. That indeed was what
he wanted to hear.

I added, 'You might be thinking about
that disease angle. You never know.'

'I sure will, Mr. Denson. You keep in
touch, now, and say hello to your redskin
partner.' Bubba Tubig rose on porcine
thighs and grabbed his cap from a peg
on the wall. His stomach, eager for the
mashed potatoes and gravy waiting at
the Pheasant Café, gurgled a thunderous
rumble.

14

Leiat Podebski, Lenora Kemiah, and I settled in at the quail booth at the Pheasant Café, which again was filled to bursting, what with tonight being the night of the long-awaited all-school reunion, the ritual rejoining of the local version of Willie Prettybird's Great Hoop.

Wallowa County had been infected by the killer anthrax, and anthrax was on the minds of the diners, but Leiat, Lenora, and I had an unspoken agreement not to dwell on the fate of Monty Hook's cattle; there was no bringing them back to life. True, Generations of Wallowa County residents had earned their living from the running of livestock, and an outbreak of anthrax was a disaster of the first order. But we could only hope that the destruction of the cattle under the supervision of state and federal health officials had stopped the disease from spreading.

It was my bet that Hook's friends and classmates at the reunion would respect his privacy and not dwell on the details of his tragedy; as curious as they had to be, and envious though some likely were of his success as a rancher, they would know intuitively that the will to overcome and endure was at the heart of the human spirit. His struggle was theirs as well.

Leiat Podebski was a sharp-looking widow tonight, dressed in a simple white dress with a double strand of pearls and her hair in a short, fashionable cut. She had had her hair colored brown, which made her look closer to sixty than seventy. She was looking forward to seeing her students from the past, and I was looking forward to an evening with Lenora Kemiah by my side.

Lenora was hot-looking in the extreme in a form-fitting black cocktail dress that showed off her elegant little figure. She wore all turquoise jewelry — earrings, necklace, and bracelets — which looked genuine and went well with her lovely copper-colored skin. She had a bright yellow ribbon in her black hair, which she had unwound from its usual pigtail and allowed to plunge halfway down her tiny back. She was obviously pleased to have emerged from her seclusion.

With a grand wave of my hand, I said, 'Ladies, inasmuch as I'm on the job tonight, listening for useful gossip from the class of '68, this is expense money. Olden Dewlapp, of Portland, is springing. When it's Olden's wallet, money is no object. He's a hateful lawyer, remember, fair game, so order whatever you please.'

'Don't you mean Monty Hook's money?' Leiat said, grinning.

'Well, yes, maybe Monty's in the end. He'll have to butcher a couple of steers to pay for this. But he's gotta expect to pay top dollar for hotshot private eyes like Willie Prettybird and me. Face it: you got Denson and Prettybird on the job, you got the best.'

Picking up the laminated plastic menu, Lenora said, 'Willie said you were a little crazy.'

I said, 'With Willie as a partner, that goes without saying. But I owe Willie one for his conniving on our behalf. I'm

226

having a T-bone steak, rare, with a baked potato and a bottle of Henry Weinhard to wash it down. Maybe even a couple of Henrys before I'm through. Do they have sour cream for their baked potatoes here, Leiat?'

'Their baked potatoes are wonderful. They do indeed have sour cream, and chopped chives and crumbled bacon if you want. Real bacon, not flavored soybeans. Incidentally, the steaks probably come from Monty's cattle.'

While Leiat and Lenora perused their menus, I studied the reunion program that Podebski had given me. 'Let's see, it says the 1920s and 1930s graduates of Enterprise High School are having a dinner at the home of Mrs. Spark Newton. That's at a ranch outside of town, I take it. They've got a map here. You interested in that, Leiat?'

'That was a little before my time. I taught from 1955 through 1990, that is, from age thirty until I retired at sixty-five. I was ready and able to continue, but the law is the law.'

'If you dated that stretch by pop

musicians, that would be Elvis Presley through the Beatles and the Grateful Dead to Bruce Springsteen and Madonna. Something like that.'

She laughed. 'By another measure, from beer drinking to pot smoking. Or from massive retaliation to the end of the Iron Curtain.'

I said, 'From Elvis Presley filmed above the waist on Ed Sullivan to X-rated channels. From the clap through herpes to AIDS.'

'Nineteen sixty-eight, the year Monty and Bubba and Lil and Thad Bonnerton graduated, was a particularly terrible year. First there was the Tet Offensive. Then Martin Luther King, Jr. and Bobby Kennedy were assassinated. Then we had riots in the summer.'

I said, 'Followed by cops beating on people in Chicago.'

'Damned fool Lyndon Johnson surrendered power to damned fool Hubert Humphrey who lost the election to damned fool Richard Nixon. Not one of them had brains enough to pour pee out of a boot with the directions written on the heel.

Oooooh, the stupidity of that war.' Leiat shook her head.

'In many respects, a year to forget.'

Leiat said, 'You know, in a way it's a relief to be seventy. I don't have to worry about such matters as career versus children or vaginal orgasms. My son is the city editor of the *Eugene Register-Guard*, takes after his mother, I think, and my daughter owns a boutique in Poulsbo, Washington. They're both still married, and I have three grandchildren who love me dearly. Not half bad. Too bad my husband isn't alive to enjoy it.'

The waitress, a pleasant, middle-aged woman in a mint-green uniform, arrived at the table, pad and pencil in hand. 'Well, hello, Leiat. Going to the big do tonight?'

Leiat said, 'I sure am, Polly. I'm on a triple date, a real score at my age.'

'Pretty kinky,' said Polly.

'I gotta keep up with the times,' Leiat said. 'These are my friends John Denson and Lenora Kemiah. Polly is one of my former students.'

Polly said, 'I get off in another hour. I'll

change my clothes, and my old man and I will head straight for the Elks Lodge.' To Lenora and me she said, 'Say, if I were you two, I'd watch my grammar tonight around Leiat. Remember to say 'completed,' not 'finalized,' and 'used,' not 'utilized.' Also, one talks, one does not 'verbalize.''

'In other words, don't try to get fancy,' I said.

'That's it. Use straightforward English, but use it correctly. Fifty-cent words don't increase the value of nickel-and-dime ideas.' She gave me a wink to please Leiat.

After we finished our orders, I continued with the program of the evening's activities. 'Okay, it says here the 1940s and 1950s graduates will be in Chuckie's Bar and Grill with Bill Davidson and the Cutups, a 1950s-style rock-and-roll band.'

'I should put in a brief appearance there, I think.'

'The 1960s and 1970s graduates are meeting in the Elks Lodge with folk singer Terry Dill and the Right Ons, and the 1980s and 1990s graduates, owing to their larger numbers, will be in the high school gymnasium with MegaTurds, a punk rock band.'

Podebski grinned. 'I suspect my tolerance for the MegaTurds will be short-lived. That kind of music, if you can call it that, just hurts my ears.'

I studied the program some more. 'Singer-impersonators Tom and Linda Beaumont and Memory Lane, here from Spokane courtesy of the Enterprise Jaycees, will make appearances at all three sites. Tom does everybody from Elvis to Mick Jagger and Bruce Springsteen. Linda can do female singers from Brenda Lee to Whitney Houston. I'm mainly interested in the Elks Lodge, but Lenora and I are at your service.'

Podebski said, 'I say a quick stop at the gym, then on to the Elks Lodge. You know, John, the body has a lamentable half-life; it's the cultivation of brains that counts in the long run. I suspect we'll see that tonight as we work our way from the gym to Chuckie's.'

'Travel backward in time.'

'We'll see, progressively, the effects of gravity and a slower metabolism. Hair

231

thins. Waists thicken.' Podebski shook her head sadly. 'But the men all say Lil Peters is still capable of turning their eye.'

'She is indeed,' I said, and received an elbow from Lenora for my comment. 'An English teacher for thirty-five years, Leiat. Were your courses considered entertaining Mickeys or were you a hateful old biddy?'

Podebski laughed. 'Closer to an old biddy, I think. I forced them to diagram sentences and memorize long lists of verbs. I do. I did. I have done. I see. I saw. I have seen. And so on. If they didn't learn the conjugations, I made them take the class again. They had to get through me to graduate, and I was real, real mean.'

'Good for you,' I said.

'They complained at the time, but in the end, I think, they appreciated my stubbornness and dedication. They know that 'hopefully' is an adverb, and for one to say 'Hopefully it won't rain tonight' is absurd.'

I said, 'Okay to say, 'I looked hopefully up at the blue patch in the gathering clouds.''

Podebski grinned. 'Very good, John. I forced them all to study Strunk and White and required them to read George Orwell's essay 'Politics and the English Language.''

'Now you've got reason to be proud.'

'I think so,' she said. 'I can tell you that even though they may be from Enterprise, Oregon, my former students don't embarrass themselves by saying 'I been' or 'it don't.' You know, a reunion of this kind has to be a disconcerting occasion for them. The pecking order was established when they were teenagers. Jocks and boobs on top. Fat boys, runts, nerds, and wallflowers on the bottom. If you don't mature early, adolescence is a harrowing time of life.'

'In your experience, what happens to students with the passing of time?' I said.

Leiat thought about her answer for a moment. 'The jocks and cheerleaders ordinarily stay around Enterprise because that's where they experienced the most glorious moment of their lives. They don't like to give it up to become one of the herd out there.'

'Out there?'

'Portland or Eugene or wherever, where the competition is tougher. High school is a closed, manageable world. After they graduate, they have to prove themselves all over again. And the competition gets tougher and tougher. Some of them are reluctant to go as far as La Grande to go to college.'

I said, 'I take it the fat boys, runts, nerds, and wallflowers are the ones who ordinarily push off for the larger world.'

'They were nothing here, and they suspect it will remain that way. There's the exception, of course, like Bubba Tubig.'

'The chief of police.'

'Correct. Bubba's done okay for himself in spite of his corpulence. But most of the fat boys, squirts, and nerds have got nothing to lose by trying their luck somewhere else. Your client Monty Hook, an all-star athlete, is a classic stay-put kind of student, but he had a head start. He took over his father's cattle ranch and has done quite well by himself.'

I said, 'He must have had something on the ball besides being a high school athlete. I bet his peers didn't elect him president of the cattlemen's association for nothing.'

'No, they didn't, it's true. He's been an active and forceful spokesman for cattlemen's causes. I'm curious — which one were you at Cayuse High School, Mr. Denson?'

'Jock, fat boy, nerd, or runt?'

She smiled.

'Yes, which was it, John?' Lenora asked. She raised an eyebrow.

'Runt. I didn't start growing until I was nineteen years old. Delayed hormones or whatever. I was so little I was called Skeeter, for mosquito.'

Lenora and Leiat both laughed.

Leiat said, 'And when did you leave the Cayuse area?'

'Straightaway,' I said. 'I went off to college, supporting myself on scholarships and by driving a truck in the wheat and pea harvests. I never went home except to visit my parents while they were still alive.' I said, 'How about you, Lenora?'

'I spent all my time on horses, I have to admit.'

'And boy, is she good,' Leiat said. 'I've seen her ride at Chief Joseph Days.'

I said, 'I suppose the drama tonight has to do with Thad Bonnerton's perception that he's showed them a thing or two with his television persona and his Cadillac limousine and yes-men.'

Leiat said, 'I think so. I saw him on television in his Food City apron. The way he sees it, success is the best form of revenge. The jocks and cheerleaders want to be on top of things again. To them, the Reverend Thaddeus Hamm Bonnerton is, and always will be, Thad Bonnerton, a pimple-faced box boy at Food City.'

I said, 'They'll be friendly to him, of course, but they won't invite him into their cliques or promote him to the top of their social order, which is what he's got in mind.'

'I don't think there's any doubt of that.'

'By the way,' I said, 'who was your best English student, Leiat?'

She smiled, thinking that one over. 'That's not an easy question. I had several good ones over the years. One of the best ones, curiously enough, was Bubba Tubig.'

'The corpulent cop.'

'He was a dancing fool and a very good writer. How he wound up as a cop is beyond me, I have to admit.'

15

As we endured the awful, echoing din of MegaTurds in the Enterprise High School gymnasium, Lenora Kemiah and I discovered we were not in the company of just another English teacher; Leiat Podebski was something of a celebrity, if not an institution. Through drilling proper English into generations of Enterprise High School students, she had made a difference in that community.

And contrary to having been a 'hateful old biddy,' Leiat was loved and even revered by her former students, who, in the end, had sense enough to know the importance of having correctly learned the English language. Thanks to her, they could travel in any company and in any city without being self-conscious.

So eager were her students to see her and thank her for her efforts in years past that it was nearly impossible for her to leave the gym. Even Roy Childress, a

1986 graduate, paid his respects.

By nine-thirty Leiat managed to say her good-byes, vowing to return later in the evening if possible. Feeling good — plus relieved at having escaped the cacophony of Megaturds — the three of us piled into my microbus for the second leg of our evening's journey, to the Elks Lodge, a redbrick building with a facade that apparently dated from the nineteenth century.

The parking lot was full, so I dropped my two dates at the front door and parked my bus down the street.

I opened the door of the Elks Lodge for Leiat and Lenora, and we stepped into the foyer, which was lined with framed eight-by-ten black-and-white photographs of past commanders. These were formal portraits, and the commanders looked solemn and stern-faced in the extreme; many of them were no doubt farmers and ranchers who did not ordinarily wear a suit, except for weddings and funerals. It was impossible for many of them to avoid looking slightly foolish wearing a necktie.

I stopped to admire the surreal quality

of the photographs, wondering if my fascination was the result of a personal quirk or if Leiat and Lenora were similarly affected.

Leiat looked amused. 'Aren't these something?'

Lenora put her hand over her mouth and giggled.

The attraction of groups, organizations, and especially fraternities was personally foreign to me, but folks in small towns apparently love them. In Enterprise, for instance, there were, in addition to Elks, Mooses, Eagles, Jaycees, Masons, and Shriners. The notion of going around calling some asshole or moron 'brother' or flashing secret signs was ridiculous, in my opinion.

But it was, I suppose, a form of immortality to be elected commander by one's fellow Elks and an honor to have one's photograph added to the foyer. No commander wanted to break tradition by allowing so much as a hint of a smile, so they looked like the soldiers in Matthew Brady's Civil War photographs.

I shook my head in bewilderment.

'Someone ought to display these pictures at the Guggenheim or somewhere, don't you think, Leiat? Is this real Americana, or what?'

'Isn't it wonderful?' she said.

'What I don't understand is why they feel compelled to wear suits,' I said. 'There's nothing dishonorable about being a rancher or a farmer. I'd like to have a ranch or farm myself. Also, I bet none of them got elected commander by being so damned solemn.'

Standing there in the hall of serious faces, I remembered what Willie Prettybird had said about the difference between Clint Eastwood and Alan Alda. The Elks commanders were pretending to be Eastwoods, whether they were or not; they were leaders, chiefs of the Elks tribe. The necktie was their version of the feathered headdress among Willie's ancestors.

After we passed through the foyer, we discovered we weren't through with photographs. The organizers of the reunion had gone to the effort of having class photographs blown up and mounted on the walls. By simply touring the Elk's large hall, strolling clockwise, one could go from class to class from 1960 through 1979. In addition to those, there were photographs of athletic teams that had won league and district championships. Below the class photographs, a small table displayed the annuals for each of the four years that that class was in high school.

Leiat, seeing the photographs, said, 'They said they were going to do this. Good for them. What do you say we start in 1979 and work our way backwards?'

'That would be counterclockwise. Fine by me,' I said.

'Let's do it,' Lenora said.

So we did. It was slow going, what with former students wanting to say hello to Leiat. If anything, these older students seemed even more passionate in their affection for her than the most recent graduates, having had time, I suspect, to appreciate the benefits of language well taught, never an easy chore.

We passed group photographs of young people who grew progressively hairier until at last we came to the class of 1968, which vied with 1969 as being the hairiest bunch of all. In keeping with the times, the boys all had sideburns and tangles of long hair spilling over their shoulders, and those who could manage beards and mustaches had them as well. The girls, in emulation of Joan Baez, also wore their locks long.

The boomers, of course, had never been Bohemians, despite their posturing. Every generation had its Bohemians — ordinarily artists and writers — but long hair and beards were simply the fashion of the time in 1968. Bohemians, ordinarily being nonconsumerist and nonmaterialist, avoid fashion.

I quickly spotted Monty Hook in the class photograph; although he had remained slender over the years, he had had an athletic look about him then, and sported a mustache and sideburns.

Then as now, Lil Peters was a hot looker.

Thad Bonnerton, afflicted by pimples, was a classic nerd.

And Bubba Tubig had, in fact, been a

fat boy from the start.

I flipped open the annual of the 1967–68 school year to the class prophecy and was not surprised to find that it had been written by Bubba Tubig. He had predicted that Monty Hook, the class president that year, would be head football coach at Eastern Oregon State College in La Grande; that Lil Peters would be a television anchor at a Portland TV station and an actress in stage productions there; that Thad Bonnerton would be a faith healer in Bartlesville, Oklahoma — pretty close, that one — and that he himself would run an Arthur and Kathryn Murray dance studio in Pendleton.

The 1967 Enterprise Savages were district football champions, and so merited a photograph. Tubig's stockiness had served him well in one respect. In a football uniform, he looked as wide as he did tall, at guard in a photograph in which the cameraman shot the offensive line straight on. When I had talked to him in his office, he'd said that in pads he looked like a human tank. He was right.

Behind Tubig and his fellow linemen were quarterback Monty Hook, fashionable long hair poking from beneath his helmet, and three halfbacks, young men who had no doubt gotten their strength pumping hay bales and their speed running after recalcitrant milk cows.

Lil, head of the cheerleading squad, looked delicious and then some in her little outfit.

As I studied the photographs, Monty Hook, saying hello to Leiat and Lenora, stepped up behind me, wearing clean jeans and a western shirt with a string tie held in place with a turquoise clip.

He was loaded — well no, not just loaded; the local expression, 'shit-faced,' more accurately covered his condition. My mother would have said he was three sheets to the wind. In this case, four sheets was more like it.

He said, 'Well, what do you think, John? My hero was Johnny Unitas. I was a Colts fan. See there, number nineteen, just like Johnny Unitas. Only thing was, I didn't go so far as to wear a crewcut. That was going too far in those days.'

'In 1968, I guess it was. You went nine and two, not bad. How could you miss with a future chief of police blocking for you up front?'

Hook wobbled and grinned crookedly. 'The stocky little son of a bitch was a hell of a football player, you can't take that away from him. He just fired off the line on a running play, and when I dropped back to pass, nobody, but nobody, got past him. He was strong and had a low center of gravity. If we'd had five Bubba Tubigs from tackle to tackle, we'd have won the state title, no question.'

Over my shoulder a man said, 'I heard that bullshit, Hook.'

I turned. It was Bubba Tubig, who had knocked back a couple of drinks himself. His sails were also full. He was wearing a jacket and tie. He wobbled uncertainly, still grinning at Hook's unsolicited compliment. 'Weren't those the days, Monty?'

Hook said, 'They sure as hell were. But my God, man, who's watching the town tonight? Your deputy?'

Tubig laughed. 'I told Duane the fun's

246

all his tonight. Have a good time with the drunks and nutballs.'

'Better lock up the women and children,' Hook said.

'The chief's got to have a turn to howl once in a while. Nothing in my contract says I gotta live like a monk all the time. Have to come and admire my picture on the football team. Days of glory and all that.'

'Gonna cut a rug, eh?' I said.

'You damned right,' he said. 'We've got most of the team here tonight, and even a few of the cheerleaders. The best-looking ones, anyway.'

'I saw the lady named Lil at the High Country,' I said. 'She's still looking good as far as I'm concerned.'

'Ain't that a fact,' Hook said.

Tubig, studying the photograph, said, 'Lil looks even better, if that's possible after all these years.'

I said, 'Who would have guessed that your friend Thad Bonnerton would return in a stretch limousine? Didn't you say he had a crush on Lil?'

Tubig and Hook both laughed.

'That asshole?' Tubig said.

'Amen.' Hook looked to the heavens in mock prayer, and they both laughed even louder.

Just as Lil herself arrived, wearing a form-fitting yellow cocktail dress with a low-cut bodice that showed off both pearls and her uh-huhs, Tom Beaumont and his wife and their group, Memory Lane, began tuning up.

I said to Lenora, 'I suppose you're going to want to dance, Lenora?'

'We Indians may not have a natural sense of rhythm, but we're not bad.'

'Does that mean I'm going to have to make a fool of myself?'

Lenora grinned.

Leiat Podebski said, 'Of course it does, you idiot. What do you think?'

★   ★   ★

The Reverend Thaddeus Hamm Bonner-ton made his entrance fashionably late, wearing an investment banker's three-piece suit similar to the one he had worn on his arrival at Food City. One could justifiably wonder: Did Ham Bone wear a three-piece suit in the shower?

Bonnerton made no immediate attempt to find the table assigned to the class of 1968, or, if he saw it, he ignored it. Instead, he appeared rather to pose, aloof, superior, more important than everybody else.

Once, Thad Bonnerton had needed the approval of his classmates. Now, by his body language, he made it clear that if they were to share in the dubious excitement of meeting the Reverend Thaddeus Hamm Bonnerton, media celebrity, they would have to come to him. By thus rearranging the hierarchy, the once-pimpled pariah of the class of '68 no doubt sought to redress the barbarous adolescent stretch of the hoop that had once tormented him.

But would such a carefully planned return ever play out as Bonnerton must have dreamed in triumphant fantasy? I didn't think so. After all, what would his classmates have to say to him and he to them? What did it really matter? And had he not proven their point by this pretentious foolishness: that he was an impossible, forever nerd? Better, I thought, to push onward and upward and enjoy life in the present.

Unfortunately, the drama of His Famousness's arrival was muted by the singer-impressionist Tom Beaumont, who took the microphone as his band struck up the familiar opening lines of 'Yesterday.'

The Beatles! This was their music.

Monty Hook immediately asked Lil to dance.

Beaumont, doing a credible John Lennon, sang: '*Yesterday, all my troubles seemed so far away.*'

The song was perfect for the Enterprise High School Class of 1968. Yesterday. Here was Monty Hook dancing with Lil Peters, just as they had more than twenty-five years earlier. *All my troubles seemed so far away.* For a sentimental moment, nothing had changed.

'*Suddenly, I'm not half the man I used to be.*'

As Monty and Lil glided by, I gave Monty a wink. 'Right on!'

'*How I long for yesterday.*'

But I noticed, out of the corner of my eye, that Ham Bone was not especially thrilled. He was, in 1968 lingo, uptight, straight. He did not think this pair was cool, hip, or groovy in any way. And if he was enjoying Memory Lane's splendid imitation of the Beatles, he didn't show it.

'*Oh, I believe in yesterday.*'

Monty and Lil's friends all clapped when the song was over and they returned to their group.

Now the inebriated Enterprise chief of police, Bubba Tubig, with a spring in his step and a grin on his round face, took a turn at asking the sexy Lil Peters to dance.

The smile on Lil's face said she was pleased to accept.

Leiat said, 'Watch this, John.'

'Huh?'

'You wait.' Podebski looked amused.

'Hey, the company's good. I'm having a good time. Let's watch old Bubba show his stuff.' Lenora gave my hand a squeeze to let me know she was having a good time too, and my mouth turned dry. Ever since she'd opened the door to Bobcat Bill's, I had been feeling sixteen years old. Inside, I was grinning as big as baby Jessica.

If Bubba Tubig felt any older than sixteen, he didn't show it. He looked downright lithe as he escorted Lil onto the floor.

If Lil had any hesitation about dancing with Bubba Tubig, she didn't show it.

On the stage, Tom Beaumont, turned John Lennon, sang 'I Wanna Hold Your Hand.'

Tubig, with his classmates cheering him on, immediately got into the music. He knew how to move that rotund body of his and did. He didn't just twist, jump, and wiggle; inebriated as he was, Tubig was fluid and graceful, confident in his moves — a Gene Kelly or Fred Astaire trapped in a fat man's body.

'Ho, I see what you mean,' I told Leiat.

'He was always a natural dancer,' Podebski said. 'Apparently born with it.'

'Now I understand the class prophecy,' I said. Bubba Tubig, the blocky guard on the football team, might indeed have become a dance instructor. Monty Hook hadn't been a bad dancer, drunk as he was, but compared to Tubig he had two left feet.

When Chief Tubig finished, everybody wanted him to take Lil for another turn, but poor Bubba, his chest heaving, face awash with sweat, was clearly winded.

Now Tom Beaumont turned into Mick Jagger, swaggering to and fro, chest out, head back. 'I can't get no sat-is-fac-tion . . . No, no, no.'

Beaumont lacked Jagger's sensual lips, but he had his wicked body language down pat.

The Reverend Thaddeus Hamm Bonnerton now headed for Lil. Was the preacher of a clean environment going to show that fat little cop a thing or two about dancing?

Why on earth Ham Bone would choose 'Satisfaction' to ask Lil to dance was anybody's guess, but he did. For one thing, it wasn't an especially good song to dance to. For another, Bonnerton looked faintly ridiculous in his three-piece suit; only a congenital nerd would go to a high school reunion dressed like an investment banker.

Lil, who was laughing and joking with her friends after her turn on the floor with the amazing Bubba Tubig, was taken by surprise. But this was a reunion, after all, and everybody was having fun. She said yes, of course she would dance with Thad Bonnerton.

The problem came when they actually danced. Lil, comfortable with her body, was loose and fluid and knew how to move with the music.

Bonnerton, who was apparently always on stage, attempted simultaneously to dance and remain The Important Man. He danced with his chin held high and his chest improbably poked out so that he looked like the Tin Man in the Wizard of Oz, or a politician with a cob up his butt. He might have compensated for his extraordinary stiffness if he'd known how to dance, but he didn't. He was apparently totally devoid of any sense of rhythm.

As a pious schoolboy and later a preacher, Bonnerton probably hadn't gotten a lot of practice dancing, but this performance slid fast to the ridiculous. He simply had no idea what to do with his body.

If Lil was embarrassed to be dancing with such a self-important nitwit, she didn't show it. Or tried not to. But it must have been the longest dance of her life.

But Ham Bone, in love with himself as he was, wasn't so stupid as to know this wasn't working out. He was supposed to be impressing Lil and his classmates, but no. He was making a fool of himself.

Monty Hook, who was still piling snort upon snort, was not as polite as Lil. He cupped his hands around his mouth and shouted, 'Go for it, Thaddie boy. Show the pretty lady your stuff.'

Bonnerton's face grew tight. He pretended not to hear Hook, and danced.

'I can't get no satisfaction.'

Hook said, 'Come on, Lil. Wiggle it. Shake your bootie.'

'I can't get no satisfaction.'

Lil's face tightened. She glared at Hook. 'Monty, shut up!'

'*I can't get no.*'

'Right on, Reverend!' Hook called.

'*I can't get no.*'

'Monty!' Lil said.

'*Satisfaction.*'

Bonnerton, aware that he had made himself the object of laughter and derision, obviously didn't know what to do. But he refused to yield until the song was finished. To quit in the middle of the dance was to admit defeat. That was impossible for Bonnerton to do.

'*No, no, no.*'

'Groovy, dude, groovy,' Hook called.

Defeat certainly wasn't what the Reverend Thaddeus Hamm Bonnerton had had in mind when he'd come rumbling into town with six tour buses and a stretch limousine, scoring immediately with his picture in the *Wallowa County Chiefain* and an interview on television. He'd see it through.

When, at long last, the sweating Tom Beaumont was finished with his Mick Jagger imitation, Bonnerton, face flushed with anger, retreated quickly from the floor and headed for the door. He had been humiliated; his long-fancied moment of triumph had turned to manure. All his fancy duds had failed to erase the past. To the sexy Lil Peters, he would always be Thad Bonnerton, pimpled one. The clock could not be magically turned back and a new entrance made. He had been mocked and ridiculed.

As Bonnerton retreated from the building in defeat, he could not conceal the depths of his anguish. His final exit, mercifully, was witnessed only by the solemn, framed faces of past commanders of the Enterprise Elks.

The silence that followed was downright embarrassing. Bonnerton's classmates weren't a malevolent bunch of adolescents out of *Lord of the Flies;* they were just loaded, most of them, and having fun, but they had gone too far, and they knew it, and they didn't feel good about it.

I had no stomach for watching anybody destroyed, but when I thought about Bonnerton's brutal and unnecessary badgering of the poor Food City manager, it was hard to work up a whole lot of sympathy for him.

Would Jesus approve of such barbarous horseshit by a minister of the gospel?

As ye sow, so shall ye reap. Wasn't that in the Bible somewhere?

Also, I wondered if there weren't admonitions in the Good Book somewhere about plain old greed. I wondered how much of Bonnerton's God Squad take actually went to improve the environment and how much went to purchase limousines and fancy tour buses and the other accoutrements of the preacher's lifestyle.

One thing was sure. The Reverend Thaddeus Hamm Bonnerton didn't get much in the way of satisfaction on this occasion. No, no, no.

★   ★   ★

Leiat Podebski began to tire about an hour after Thad Bonnerton's untidy exit. We had a cup of coffee in the Pheasant Café and I drove back to the Wallowa River Inn. I dropped Lenora and Leiat off at the manager's unit, and had no sooner stepped into my unit than the phone rang.

It was Willie, calling from Bobcat Bill's house on our cellular phone. 'Got it figured,' he said.

'Lay it on me,' I said.

'We isolated the trail of the two horses. It was obvious one was leading the other, a lead horse and a pack horse.'

'A lone rider?'

Willie said, 'Correct.'

'Carrying what?'

'Salt licks.'

'Say again?'

Willie said, 'Salt licks, poisoned with anthrax. When we found the first salt lick, we could see it was no ordinary block of salt. An outer layer of the usual mineral salts had apparently been licked away, revealing a core of something else. Neither one of us had ever seen a salt lick like that, and it sure as hell hadn't been put there by one of Bobcat's hands. We called the communicable-disease people on our cellular phone. After they came in their four-wheel-drive to pick it up, Bobcat and I split in separate directions and kept riding. We eventually found eight similar salt licks, placed in isolated arroyos, probably a couple of nights' work by one rider working by moonlight. By the time we got back, the state vets had analyzed the core of the first salt lick in their portable lab: it contained a little of this, a little of that, and a whole lot of anthrax spores.'

'Whoa!' There was hardly an adult in Wallowa County who didn't know cattle love salt licks. Cattle go for salt licks like little kids after ice cream cones.

'We knew they had to catch that shit some way,' Willie said. 'Didn't you say McAllister had been chasing poachers? Poachers know their salt licks, don't they? Maybe our man's a poacher.'

I said, 'What poacher in his right mind would use poisoned salt licks? Deer like salt licks too.'

'Unfortunately, and a deer can smell those things from miles away.'

'Whoops!'

'Right. We've got deer tracks leading away from several of the poisoned salt licks, which means we've got infected deer on our hands. A dead deer doesn't just rot out here. It's food for another animal. Part of the hoop.'

'Ooof!' I said.

'Bobcat and I have spent the last few hours phoning friends on the Umatilla and Nez Percé reservations. We gotta track the sick animals down and dispose of them properly, or that shit will spread like wildfire.' The Umatilla Indian Reservation was a two-hour drive from the west, near Pendleton, Oregon. The Nez Percé Reservation was three hours to the northeast, near Lewiston, Idaho.

'I take it you'll have to skip the rodeo tomorrow.'

Willie said, 'No, we'll put the trackers to work in the morning and come in and join you and Lenora for the rodeo tomorrow night. Can't track after dark anyway, and there's no sense sitting around pissing and moaning. That won't solve anything.'

'You think you can run down all the sick deer?'

'We'll get 'em. We won't stop until every set of tracks is accounted for. It's as simple as that.'

'See you tomorrow, then.'

'Tomorrow, Kemosabe.' Willie hung up.

I sat back on my bed. Salt licks. If you wanted to infect somebody's herd with anthrax, a salt lick was a simple solution. Diabolic perhaps. Demonic. Chickenshit in the extreme. But effective.

Willie Prettybird and Bobcat Bill had stumbled onto the trail of a genuine, world-class asshole. No doubt about it.

★   ★   ★

When Willie and I had checked in at the Wallowa River Inn, Leiat Podebski had said that the folks in unit eight, an end unit around the interior corner from six, were real partyers. Boy, was she right tonight. The music inside was thumping and rocking. The people who had set up the Reverend Bonnerton's revivals in Enterprise were partying out. Boogying.

That didn't bother me a whole lot. My mind was on salt licks and Lenora anyway, so I decided to wait them out. I flipped on the idiot box and there was Ronald Reagan in *Navy Hellcats*, one of his preliminary roles leading up to his eight-year run in the White House. But the vintage Reagan, in my opinion, was the guy who hustled 20 Mule Team Borax on *Death Valley Days* in the 1950s.

I got out some screw-top red and kicked back to enjoy the movie. To hell with the idiots in unit eight.

A few minutes later there came a rapping, a tapping at my motel door. Were the partyers after more ice or a can opener? I opened the door.

Lenora Kemiah.

She said, 'I couldn't sleep.'

'Neither could I,' I said.

'I saw your light on.'

I said, 'Won't you come in?'

She hesitated, then stepped inside. 'I don't see how anybody could sleep with the music blasting like that in the end unit.'

'I probably wouldn't have been able to sleep under any circumstance,' I said.

She said, 'I wanted to tell you, I sure did have a good time tonight.'

'So did I, part of the reason why I couldn't sleep. I don't have much to offer, screw-top red and Tillamook sharp cheddar.'

'Jug wine is all Bobcat ever buys. All he can afford.'

I unscrewed the wine and poured us each half a water glass, and got the cheese out of the refrigerator. I said, 'No couch, but the carpet looks clean.'

I gave her the remote, and she squatted on the carpet.

I said, 'I got a call from Willie when I got back. Progress report.'

'Oh?'

I told her what Willie and Bobcat had found.

She blinked. 'Salt licks?'

'That's right. Whoever put them there poisoned some deer along with Monty's cattle. Willie and Bobcat have been calling Umatillas and Nez Percés all evening. Tomorrow they have to track the infected deer down and burn their corpses, just like the cattle.'

Lenora was stunned. 'Who on earth would do such a thing?'

I said, 'Beats hell out of me. But there's not a whole lot we can do about it tonight, I suppose. You want to find something else besides Ronald Reagan?

We've got cable, so there should be some choices.'

Lenora Kemiah, her mind on poisoned salt licks, took a sip of wine and aimed her remote at the television set. She began clicking through the channels.

16

The bacon smelled wonderful; even the cholesterol-laden grease sounded good as it popped and cracked in the frying pan. It was nice watching Lenora Kemiah cook as I munched on whole wheat toast and drank the good, strong coffee she had made. We had shared the hormonal other and it was splendid in the extreme. Now Leonora was showing me her cooking skills, had me thinking about a place down in Klickitat that I had been eyeing. Life was good.

She said, 'I need to drive out and see Jessica today, so I can come back and watch the rodeo with you tonight. What'll you be up to, Mr. Detective?'

'Now that we know how Monty's cattle got infected, we have to find whoever was behind the salt lick. Somebody put the salt licks on the north spread. It wasn't little green people popping out of UFOs.'

She laughed. 'I don't imagine it was.'

I said, 'You know, I bet the Reverend Thaddeus Hamm Bonnerton is as good a businessman as he is a preacher or he wouldn't be so successful. He has all those advance men and technicians and yes-men. And he even brought along a camera crew to record the fun when Monty had to burn his cattle. That all has to cost a fortune.'

'I bet it does.'

'His revival today is just a tune-up for his televised extravaganza on Sunday. Do you really think he would go to all this trouble without a good chance of a payback at the end? Strikes me as he could use something dramatic to get the maximum number of people to tune in.'

'Maybe he thinks the Lord will provide.'

'I suppose he does. Still, I probably ought to have a talk with him, don't you think? Just in case he has something to do with the salt licks. That's assuming he hasn't left town after his unpleasant exit from the reunion last night.'

'Wasn't that awful, poor man.'

'All that resentment built up over the years to what end? A piss-poor climax, I'd say.'

'How do you propose to get him to talk to you?'

I shrugged. 'Oh, I don't know. Over the years I've learned there are ways, if I use my imagination. You know. I might try this. I might try that.'

She grinned. 'Like this and that what? If it isn't some kind of trade secret.'

'With someone like Bonnerton, I'd say ego's probably my best bet.' I dug into my travel bag and retrieved a bundle of business cards.

'What're those?' Lenora said, looking puzzled. I handed her a card from the top of my collection. She looked at it and said, 'Really?'

'People like to talk. I don't mind listening.'

She began flipping through the cards, reading them. 'Oh, you are the naughty one, aren't you? How long have you been doing this?'

'I don't know. A few years. Whenever the occasion calls for it.'

'You think it'll work this time?'
'I don't know. We'll see,' I said.

★   ★   ★

The Reverend Thaddeus Hamm Bonnerton's entourage was encamped just outside the Enterprise city limits on Ant Flat Road. It was my bet that permits and permissions were fewer in number and easier to come by from the county than the city, but never mind. After a couple of inquiries at the Bonnerton compound or wagon train — five smaller tour buses were literally circled around the one obviously occupied by the Important One — I was directed to the bus where, I was told, I would find Loretta Mannsen, the Reverend Bonnerton's 'media affairs spokesperson.'

Were the buses merely circled against pagans and humanists, or were papists and Calvinists also excluded? Halfway expecting Charlton Heston to stride forth as the wagon master, I headed for the media bus.

I thought the title 'media affairs

spokesperson' was a bit much. I preferred the straightforward old newspaper reporter's title for such people — flacks, in the sense of shooting down incoming bombers. But I understood few people wanted to be called flacks, a title lacking the ring of importance which was sometimes substituted for a fair salary. I rang the buzzer.

The door was answered by an earnest young man in the ubiquitous God Squad T-shirt. 'Yes?'

'I would like to speak to Loretta Mannsen, please.'

He looked surprised. 'Ms. Mannsen is quite busy this morning. May I ask your business?'

I gave young Mr. God Squad the card.

He read it and blinked. He was Sticksville. *New York Times Magazine* was New York, the Big Apple and all that manure.

'*New York Times?*'

'The Sunday magazine, not the daily. Ms. Mannsen is the reverend's press secretary, is she not?' I thought better of calling her a flack; better to meet her halfway.

'Media affairs spokesperson,' he said.

Twit, I thought. I said, 'Whatever. I'm after whoever it is who deals with reporters.' If I had tried to palm myself off as a writer for *Time* or *Newsweek*, it would have been easy enough to grab a copy and check my bona fides by looking at the list of editors and writers in small print at the beginning of the magazine. It was my bet that in Enterprise, Oregon, a copy of *The New York Times Magazine* was not easy to come by.

'One moment, please.' Then he was gone, taking my card with him.

A moment later, a good-looking blonde with an air of self-importance was at the door. Her body language said clearly: she was busy, busy, busy. And a big shot. A big, big shot. She was not impressed by someone from *The New York Times*. Reading from the card, she said, 'Mr. John Denson?' She screwed up her face. Whether this expressed disapproval or bewilderment, I couldn't tell.

'That's right,' I said. 'With the San Francisco bureau of the *Times*. Of course you know Bob James.' A man named Bob

James was, in fact, the head of the *Times's* San Francisco bureau.

'Loretta Mannson.' We shook. She said, 'And this has to do with?'

Salt licks, I thought. I said, 'A profile of the Reverend Bonnerton. Bob James knows I'm from Cayuse originally. When he read about Bonnerton's attending an all-school reunion, going home, so to speak, he dispatched me here to write a profile. I'm supposed to know the area and everything. Here I am. Old home week for me too.' If she wanted to paw through old annuals of Cayuse High School, let her.

She studied the card again.

'You know Bob, of course,' I said, old pro to old pro. Sure.

She hesitated. 'I can't say I really *know* him. I've talked to him on the phone a couple of times.'

Right. *Liar*, I thought. This is like people who never read books, or only best-sellers, saying, I don't get a chance to read much anymore, or I read it years ago. I had read enough of Carlos Casteneda to get the gist of Don Juan's concept of inner and outer tonal. I was inner; I read books, and wondered who I was. She was outer, and turned this way and that in the mirror every morning, making sure she looked right. As I think, so I am, versus as I look, so I am.

I said, 'You may have seen me at Food City when you first arrived. I came early so I could see some old friends in the area. Lucky I was there when the good Reverend Bonnerton rolled in. Gave me some good, spontaneous stuff. The reverend having a chat with the store manager at the vegetable display. The reverend bagging an old lady's groceries.' I thought, *The reverend deliberately squashing the old lady's tomatoes.*

'A profile in *The New York Times Magazine?*' She suppressed her excitement; the Reverend Thaddeus Hamm Bonnerton was a serious Christian environmentalist, not some fly-by-night egoist who locked himself in the toilet to savor his press clippings in private. To make *The Times Magazine* was to have one's bona fides stamped with the seal of establishment recognition, sort of a Billy

Graham border chop. Preachers with the proper chop got to lecture presidents on Sunday morning and pretend the president actually listened.

I looked chagrined. 'To tell you the truth, I suspect the magazine's sensitive to charges that we don't pay enough attention to Christians.'

She gave me a you-got-that-right-brother raise of her eyebrows.

I said, 'They're worried about being Jewish and uppity New York and all that. They're a lot more broad-minded than you give them credit for, they really are.'

'Oh?' She suppressed a grim smile that said Jews were odious intellectuals with yucky noses, and she didn't like them.

I plowed right onward. 'But to tell you the truth, I think in this case the environmental angle is what's got 'em juiced. Good grist for a makeup piece.'

'A makeup piece.'

'So to speak. I don't think they'd put it quite that crassly.'

'I bet they wouldn't.'

'But I'm the guy who has to get the story,' I said quickly.

She seemed to calm, if not exactly soften. She said, 'As you might imagine, the reverend's quite busy this morning, preparing for a revival this afternoon. He's quite meticulous about his revivals, even those that aren't televised. He personally sees to it that everything is done properly.'

'That's why I'm here, to find out what's on his mind and how he gets ready for one of his revivals. Gotta have all the details.'

She gave me a they-all-say-that look, no doubt having seen Bonnerton dumped on many well-deserved times in addition to a few casual cheap shots, as though his being called an asshole, crook, or con artist made a difference to his followers. The fundamentalist high rollers regarded mainstream reporters as atheist humanists, one step up from horse thieves and child molesters.

I said, 'That's the stuff that makes a magazine profile really sing. Details, details, details. Pioneered by *Time* magazine. You know the drill. If the Reverend Bonnerton could give me just a few minutes this morning for a get-acquainted chat, I could come back tomorrow for a longer talk.'

With all the courtesy she might have extended to an infected prick, Ms. Mannsen stepped back and gestured for me to come inside. 'Won't you come in and have a cup of coffee, Mr. Denson. I'll talk to the Reverend Bonnerton, and we'll see what we can do.'

★　★　★

The Reverend Thaddeus Hamm Bonnerton eyed me over a cup of tea. Preachers like Bonnerton could not understand why they were not regarded as cultural heroes; in their Manichaean good-guy, bad-guy world, they were the goodest of white-hat good-guys in mortal combat with the shits of the world.

While Bonnerton did not appear overtly suspicious, he had to be wary of highly paid, cheerful skunks from news magazines trying to pin him as an overt hustler, if not an outright crook. Looking about his spacious tour bus, I thought that only a hustler or crook could go for such horsepucky ostentation. But never mind.

When Willie and I had checked into the Wallowa River Inn, Leiat Podebski, I was convinced, had been about to tell us a revealing secret from Bonnerton's past, but had checked herself. Telling us that Thad Bonnerton was a pimple-faced nerd infatuated with a hot-looking cheerleader was fair enough. But Leiat had stopped short of revealing the entire arc of Bonnerton's hoop through his high school years.

A terrible business, was the way Leiat had phrased it.

A terrible business . . .

A man like Bonnerton would not share any kind of terrible business with the gophers, yes-men, and press agents around him. I had sense enough to know that. The trick for me — if I was to learn anything useful — was to convince Bonnerton that I was genuinely neutral with regard to ripoff egoists, a sympathetic figure because I went to high school in Cayuse. A city boy from the East Coast couldn't fake being from Cayuse. It took a real dork McCountry kid to pull it off.

Even better if I had been a nerd, fat boy, or runt — same difference in the unforgiving world of teenagers. Bonnerton might warm up to an ex-runt from Cayuse, but maybe not a jock or class president. There were high school class presidents who spent their entire lives proving they were above people like Bonnerton. If they were from someplace like Cayuse, it was an embarrassment to them, and they kept it a secret.

'Denson? Denson?' Bonnerton bounced his teabag up and down in his cup. He pursed his lips and furrowed his eyebrows, trying to remember my name from the fog of the past.

'The Broncos never played ball against Enterprise, but we did tangle with Joseph a couple of times. Small world, I know.'

'Denson? From Cayuse? Mmmmm.'

'Helluva place to be from, I admit. The truth is I was an easy-to-forget little runt.'

Bonnerton looked surprised.

'I was a late grower. Shot up like a weed when I was nineteen. Too late to be a big man on campus. When I was a freshman, I remember, I figured if I made it to five six and a hundred and thirty pounds, I'd be satisfied. I ended up five eleven and one seventy-five, Mr. Medium-sized.'

He smiled. 'A runt from Cayuse winds up with *The New York Times*. Isn't that something?' It wasn't clear whether he believed that or not.

I plunged forward with my gambit. 'I was too small to be any kind of jock and too poor to own a car. But I earned a few extra bucks phoning in game stories to the *Hermiston Herald* when we were on the road. A writer has to start someplace. If we were hopelessly behind or twenty points ahead, I actually got to play a half minute. Long enough to hack someone on the arm and get my name included in the stats. Denson, J., one foul. If they had kept a stat called screwups, I'd have had big numbers.'

Watching me, Bonnerton laughed. Was he warming? Hard to tell.

I said, 'When I was a freshman we rode all the way to Athena to play a baseball game, but the flu had been through, and they could only field eight players. Coach asked for a volunteer from those of us who never got to play, and I got my hand up first. I played right field for Athena.'

He laughed. 'Hey, that's the spirit.'

'Better to play right field for Athena than to sit on the bench for the Broncos, was the way I saw it. I showed them I could strike out for anybody. I didn't discriminate. Did you ever play basketball at Lexington?'

He smiled. He liked my suggestion that he might have played basketball. 'No, I don't believe I did.'

I said, 'The dressing room was in the building next door to the gym. One night, we had to run through a snowstorm to get to the gym. The gym had a low ceiling so you couldn't shoot a shot with any kind of arc. They had an oil stove that stuck out onto the floor. It was protected by a wire cage, and it was legal to dribble close by it to scrape off the player guarding you. Sort of a permanent pick. The Jackrabbits were good at it.'

Nobody who hadn't played at Lexington would remember details like that. I figured I had him, but just to be safe, I said, 'I was playing on the B team one night, and the Jackrabbits apparently couldn't afford proper jerseys, so they wore white T-shirts with numbers stenciled on them. The man guarding me wore number three thousand seven hundred and thirty-six.'

Bonnerton said, 'I spent most of my time bagging groceries at Food City. Ms. Mannsen said you saw me there.'

'Yes, I did. Got to see you bagging groceries for the television cameras. Lucked out.' I checked my notebook. 'Your father is originally from Oklahoma, as I understand it. How did he happen to end up in Enterprise, Oregon?'

'Good question, Mr. Denson. My father's sister lived here in Enterprise. She was married to the owner of a hardware store, and suggested my father to the committee of the local Baptist church that was then searching for a new preacher, their old one having passed on.'

That is, he died, I thought. Joe Montana might be said to pass on. Or pass forward. The rest of us plain old die.

Bonnerton said, 'My aunt later passed on as well, I'm sorry to say. Cancer.'

I bunched my face, a gesture of sympathy. Only then did I realize what they meant by that phrase. Passed on to heaven.

'My father just loved it up here, such beautiful country.'

'A far cry from Oklahoma scrub. How is it your family moved back?'

Bonnerton blinked. With this question I had struck some kind of bull's-eye. If he had been wired to a polygraph, the needles would have been hopping like Mexican jumping beans. 'My aunt died, as I said, and my grandfather was ailing back in Tulsa. My mother wanted to be near him and to help care for him.'

'Oh, I see.'

'She was a loving Christian woman.'

'Do you have any family left in these parts?'

'No, I'm afraid they're all gone now.'

'But surely you must have had some contacts here. It must take a lot of organization and advance work to set up a revival. You surely must have someone local helping you out. Did you get some help from your former classmates? I note that one of your classmates, Bubba Tubig, is chief of police. The chief of police would be a good contact, I'd think.'

Bonnerton looked startled at the mention of Tubig's name. 'That little fat boy?' He narrowed his eyes malevolently. 'Did you talk to him about me?'

I blinked.

'Do you know Bubba Tubig was in love with the best-looking girl in high school? The class fat boy. Talk about ambition exceeding your grasp.'

I did my best to appear shocked. Such gall!

Bonnerton said, 'Oh, he was just crazy about her, as if she would have anything to do with a fat toad like that. Corpulent fool.' He spit the words 'fat' and 'corpulent' out like they were bullets. 'She was the best-looking girl in school. It was flat ridiculous.'

Bonnerton seemed to feel that Tubig's feelings for Lil were not just in bad taste, or annoying, but outrageous. The nerve of a fat boy falling in love with Lil Peters.

Were fat boys beneath nerds in the

high school pecking order? Were they at the bottom of the totem, demonstrably not entitled to high school infatuations? Was that the reason for Bonnerton's vehemence?

He cleared his throat. He wanted to get past these questions. He said, 'To answer your question, my chief contact has been a good Christian woman who is a lover of nature. She dearly loves the Lord Jesus Christ, and has been following my environmental crusade on television.'

'I see.'

'It turns out she lived just down the street from my family, but she was just a toddler then, and I was a teeager. She's a Tupperware distributor, you know. She's quite popular, I'm told.'

On my notepad, I wrote *good Christian woman, loves nature*. Ordinarily nobody can read my scrawl, but me. But this time I took care that it was legible and large enough for Bonnerton see. I tried to look thoughtful.

Bonnerton, seeing *good Christian woman, loves nature* looked pleased.

I said. 'You know, perhaps I should talk

to this woman. Make a more rounded portrait.'

Bonnerton looked perhaps not so pleased at that suggestion.

I pretended to study my notes. 'People think all we're after is the negative. In digging up dirt on someone. It's a nice change of pace to run into one of life's givers.'

Bonnerton licked his lips. 'She is a giver, that's a fact. A good Christian woman.'

I readied my pen and glanced up. 'And her name?'

He hesitated. 'Uh, Opal Wiggen.'

Opal Wiggen! I thought *well* . . . I said, 'And Ms. Wiggen can be located where?'

He licked his lips. 'You might check with my advance crew. They're staying in a motel just outside of town. The Wallowa River Inn, I think it's called.'

'I truly can understand your reservation, Reverend Bonnerton. You must have taken a lot of cheap shots from the press.' I tried to look sore at cheap-shot writers.

Bonnerton said, 'It is a pleasure talking to a responsible journalist for a change, I can tell you.'

'I want to do this right, Reverend

Bonnerton. Something I can be proud of and you can read without wanting to bomb the magazine. Let's face facts: it would be in bad taste for a Cayuse boy not to do right by someone from Enterprise. Hey, where's the loyalty?'

He smiled. 'I do want to help you out all I can, you understand. It is a foolish preacher indeed who would blow off *The New York Times*. You will be at the revival today, won't you? We might hold a short press conference afterwards if there's enough interest.'

'Oh, yes,' I said. 'Wouldn't miss the revival for the world. I might skip on the press conference, though. My editors don't want to see quotes in the magazine that their readers saw in the newspapers. They want to treat their readers with candid stuff, the real Reverend Thaddeus Hamm Bonnerton.'

'Bonnerton with his hair let down.'

'In a manner of speaking, that's exactly it. I thought I should start by introducing myself and getting to know you as a person, not as some phantom on a television screen.'

Bonnerton was pleased. 'It's been

pleasant talking to you, Mr. Denson. It really has.' His manner of saying this was ex-nerd to former runt, fellow conspirators against former hotshot jocks, class presidents, and cheerleaders.

I suspected, without knowing it for a fact, that this spur to ambition accounted for more successes by nerds, fat boys, and runts at the adult end of the hoop than was achieved on the adolescent stretch by hormonal jocks, tah-tah class officers, and top-heavy cheerleaders.

I also wondered if a former nerd like Thad Bonnerton, whose desire seemed driven more by high-octane malice than a need simply to prove himself, might not risk some kind of awful flame-out. His attitude toward Bubba Tubig, in particular, seemed of doubtful Christian merit. Better a fat body than an empty head.

I drove off in my microbus, thinking of the common-sense advice of the animal people to keep a watchful eye on the path of the Great Hoop. I noted that no vengeful bolt of lightning issued forth from the wrathful hand of God to punish me for my wayward thought.

17

The Reverend Thaddeus Hamm Bonnerton's green revival tent was maybe fifty yards long and fifty yards wide, with sides that could be rolled up on a warm day to let in fresh air, and the sides were up today. The winters were vicious in Wallowa County, but the summers were exquisite, and this was a gorgeous summer day; the air was crisp and warm and smelled good. The pasture along Ant Flat Road was covered with dandelions, and meadowlarks could be heard giving their mellow riffs as they had when Monty Hook destroyed his cattle.

On the outside of the tent, above the raised flaps, lest we forget his name, THADDEUS HAMM BONNERTON was written in the reverend's distinctive signature script, with each yellow letter close to three feet high. Below that, in more modest block yellow letters, was THE INSTITUTE FOR THE RESTORATION

OF CHRIST'S BOSOM.

It looked as though several hundred of the faithful had arrived in large, air-conditioned, chartered tour buses. In addition to the buses, the parking lot outside the main tent was filled with pickup trucks, station wagons, and older cars, reflecting the rural, working-class religious faithful who were attracted to tent-pitching revivalists. It was people like this the Baltimore newspaperman H. L. Mencken in the 1920s had dubbed the American booboisie. In fact, they were found not just in the Appalachians and the American South, but in rural areas all over the country. These were hardworking, God-fearing people; unfortunately, their love of literal interpretations of the Bible, plus their fear and suspicion of education in general, made them natural prey for fast-talking preachers.

The vehicles of those who had driven in included a scattering of license plates from Washington and Idaho, in addition to Oregon, come down from the Tri-Cities and Walla Walla to the northwest, I supposed, and up from Payette and Boise to the southeast. A few of the faithful had even made the long drive from western Montana. On the surface, the size of the gathering contradicted the repeated polls and studies that showed Alaska, Oregon, Montana, and Washington, in that order, as the least religious of the fifty states. Idaho was a different matter; the bottom of that state was heavily populated by Mormons spilled northward out of Utah.

The trucks of the Institute for the Restoration of Christ's Bosom that Willie and I had seen at Food City when Bonnerton made his grand arrival were now parked to the left of the main tent. Under awnings in front of the trucks, in front of six-foot-high blowups of Bonnerton giving his signature high five for Jesus, wholesome, freshly scrubbed young men and women in 'Cleaning the Bosom of Christ' T-shirts were selling those T-shirts, plus God Squad baseball caps and trash bags and autographed copies of *Heavenly Scrubbing*.

A crowd had gathered at the tables, with the menfolk pulling out their beleaguered wallets while their wives and children pawed through the T-shirts looking for the right sizes. These didn't appear to be people who had a lot of money, and for them to spring thirty bucks for a T-shirt was no small matter, yet there they were, turning their hard-earned money over to Bonnerton's underlings. To me this was a dismaying spectacle, but I supposed people had a right to peculiar follies as long as they didn't infringe on the rights of others. It wasn't that I didn't have peculiar follies of my own.

Inside, people were already gathering in bleachers, many of them flipping through the pages of *Heavenly Scrubbing* while they waited. These bleachers were arranged in a semicircle around the small stage where, flanked by six-foot-high speakers on either side, Bonnerton was to perform his Christian environmental number.

I didn't want to go through Loretta Mannsen and have to deal with media assistants, or whatever her assistants were called. I didn't want to deal with the ass-kissing and kowtowing that would inevitably be bestowed on John Denson of the *Times*. I wanted anonymity, although I took a notepad in keeping with my writer scam.

After cruising by the sales tents to scope the action, I slipped quietly inside the main tent, there being no charge for admission. I occupied my time reading that day's edition of the *Oregonian* while I waited for the tent to fill up and the action to begin.

It was a wait that, I thought, was a trifle longer than was necessary, forcing me to read even the *Oregonian's* editorials, never much fun because they were so predictably Republican and uptight. It wasn't that I was a hidebound Democrat, or that Republicans were congenitally uptight and Democrats loosey-goosey, only that I thought most interesting reading, from whatever perspective, was independent and unpredictable.

The large screen behind the stage was presumably going to show the slaughter that had been denied Bonnerton's camera crew. There was no action, no testing of the sound system or preliminary announcements until a full half hour and then some after the bleachers were packed.

Then, as the assembled butts began to grow weary — with the heads above the rumps listening to birds twitter in the fresh air outside the tent — the sound men began the tease: 'Testing, testing, one, two. Testing, testing, one two.' For Bonnerton to make his appearance too early would have suggested that he was eager and thus detract from the drama and mystique of The Great Man. The more impressive His Wonderfulness, the longer he made people wait.

At last Bonnerton strode resolutely onto the raised stage, and the assembled faithful, grateful that their boring wait had ended, rose as one and applauded as though he were a famous singer or storied juggler. As a celebrity preacher, Bonnerton was only part religious man. He was all entertainer and understood the requirements of timing.

The applause continued for what I regarded as an inordinate if not downright embarrassing length of time. What on earth had this man done to deserve this kind of applause? He was not Gandhi or Gorbachev. When it ended at last, possibly because of sore hands, Bonnerton, Bible in hand, affecting a simple, modest dignity, said softly, 'Those of you who have brought your Bibles with you today, and I hope you all have, can follow along with me at the beginning of chapter nine in Exodus of the Old Testament.'

Bonnerton waited while his audience flipped through their Bibles. Then he read:

' 'Then the Lord said to Moses, go to Pharaoh and say to him, this is what the Lord, God of the Hebrews says, Let my people go, so that they might worship me. If you refuse to let them go and continue to hold them back, the hand of the Lord will bring a terrible plague on your livestock in the field — on your horses and donkeys and camels and on your cattle and sheep and goats. But the Lord will make distinction between the live-stock of Israel and that of Egypt, so that no animal belong to Israelites will die.''

Bonnerton paused, and waited in silence for his listeners to digest the passage. Then he said, 'Now the Lord is not talking here about human beings or about leprosy or consumption or syphilis. He's talking about animals. He's not talking about fleas or ticks or distemper. He's talking about anthrax, isn't he? This loathsome affliction was a plague upon our animals in biblical times as it is now. I will finish the passage:

''The Lord set a time and the next day the Lord did it: all the livestock of the Egyptians died, but not one animal belonging to the Israelites died. Pharaoh sent men to investigate and found that not even one of the animals of the Israelites had died. Yet his heart was unyielding, and he would not let the people go.''

Bonnerton looked at the top of the tent as though studying it, his face bunched with what was no doubt intended to be deep concentration. 'Now then, I want you to think about that for a moment. 'Yet his heart was unyielding, and he would not let his people go.' Let go from what?' Bonnerton looked grim-faced. Then he shouted as loud as he could: 'From pagan idolatry, my friends, from greed!'

A ripple of amens rippled through the crowd. He lowered his voice and said calmly, 'But we will come back to that passage. Now, I would like you to skip down a few paragraphs to Exodus nine-eight.'

As the faithful turned to Exodus, on the screen behind Bonnerton the black smoke rolled above the ponderosa pines on Monty Hook's spread. Bonnerton's camera crew might have gotten screwed out of the shooting and the burning of infected corpses, but the black smoke, shots I had already seen on television, was dramatic as hell.

Standing in front of the billowing smoke, Bonnerton stripped off his jacket and flung it dramatically offstage. Then he jerked loose the double Windsor knot of his necktie and rolled up the sleeves of his shirt, which by then had great moons of sweat under the armpits. This was Bonnerton's trademark let's-get-down-to-business-and-really-give-'em-hell gesture, and the faithful below him, having seen him do this many times on television, knew what they were expected to do and did it with enthusiasm: they rose as one to their feet, applauding wildly. Now was the time for their man to shake, rattle, and roll, and they urged him to do it — defend Mother Earth, bequeathed to them by the Lord — with individuals crying out 'Yes, yes, do it!' and 'Go for it, Reverend!'

Bonnerton shouted above the din, ''Then the Lord said to Moses and Aaron, Take handfuls of soot from a furnace and have Moses toss it in the air in the presence of Pharaoh. It will become fine dust over the whole land of Egypt, and festering boils will break out on men and animals throughout the land.''

Having said that, he waited for the tumult to subside and people to settle back in their seats.

Then he said, 'Well, now!' He stepped back on the stage, arms outstretched and mouth open. 'I ask you, friends, what was the Lord referring to in that passage? Soot from a furnace. A fine dust over the whole land. Festering boils breaking out on men and animals. Why, he was clearly referring to filth, wasn't he? He was referring to the evil smoke and pollution that daily fouls the air we breathe and the water we drink. You ask the people of Mexico City or some of the industrial cities of China about filth in the air and boils on the skin. There are cities on this earth where the children never see the sun! So what happened, you ask?' Bonnerton paused, waiting for an answer. There was none. 'What happened?'

Silence. The script called for the faithful to keep their mouths shut; their man was about to give them the word.

Bonnerton did not disappoint them. 'Well, the Good Book tells us they took soot from a furnace and stood before the pharaoh. And here, friends, is the lesson for us today. Moses tossed the soot into the air, and festering boils in fact broke out on men and animals. 'The magicians could not stand before Moses and Aaron because of the boils that were on them and on all the Egyptians.'

'And what smoke is this behind me? What manner of soot? You may have seen it on television, but that was shown to thrill. The smoke we see today is for a lesson. This smoke is coming from the burning bodies of three hundred cattle right here in Wallowa County that were infected with anthrax. Look at this smoke and weep. Look at it and know that if we don't change our ways, the end of our beloved earth is truly near!'

Bonnerton mopped more sweat from his brow. 'The Bible teaches us we are the children of Jesus. It follows, does it not, that the earth is the bosom of Jesus? Yes, we are literally cradled by the bosom of our lord. We share that bosom with the soulful animals in the field and forests.'

Soulful animals? I noted that Bonnerton didn't outright say animals had souls. When I was a kid in Cayuse, a Presbyterian minister once told me I had a soul because I was born in the image of God, but my beagle, Omar, did not, because he was a dog. Ordinary beasts did not have souls, while we big-deal humans did. It followed, according to this man's logic, which was the standard Calvinist argument, that I might qualify for heaven, but there was no hope for

Omar. He spent his life sleeping and running around smelling things, and one day he croaked, and that was it.

Was Bonnerton some sort of revisionist on the issue of animals and souls? It struck me that the poor Christians had been forced to do a lot of revising in their time. Copernicus had really pissed them off by suggesting the earth was not flat. In the good old days when the Church ran everything, people were flogged and burned alive for agreeing with Copernicus.

Bonnerton lowered his voice. Mr. Sincere. Mr. Thoughtful. Mr. Concerned. Mr. Devoted. 'You know, friends, I recently went to Canada where the Canadians had to destroy thousands of lovely buffalo because they had contracted anthrax. We all know those beautiful creatures did not infect themselves; the disease came from the outside. From us. We are to blame!'

'Amen,' said the faithful.

'These lovely creatures of God are dying because of our sinful ways!'

'Amen.'

Bonnerton pleaded to the heavens with outstretched arms. 'They are dying because we foul the earth!'

'Amen.'

'They are dying because we refuse to acknowledge the word of God and respect the works of God. We have become as the pharaoh.'

'Amen.'

'We foul our environment like babies unable to hold their bowels.'

'Amen.'

'The soot in the air reeks with the stench of greed and decay.'

'Amen.'

'We have lost our way.'

'Amen.'

'We lack discipline.' He pronounced this dis-cip-line, with the accent heavy on the second syllable.

'Amen.'

'These dead bison are clearly the first step toward Armageddon, and if we do not recognize the error of our ways and change them, we too are doomed.'

'Amen.'

'We will perish amid the rot and stench

of our own decadence.'

'Amen.'

'It is all there in the Scriptures. The message is clear.'

'Amen.'

Bonnerton paused. He knew he had worked that line to its limit. He mopped more sweat from his brow, and dropped the pitch and timbre of his voice. 'What do we do?'

'Amen.'

I agreed with the amen chorus. What were we supposed to do now?

'How do we act?'

'Amen.'

You tell us, Thad baby, I thought.

Bonnerton said, 'The Old Testament tells us in the sixth chapter of I Samuel that the ark of the Lord had been in the territory of the Philistines for seven months, when the Philistines asked the magicians and diviners how they should go about sending it back home. The magicians and diviners told them they should load the ark with an offering of guilt. This should be five gold emerods which means hemorrhoids and five gold mice, modeled after the plague that then afflicted the land and according to the number of Philistine rulers — one gold tumor and one gold mouse for Ashdod, Gaza, Ashketon, Gath, and Ekron.'

''Make models of the emerods and the mice that are destroying your country, and pay honor to Israel's god. Perhaps he will lift his hand from you and your gods and his land.''

His voice rising with each sentence, Bonnerton said, 'What gods does the Bible refer to in this passage? Why, pagan gods, my friends. Keep in mind, these are worshipers of Mammon. Is it not worshipers of Mammon who are running their cattle on public land, land that belongs to you and to me and to our children and grandchildren, and eating our beautiful land to the bare dirt?'

He paused.

We waited.

He said, 'Is it not, in fact, worshipers of Mammon who have brought anthrax to Wallowa County?' He paused again. 'You saw for yourselves on television what the Canadians had to do with the infected buffalo.' Finally, pop-eyed, sweaty, he shouted, 'They were forced to shoot them, shoot those magnificent beasts, and soak their poor bodies with gasoline and burn them in a pyre!'

Bonnerton sighed and mopped the sweat from his forehead. He gazed out at his audience, looking so very sad and disconsolate. Was he about to weep? He said, 'Talk about soot thrown into the sky by Moses! This is a lovely day and the air appears clean, but we can yet smell the stench of those burning buffalo, can't we? The odor lingers. What about the terrible soot that will soil the azure sky of this beautiful high country if you're forced to burn the bodies of all your cattle and horses and deer and elk? What manner of boils will that bring to us all? What vile suffering will we visit upon our children and grandchildren? Ask yourself those questions and humble yourselves before the Lord.

'You say, well now, Reverend Bonnerton, it's hardly within our means as individuals gathered here in Enterprise, Oregon, to fashion gold tumors and gold mice, is it?

How, then, do those of us who are concerned about the bosom of Christ pay honor to the Lord so as to secure his blessing? How do we responsible Christians make a proper offering to the Lord's ark in this critical hour of need?'

Bonnerton boomed out the answer to his question: 'The answer, my friends, as the answer to everything, is in the Good Book. Oh, yes. The answer is in the number five, representing the Philistine rulers. Place in the Lord's ark just five dollars, or fifty dollars, or five hundred dollars, or five thousand dollars, according to your ability to give, and together we will rout the Philistines who are destroying our beautiful land.'

Well, here was a simple enough message, I thought: just deliver any amount of money beginning with the number five to the ark of the Reverend Thaddeus Hamm Bonnerton, the stalwart, indefatigable enemy of Mammon, and he will see to it that you won't have to make a bonfire out of your livestock.

I quietly exited the tent. I was not in the mood to watch him do his famous high five for Jesus, striding into the crowd like he'd just won the Super Bowl.

A man like Ham Bone had a real ego. Had some of those boils imagined by the author of Exodus somehow affected his brain and therefore his imagination? Had he been jerking off all these years to private visions of a naked Lil? We knew from the Reverend Jimmy Swaggart and other fallen preachers that hormones respect no title or position. Would Bonnerton have gone so far as to murder Lil's state cop boyfriend because he couldn't let go of a boyhood infatuation?

Then there was the matter of anthrax-infected salt licks.

Leiat Podebski had said Bonnerton's advance crew, including the partiers in unit eight, had been living in the Wallowa River Inn for more than a week setting up the electrical and water connections for his revival tent. Somebody had to secure the necessary permits in advance. Even if Opal Riggen had been helping them out, that all cost money. Bonnerton no doubt had a grab bag of biblical quotes for his sermons and calls for loot, but the drama and potential profit of his Enterprise revival clearly rested on the local infection of hoof-and-mouth disease.

Would Thad Bonnerton go to such lengths as to infect Monty Hook's cattle with anthrax to give himself a dramatic, and therefore profitable cause? He was possessed by righteousness, and the emotion of righteousness, taken to the logical extreme, often convinced otherwise sane men that whatever they did was justified in the name of a higher good.

The Reverend Jim Bakker maintained his righteousness right up to the moment he was convicted of scamming people in his Christian resort enterprise. David Koresh was righteous in Waco, Texas, even as he collected automatic weapons to shoot his way into Armageddon. The cultists who lived at Rajneesh Puram were no doubt feeling righteous when they poisoned a salad bar in The Dalles, Oregon.

Rightness on that order was as addictive as any narcotic. Was Bonnerton so crazed that he felt justified in doing whatever he pleased, above the rules of civilized conduct that governed the rest of us ordinary mortals?

The Reverend Bonnerton, screwed out of everything but billowing black smoke by the hardheaded Monty Hook, had managed to find a passage in which Moses and Aaron threw soot in the air before the pharaoh to teach him a lesson from God. It was my bet that Bonnerton could find a passage in the Bible to demonstrate anything he wanted.

I climbed into my VW bus, thinking. There were any number of places I could spot on a map that were more accessible to the faithful than Enterprise and so could promise a full tent every night. A current controversy in Arizona had to do with the destruction of prime vegetable-growing land that, owing to repeated irrigation over the years, was being destroyed by a buildup of salt. A revival down there presumably would draw the concerned in from both Phoenix and Tucson.

Also, water sucked out of the Everglades to irrigate winter tomatoes in south Florida was destroying that state's prized swamp and all the animals that lived in it. A Bonnerton revival there would draw animal lovers from Miami and Florida's populous Gold Coast.

The sun was now low in the west. My mind spinning with tales of Aaron and Moses, I headed for the rodeo, where I would join Willie, Bobcat, Leiat, and Lenora to watch the cowboys do their macho thing under the lights at the Chief Joseph Days rodeo.

18

In Portland and Seattle, some owners of small cafés vented the smell of frying onions onto the streets to lure in the customers. But the competition from city smells and exhaust fumes debilitated onion action as *eau de* horse dumplings somehow did not. County fairs and rodeos were proper onion venue, whether it was the lofty Pendleton Round-Up or the more modest productions by the folks at Joseph or the Umatilla Sage Riders. Deep-fried onion rings — lacking a killer odor — were culinary mortars in the action, whereas heaps and mounds of onions browning slowly on a vast grill were proper siege guns; the smell wilted rodeo goers with desire.

Behind the rodeo stands at the Chief Joseph Days, competing Jaycees, Elks, and Eagles joined in culinary combat. As Leonora, Leiat, Bobcat Bill, Willie, and I waited for the evening's competition in saddle bronc riding to begin, the killer smell of frying onions wafted up through the bleachers.

Willie and Bobcat Bill had spent the day tracking down infected deer with their Umatilla and Nez Percé friends, and there wasn't much to do now but wait until every set of deer hoofprints leading from every infected salt lick had been tracked down and the animal or corpse properly burned and buried.

Now, under the dim yellow night lights at Chief Joseph Days, it was time for fun. 'Dumsht, you smell those onions?' Willie said.

'How can I not?'

Bobcat rubbed his stomach. 'I can hardly stand it.'

'Lenora?' I said.

She grinned. 'They do smell good, I have to admit.'

Willie said, 'What do you think, Dumsht?'

I grinned. 'I say we go for it, Tonto.'

'Me too,' Willie said.

We climbed down from the bleachers, stomachs growling. Choosing which stand to buy your hamburger from was never an easy matter. Rodeo and county fair food stands were always big money raisers for small-town fraternal organizations; members always ate at their own stands, so the competition was for non-members like us.

We settled on the stand run by the Jaycees, because their hamburger buns seemed more generously studded with sesame seeds than the competition's. When these stands were side by side in a hamburger-hot-dog-and-onion-ring row, victory lay in the details. It went without saying that the buns were well slathered with butter and left on the grill until they were golden brown and crunchy. Any stand with the gall, or outright stupidity, to try to sell hamburgers by clapping a piece of meat in an ungrilled bun — the way they did at big-city ballparks — was limiting customers to its own club members, and even those might bolt.

We each got ourselves a plastic glass of foaming Henry Weinhard beer. Leiat, who was on the far side of the hoop, seemed to especially enjoy her beer. Willie would no doubt say that she had learned that the most important part of the hoop was the current stretch, which was to be enjoyed to its fullest. We watched the cook scrape the grill clean with the edge of his spatula and begin cooking our hamburgers.

Standing there sipping my Henry Weinhard and enjoying the frying onions, the wonderful mountain air, and the delightful ambience of Chief Joseph Days, I felt something squishy under my foot. I looked down, knowing what had happened; I had stepped on a fresh horse dumpling. Yuch! As I looked around for someplace to clean the bottom of my Adidas, I spotted a hoofprint with a knick in the corner of one shoe. Staring at the hoofprint, I scraped the bottom of my foot on the edge of a four-by-four that supported the roof over the Jaycees' food stand. The salt-lick man had been riding a horse with a knick in one shoe. Could this be it? Had I stepped in manure and come up with a puzzle-solving rose?

I used the toe of my freshly cleaned shoe to nudge a horse dumpling beside the hoofprint. 'Did the salt-lick rider's hoofprint look anything like that?' I asked Willie.

Looking surprised, he squatted and studied the impression in the dirt. Bobcat examined it too.

I said, 'Another beer, please.' I gave an aproned Jaycee my empty plastic glass. I knew it was the same print. Had to be. The description was too similar. I tried to remain extra cool so as to take maximum advantage of my coup. The eagle-eyed Chief Dumsht had come through!

Willie looked up, amazed. 'By God, Dumsht, just when I'm about to give up on you as another hopeless white-eye, you somehow manage to redeem yourself. I don't know how you do it. I really don't.'

'That's the one, then?' Lenora asked.

'That's it,' Bobcat said. 'The left rear hoof of the lead horse.'

Willie said, 'Our salt-lick rider is ambling around here big as you please. We're gonna have to make you an honorary Injun, Dumsht, eyes like those.'

I said, 'Our salt-lick rider and maybe our murderer, too. While Officer McAllister was investigating the poaching, he was shacked up with Lil Peters. Maybe Lil overheard loose talk at the High Country

314

Inn about poaching and passed it on to McAllister.'

Bobcat said, 'Especially if the talker was poaching big-time. People around here can live with somebody who knocks down an animal to feed his family, but the ones who are in it to make money are another matter.'

'Maybe you should have a talk with Lil Peters, Kemosabe,' Willie said. 'There's gotta be a lot of flapping mouths at the High Country.'

'I agree. First thing in the morning.' I took my refill of beer and gave the Jaycee a buck.

Willie said, 'The sheriff and the state police have probably talked to her already, but who knows what they might have overlooked?'

I said, 'Yeah. Or maybe they just didn't ask the right questions. You have to remember, they didn't know about the salt licks then.'

'Maybe the salt licks will jar her memory,' Willie said.

I said, 'What do you think? Can you and Bobcat follow these prints in a place like this?' The soil surrounding the rodeo was a jumble and hodgepodge of hooves upon hooves.

Willie frowned. 'Impossible in this mess, but we'll get him.'

'How?'

'Bobcat and I'll get here first thing in the morning, and when the cowboys arrive and unload their horses from their trailers, we check each horse out, one at a time. There'll be plenty of people, including redskins, hanging around. We'll blend right in.'

Bobcat nodded his head in agreement. 'That's the only way, I agree. As it stands now, we can spot a hoof here and a hoof there, but there are too many horses for it to make any sense. We'll get him if we come early tomorrow and are patient. The trackers chasing sick deer don't need us. They know what they have to do.'

Willie said, 'A lot of work for us all tomorrow.'

I said, 'I'll check with you after I talk to Lil, and we'll see if we learn anything that comes together.'

Bobcat said, 'I can drop my pickup off

at your motel on the way back tonight so Lenora has her own wheels if she needs them. I can go with Willie.'

'Thank you,' Lenora said.

'Good thinking,' Willie said.

I said, 'Well, what do you think, Lenora, don't those onions smell great?'

Lenora said, 'They're smelling better every minute.'

'They sure as hell are,' Bobcat said.

'I like 'em a lot,' Willie added.

I said, 'Shall we throw all caution to the wind and go for more?'

Bobcat Bill and Willie both grinned broadly. A person could only get a hamburger like this at a rodeo or a county fair. Fried onions and grilled buns. Yes! They were for it.

Lenora laughed. 'You guys! Oink, oink!'

★　★　★

When we got back to our seats, having stifled our gurgling stomachs, the folks running the rodeo were ready to start the saddle bronc competition. It felt wonderful to be sitting beside the extraordinary

Lenora Kemiah knowing the pleasure was mutual. Willie Prettybird and Bobcat Bill, aware that Willie's conniving had kindled a romantic spark, seemed equally pleased.

The mellow-voiced announcer, a gentleman named Zoop Dove, said, 'But before we have our first ride, we'd like to call attention to a special guest here this evening, fresh from a Christian environmental revival this morning. If you'll all look at the center grandstand on the west side, will you welcome, please, the Reverend Thaddeus Hamm Bonnerton of Bartlesville, Oklahoma, a 1968 graduate of Enterprise High School, here also to attend the many activities surrounding the all-school reunion.'

The folks all applauded Bonnerton, who stood, smiling broadly and waving a high-crowned, white cowboy hat.

Dove said, 'Thank you for joining us this evening, Reverend Bonnerton. We hope you enjoy the show and tell all your many friends around the country.'

Bonnerton energetically waved his hat again to a second round of applause.

'It's to vomit,' I said.

Willie said, 'Control yourself, Dumsht.'

Dove said, 'Okay, folks, if you'll keep an eye on chute number two, Roy Childress, a cowpoke from right here in Wallowa County, a 1986 graduate of Enterprise High School and a two-time saddle bronc champion here at the Chief Joseph Days, is getting ready to ride a big bay named Slippery Dick. We have to tell you, Slippery Dick is a notoriously mean piece of horseflesh. He just plain doesn't cotton to folks sittin' on his back. He's thrown the last twelve riders to get on him, so this'll be a real challenge for Childress.'

A bronc was easier to ride saddled than bareback, and a rider had to impress the judges as well as stay on him for a full ten seconds. The rider scored points by keeping his free hand high and his spurs digging into the animal's flanks.

This wasn't easy with a pissed-off horse like Slippery Dick, who was twisting and struggling in the chute. But if a rider could stay on him and show good form, it was possible to score more points on a horse like Slippery Dick than on an easy draw.

As I watched Childress lower himself

onto the furious animal, I sang that old cowboy song:

He sure was a frog-walker, he heaved
  a big sigh
Turned all four feet straight up to the
  sky

A frog-walker, as I understood the term, was a bronc who leaped up and came down on four feet at once, a tactic that jarred the mustard out of the most determined rider. A horse who heaved a big sigh went sideways, whoops!

Willie, enjoying himself, picked up the song:

He was a sunfishing son-of-a-gun
Turned his old belly right up to the sun
Oh, that Strawberry Roan
Oh, that Strawberry Roan

A sunfisher was a bronc that twisted this way and that like an out-of-control fish, a real challenge to a cowboy who wanted to stay on board and demonstrate good form at the same time.

Across the way, the spring-loaded door to chute number two whipped open with a dramatic *ka-whack!* and Roy Childress was on his way, right arm high holding his hat, spurs digging hard. He might have been an asshole personally, but he was a skilled and determined rider, I had to give him that.

Slippery Dick, a sunfisher if there ever was one, twisted his torso this way and that.

If Childress was handicapped by a hangover, he didn't show it. Despite Slippery Dick's determined sunfishing and frogwalking, Childress stayed on him, doing a beautiful job of spurring — with his hand high the whole while, waving his hat in a dramatic circle.

When the whistle blew, Childress swung one leg over Slippery Dick's back and leaped lightly to the ground, landing neatly on both feet, and put his hat back on his head, extra cool.

As the cutters moved in to herd Slippery Dick out of the arena, Zoop Dove said, 'What do you say to that ride by Roy Childress, folks? Wasn't that something? You see that free hand up there and those spurs moving? Let's give Childress a big hand.'

Willie and I both agreed that it had been an extraordinary ride, and we joined in the applause with enthusiasm. When the numbers came up on the scoreboard, Childress scored a 93, offering a real challenge to his competitors in the first round.

I couldn't help but notice that Thaddeus Hamm Bonnerton completely went off his nut at Childress's ride, leaping up and down screaming and waving his white hat. A real rodeo fan was Thad Bonnerton. The members of his entourage, taking their cue from their Maximum Leader, all jumped up and down to demonstrate their enthusiasm for Roy Childress's accomplishment.

Even the announcer noticed the fuss from Bonnerton's section. 'We see the Reverend Bonnerton appreciated that ride. As you know, folks, the reverend is from Oklahoma. The National Cowboy Hall of Fame is located in Oklahoma City, where they hold the national rodeo finals. Will you tell us again how you liked that ride, Reverend Bonnerton?'

Bonnerton popped to his feet yet one more time and eagerly, if not frenetically, waved his cowboy hat. Yes, sir, that was a hot damn ride if ever there was one! Even at a distance it was clear that Ham Bone was grinning like a manure-eating dog. The members of his entourage, taking their cue again from their main man, sported similar if not identical excrement-eating grins. Their apparent determination to ape Bonnerton in all respects was downright amazing.

The next rider scored a credible 91 on a ride I thought was as good as or better than Childress's, but I noted that Bonnerton and his Christian rodeo fans across the way — perhaps having shot their hat-waving wad on the first cowboy — appeared almost uninterested. In fact, several of them, perhaps drawn by the wonderful smell of frying onions, had left their seats.

Bonnerton's enthusiasm no doubt stemmed from the fact that Roy Childress was Opal's current beau, and Open Hole, good Christian that she was, had been helping the revivalist's advance men. If that was so, the Reverend Bonnerton was loyal to his supporters, I had to give him that.

Monty Hook had said Opal Riggens had started out as a schoolteacher in Milton-Freewater before her hormones tripped her up. Taught what, I wondered?

19

After we finished with the last of the rodeo events at ten o'clock, we dropped by for a late-night snack of chicken-fried steaks and french fries at the Pheasant Café. After our dinner, we lingered over coffee and listened to jukebox music for the better part of an hour. On the way home, I slowed the bus as I neared Wilson's Big E Drive-In on the edge of town. 'Do they make banana splits at this place, Leiat?'

Lenora said, 'My God, are you still hungry?'

'I've got a hankering for a banana split, if they have them. We didn't have dessert, remember? We're entitled.'

Leiat said, 'Yes, they do have banana splits, and good ones they are, too. They make them with hard ice cream. Chocolate, strawberry, and vanilla.'

'Really? Classic banana splits?'

'With pineapple goo, strawberry goo, chocolate syrup, whipped cream, and a disgustingly sweet maraschino cherry on top.'

'Whoa. We'll have 'em,' I said. I wheeled into Wilson's and parked my 'bus by a call box mounted on a metal post. One ordered the food through the call box and it was delivered by a girl in a fetching outfit. A drive-in like Wilson's would be lost elsewhere in the parade of passing fashion — grist for sentimental movies — but somehow it persevered in Enterprise.

As we were enjoying our banana splits, we heard two shots fired from the direction of the Wallowa River west of town. A few minutes later, the Enterprise city squad car raced by, siren squealing and blue light flashing.

I said, 'Looks like Bubba Tubig's deputy has his hands full tonight.'

Leiat sighed. 'This is Friday night, so that'd be Duane. Not surprising to hear gunshots in the middle of Chief Joseph Days. Guns and alcohol just don't mix. Throw an all-school reunion into the stew, and you've got problems.'

Lenora said, 'You want to find drunks,

just go to an Indian reservation some Friday or Saturday night. It's terrible. I just hate it.'

A couple of minutes later two white squad cars from the Oregon State Police whipped by in the same direction, lights flashing and sirens wailing.

★ ★ ★

The partyers in unit eight were at it again, louder than the previous night, if that was possible. Lenora Kemiah and I didn't mind. We were in the middle of a sweet and lovely encounter that would be memorable one day at the far end of our personal hoops. No matter what the next curve held for us, this stretch was perfectly grand; there was no other way to describe it.

While I poured Lenora some screw-top red and cut some more Tillamook sharp cheddar, behind me on television Bing Crosby began singing to Grace Kelly.

Well, I give to you
And you give to me
True love, true love.

I said, 'You like that song?' She looked splendid squatting there on the floor in front of the tube.

She grinned. 'I like it a lot. You want to watch this movie?'

'Sure,' I said.

So on and on
We will always be
True love, true love.

'You like this song, John?'

I said, 'I think a person would have to be brain dead not to like that song. That's why it's held up all these years.'

Lenora Kemiah looked pleased. She took a sip of Carlo Rossi while we waited for Bing and Grace to finish their song. Then she said, 'Say, this wine does taste good.'

I agreed. 'Not as good as Willie's elderberry wine, that's so. It may be cheap swill, but right now I think it's the best wine I've ever tasted.'

She held her glass up. 'A toast to Willie Prettybird, that clever rascal.'

'A toast to Willie. Yes, isn't he a nice

man? Thoughtful.' I grinned wickedly, if
not lasciviously.

After we watched mellow Bing and
elegant Grace launch their lives in the
presumed direction of heaven on earth,
we lucked onto another kind of romance,
this time between Don Murray and
Marilyn Monroe in *Bus Stop*. This was
rather more rowdy and tormented, but
since it took place out west and had
modern cowboys, the cowgirl Lenora
Kemiah liked it a lot.

By the time we got to *Bus Stop*, Lenora
was leaning back against me, and her
scent was flat intoxicating. This would be
my second night with her, and she yet
smelled so sweet and felt so grand I could
hardly breathe.

But I wasn't nearly as intoxicated as the
driver of a vehicle that wheeled into
the interior parking lot of the Wallowa
River Inn at about two o'clock. Lenora
and I peered between the curtains to see
a fancy new Ford pickup, one of those
outsized models with a macho-man engine,
four-wheel-drive, an outsized double cab
with four doors, a CB antenna on top,

and knobby, all-terrain Goodyear tires.

Out of this impressive rig piled Roy Childress and his lady-friend, Opal Riggen. Childress scooped up two cases of Olympia beer from the rear seat, and Opal had bottles of something in three state liquor store paper bags — whiskey or vodka or whatever. Both Childress and Opal were, as they say, feeling no pain.

Childress, smiling broadly, poked his head back inside the cab and inhaled deeply. 'Don't you just love that new car smell? It's just wonderful.'

'Enjoy it while it lasts,' Opal said.

'You're damned right.'

'Hog heaven,' Opal said.

'May not smell as good as a willing pussy, but it has to be right up there.'

Opal laughed.

Childress said, 'You know why women have legs, don't you?'

'Why's that?'

'So they won't leave a trail like a slug.' Childress, momentarily losing his balance, looked amused.

Opal pretended to swing one of the

bottles at his jaw. 'You shit!'

Childress said, 'What makes this rig smell even better is it's paid for. Any asshole can turn his paycheck over to the bank every month. Fuck that payment shit!'

While Opal giggled, Childress flopped the two cases of beer on the trunk of the car next to my unit. He said, 'You know, I think I just might buy myself a place and run a few cows myself. Be a gentleman rancher. Ring the bell at the High Country every night if I want.' He reeled out his cowboy yardage, the better to piss into one of Leiat Podebski's planters.

Beside me, Lenora said, 'Yuch!'

Childress said, 'Under the circumstances, there ought to be plenty of money where this came from. Don't you think?'

Circumstances?

'What's he going to do?' Childress said.

What was *he* going to do? Who was *he*? I wished to hell Childress would be more specific.

Lenora gave me a nudge with her elbow. She was thinking the same thing as me.

Childress said, 'I'd piss on this guy's car or on the pavement, but I don't want it bouncing back on my pants. Don't want people to think I'm not civilized.'

Opal said, 'Water the flowers. Help out with the environment.'

'Beer piss builds up fast. Ohhh, does that ever feel good!' Childress stuffed his yardage back into his jeans and zipped himself up. 'Oh, hell yes. Gotta take care of the precious fucking environment.'

Childress moved the cases of beer to the trunk of a car in front of unit eight, where the party was still going strong, and used his fist to hammer loudly on the door.

Boom, boom, boom!

Boom, boom, boom!

A man opened the door cautiously and peered out. Seeing it was Roy, he looked relieved.

Roy said, 'Open the goddamn door. What do you think we are, cops or something?'

The man grinned. 'Well, goddammit, Roy, I see you and Opal managed to show up at last. What's been keeping you two?

We've been countin' on you. We're fast running out of fuel in here, and all the grocery stores are closed tighter than a bull's butt in fly time.'

'Are we too late?' Childress pretended to leave with his two cases of beer.

The man laughed. 'Oh, shut up and get your asses in here. The night's just started.'

'Got another two cases in my rig. Be right back.'

'Well, big spender from the west.'

'Fuckin' A. John.' The happy Roy gave the man his two cases and returned to his truck for the remaining two. Then he and Opal joined the revelers inside.

As the man let them in the door, he said, 'I thought everybody was supposed to be partying on account of Chief Joseph Days. Talk about the sticks. These people must get off on watching paint dry. Shit!'

Well, Roy Childress could have all the new car smell he wanted, if that's what turned him on. Lenora and I had something far better going for us. We snuggled back up, luxuriating in one another's delicious aroma, and returned to the saga of Don Murray and Marilyn Monroe.

Had Childress paid cash for his fancy rig? How in the hell, if he was supposed to be a shiftless no-account, had he come by that kind of money?

20

As I watched Lenora cooking breakfast, I punched up KBMT in LaGrande for the local news. 'They'll be sure to have something on about the rodeo results.'

Lenora turned the bacon. 'More coffee?'

'Sure,' I said and held out my mug for a refill. Oooh, was she ever cute. I was ecstatic at my good fortune, thanks to Willie Prettybird.

On the tube a serious-faced young woman said, 'At the top of the news this morning, tragedy struck Enterprise last night after the long-planned all-school reunion. Lil Peters, a graduate of the class of 1968, was found murdered in her small house on the Wallowa River shortly after midnight.

'Enterprise Police Chief Bubba Tubig, who himself had been attending the reunion activities, said his deputy, Duane Marshall, responding to reports of gunfire, found Ms. Peters dead on her living room floor, strangled. A preliminary search revealed no weapons at the scene.

'Monty Hook, president of the Oregon Cattlemen's Association, was found passed out in his pickup parked outside Ms. Peters's house. Tubig said Hook, who had been drinking heavily, claimed to remember nothing.

'On Wednesday, Hook, an outspoken figure in the controversy over grazing rights on federal land, was forced to destroy more than four hundred head of Herefords that were infected by highly infectious anthrax. Ms. Peters, a longtime friend of Hook's, worked as a bartender in the High Country Saloon in Enterprise.

'Chief Tubig said no arrests have been made. He said the investigation, with the help of the Oregon State Police, will continue.'

Lenora Kemiah, staring transfixed at the television set, said, 'My God!' She scooped the bacon out of the frying pan. 'What now?'

I took a deep breath and let it out between puffed cheeks. 'Now I've got to hustle my buns.'

'There'll be no talking to Lil Peters now.'

'That's probably what the killer had in mind.'

Lenora said, 'Bobcat and Willie will hear the news when they come in to check out the hoofprints at the rodeo grounds.'

'The first thing I have to do is check in with Olden Dewlapp.' I picked up the phone and dialed Dewlapp's home number in Portland.

On answering the phone, Dewlapp made a noise in his throat. 'I was waiting for your call.'

'You know what happened, then?'

'Hook phoned me a few minutes ago. Chief Tubig let him sleep off his hangover in jail.'

'Did he arrest him?'

'Releasing him without charges pending further investigation.'

I said, 'What's Monty's story?'

'He says he skipped on going to the rodeo last night in favor of a little drinking at the High Country Saloon. You know that place?'

'I've been there a couple of times.'

'He says Lil Peters was an old friend.'

'That's true.'

'He claimed he drove to her house afterwards with the idea of getting laid — this was with her implicit consent, he says — but he doesn't remember anything after leaving the tavern.'

'Wonderful.'

'He says he was slumped over in his own puke on the front seat of his pickup when Tubig's deputy shook him awake. His Buntline pistol had been taken from its rack behind the seat. He has a terrible headache this morning.' Dewlapp made another noise in his throat. 'Coming down with something.'

'Did he tell you about the salt licks?'

'Yes, he did.'

I told him about the hoofprints we had spotted at the rodeo grounds. 'I was going to talk to Lil this morning to see if the business of salt licks would jar her memory. Willie and his friend Bobcat Bill think they can run the hoofprint down today.'

'Let's hope to hell they score. Can they give odds?'

'No. But these are two pretty damned

stubborn redskins. They won't give up.'

'Let's hope not,' Dewlapp said. 'First McAllister, the boyfriend, now Lil, the longtime ladyfriend.'

'It doesn't look good for our side, does it?'

He said, 'No, it doesn't, to be frank. Cops love hormonal motives.'

'You don't think Monty did it, do you?'

'Oh, hell no. Poor bastard's all shaken up, and I don't think it's an act. If I were the killer I believe I'd stay well clear of him until he calms down.'

'It's the salt-lick man. Has to be. Find the salt-lick man, we've got the killer.'

Dewlapp said, 'Hard to believe they're not connected, I agree.'

'What does Chief Tubig think?'

Dewlapp said, 'He's pretty close-mouthed, but I don't think he believes Monty had anything to do with it either. He said they played on the same football team together. Is that true, do you think?'

I said yes it was, and gave Dewlap a summary of what I had learned so far. 'I think I should have another talk with Chief Tubig.'

Dewlapp sighed.

'You never know,' I said.

'You sure as hell don't,' he said. 'Well, whatever. I gotta drive up there and watch out for the best interests of my client. They tell me the nearest motel vacancy is in La Grande. Good God almighty!'

'You're looking at Chief Joseph Days, Olden. If you laid off advertising on television maybe you wouldn't wind up in places like this. Lucky you don't have to stay in Baker City or Boise, someplace like that.'

Olden made another noise in his throat.

'Gargle with hot salt water,' I said.

'What?'

'And drink lots of fruit juice. The idea is to flush your pipes by pissing a lot. Gets rid of what ails you. That, and your system can use the vitamin C.'

'You sound like my wife.'

'Willie would make you drink pine-needle tea.'

'Jesus.'

'It's good, really.'

'Right.'

I said, 'When you get settled, let me

know where I can find you. You can leave word with the manager of the motel here. Her name's Leiat Podebski, and she's a friend of Monty's.'

'Looks like he's going to need a few friends before this is over.' Olden hung up.

I peered outside to see if Roy Childress's fancy new Ford was still there, but it was gone.

21

I drove slowly out of town heading east, looking along the Wallowa River for a small house with squad cars outside, which would be Lil Peters's residence. This was an easy enough chore; the house, about a quarter of a mile from the drive-in where Lenora, Leiat, and I had pigged out on banana splits the previous night, was surrounded by five white cars from the Oregon State Police and one from the Enterprise city police.

Lil Peters was not just another corpse among many, another ho-hum killing as might have been the case if she had been murdered in the anonymity of a city. She had lived her entire life in Enterprise, and she was the well-liked, sexy bartender at the High Country Saloon — full of jokes, wry comments, and a love of life. Since her murder had been on the radio and television all morning, the traffic on the state highway flanking the river had slowed as people gawked and speculated; it was no secret that her state cop boyfriend had been murdered just ten days earlier, so this was the highest of high drama.

A state trooper was posted at the entrance to the fenced lane that went from the highway to Lil's house. On either side of the lane, milk cows placidly chewed their cuds, indifferent to the goings-on. I drove down the highway until I could find a safe place to park and walked back.

As I drew near, the cop said, 'Sorry, we've got an investigation going on here this morning.' He was polite enough.

Somewhere in their training, Oregon state cops were taught that being civilized didn't cost anything, and I appreciated that. I dug out my private investigator's license and gave it to him. I said, 'If Chief Tubig is here, he knows me. I'm working for Monty Hook's lawyer.'

'Hook's the guy they found passed out in the pickup?'

'That's right. Not the best place for him to pass out, I admit, but I truly don't think he killed anyone. He was a lifelong friend of the dead woman.'

The cop studied my license, then said, 'Wait one moment, please. I'll see what they have to say down at the house.'

'Oh, sure,' I said.

He strolled to his squad car, and I watched him use his radio to talk to the people inside. He nodded his head and returned, satisfied that he had done his job. 'You can walk on down, Mr. Denson, but please stay on the grass to the side of the road, and avoid the area where Ms. Peters and her guests parked their vehicles. We have prints to take. Regular circus out here this morning, and we have to do the best we can.'

'I understand,' I said. Whoever had killed Lil Peters had likely murdered a fellow state cop, and the state cops wanted the son of a bitch in the worst way. I didn't blame them. In their shoes, I'd feel the same way. I was careful to do as I was told.

I went through the drill of showing my license again to another state cop when I got to the front door of the house.

This time, in response to the cop's

inquiry, Bubba Tubig, looking stricken, poked his head out the door. Lil had been his high school heartthrob and it showed.

'Well, Mr. Denson!' he said, clenching his jaw. 'Olden Dewlapp's man is Johnny-on-the-spot. As advertised on TV.'

'Morning, Chief. Bit of action for you this morning, I see.'

Tubig shrugged. 'Duane got the action last night, I get it today.'

'You get Friday off.'

'Friday and Saturday nights are old Bubba's time to howl. Say, the state cops told me about the salt licks. Pretty slick work by your partner.'

'No sweat for Willie and Bobcat.'

'You think that's connected to this? The same man who killed McAllister and Lil poisoned Monty's cattle?'

'Don't you?'

Tubig didn't say anything.

I gestured toward the house. 'Your people find anything in there?'

Tubig looked inside, where state forensics investigators were looking for clues. He said, 'They're lifting prints now, but we won't know for a couple of days if we've found anything worthwhile. It all takes time and patience.'

'The radio said Lil had been strangled, then the murderer fired two shots. Is that right?'

'That's it.'

I said, 'Why would he fire shots if he'd already strangled her?'

'We don't know which came first.'

'Either way, the question remains.'

'We don't know.'

'Had Lil been raped?'

Tubig said, 'Her clothes were torn, but we don't think she had sex with anybody. They haven't finished the autopsy.'

'I see. I bet Monty had sex with her dozens of times over the years, and he told Olden Dewlapp he was going with her okay. Why would he have to tear her clothes?'

Tubig shrugged. 'Rape games?'

'Oh, shit, Chief.'

'People are capable of doing the damnedest things when they're loaded.'

'If he was that damned drunk, he probably couldn't get it up in the first place.'

'That's occurred to me.' Tubig pursed his lips.

'Are you going to arrest him?'

'Not yet.'

I said, 'Did you find the weapon that fired the shots?'

'We found a weapon that probably fired the shots.'

'Oh?'

'Texas Buntline.' Tubig sniffed.

'Monty's?'

'Looks that way. Monty carried that Buntline of his in a rack by the window of his pickup. It wasn't there when Duane showed up last night.'

'Where did you find it?'

'In the river out back.'

'Duane called you?'

'He's under standing orders in a case like this.'

'At home?'

Tubig nodded. 'I'd just got back from the Lariat Room. I came over.'

'What'd Monty say? Or was he sober enough to make sense?'

'Barely. He told me he had the pistol in his truck, but doesn't know what happened to it. He was passed out.'

'Well, that's possible, isn't it?'

'Yes, I suppose so,' he said.

'Suppose it was Monty's Buntline. She was strangled, not shot, right?'

'That's right.'

'If he'd strangled her, why would he wake up half the town by firing his pistol? Why didn't he just drive away? Get away from the scene as soon as possible?'

Tubig said, 'Drunk, maybe. Strangled her after an argument. Stupidly fired his gun because he was drunk. Puked all over the inside of his pickup, then passed out. The smell is enough to knock a dog off a gut wagon. Jesus.'

'Want to show me where you found the gun?'

'Sure.' Tubig walked around the edge of the house, and I followed him.

We stood on a rocky bank overlooking the rippling water. The river started in Wallowa Lake, not far away, so at this point it was swift, shallow, and not more than fifteen or twenty yards wide. What's more, it was crystal clear.

'There,' he said.

I said, 'The water's clear and shallow. Stupid place to throw a gun you don't want anybody to find.'

'I agree. Don't see how we could have failed.'

'Even drunk, Monty Hook would know that.'

'You'd think so,' Tubig said.

I squatted on the river rocks, thinking it over. Monty Hook had said that over the years Lil had collected a shoebox of poems and love letters from her shy admirer. That kind of obsession was suggestive of real nut country, in my opinion, but I didn't mention that to Bubba Tubig. Lil Peters had been Bubba's high school heartthrob as well. It wasn't beyond the realm of possibility that pudgy Tubig, Leiat Podebski's ace student and the author of the class prophecy, was the frustrated lover.

Tubig had just returned from the Lariat Room when he got the call. Was he drunk? I wondered. If the folks in Wallowa County smoked cannabis, which encouraged introspection and contemplation, rather than drinking alcohol, which promoted aggression and action, everybody would have been better off, but that was a cultural no-no; these were cowboys and men of action, not intellectuals and artists.

I said, 'Let's see, now. The shots were fired. Duane responded. He called you. You showed up. Who took Monty to jail?'

'Duane.'

'While you stayed with the corpse?'

'Correct.'

I looked up and down the river. When the snows melted in the spring, the runoff began, and high water was in May and June. Beginning in July the water receded until it was at its lowest in August and September. The previous night had been a full moon, plenty of light to walk along the smooth river rocks. I said, 'The killer didn't have to use the lane to get to Lil's house.'

Tubig looked puzzled. 'What?'

'Easy matter to walk along the river here and get to her place the back way. No telltale car out front. No tire prints. All he'd have to do is crouch down, and he'd be shielded by the river bank.'

He blinked. 'That's so.'

I started to say it didn't take Sherlock Holmes to figure that out, but thought better of it. 'Do you think Monty Hook did it? I'm asking you as Bubba Tubig who played football with Monty in high school, not Bubba Tubig chief of police surrounded by pissed-off state cops who are determined to find the son of a bitch who killed a fellow cop.'

'It's hard to imagine he did, but you never know.'

'You think Lil's death is related to McAllister's murder?'

'We don't get a whole lot of murders in Wallowa County, Mr. Denson. First somebody shoots Lil Peters's state cop boyfriend. Then somebody strangles her. We'd be proper fools not to suspect a connection there somewhere, wouldn't we?'

'It's connected to the poisoned salt licks,' I said flatly.

'Oh?'

'What else?' I said.

'Good question.'

I said, 'How about her personal belongings? Find any clues there?'

'Like what?'

I shrugged. 'Oh, I don't know. Letters, photographs, something like that.'

'We looked through everything. We didn't find anything obvious that we know of.'

I looked him in the eye. 'What do you think of the poetry?'

Tubig blinked. 'Poetry?'

I said, 'They're still going over the place. Who knows what they'll find.'

Tubig regarded me with a curious look on his face. Was he worried? It was hard to tell.

Finally he said, 'You know something we don't, Mr. Denson? If you do, you better spill it.'

I rubbed my chin, thinking it over. 'Monty said somebody had been sending Lil love poems, posted from various places in the country.'

'If she's got poems hidden in there, we'll find 'em,' he said.

'Well, I'll keep in touch. Thanks for your help, Chief.' Then, as an afterthought, I said, 'Tell me, Chief, do you attend the annual conventions of the National Association of Chiefs of Police?'

He looked puzzled. And his face looked flushed. 'Why, yes, I do. Why do you ask?'

I shrugged. 'No reason. It's good to

know towns like this are represented as well as the biggies.'

'You ... ' Tubig decided to leave unfinished whatever it was he was going to say.

Then, as I started to leave, he said, 'Who do you think did it, Mr. Denson?'

I said, 'I don't have any idea at all, Chief Tubig, and that's the truth. I do think if we can find whoever it was who poisoned Monty's cattle we'll be a whole lot closer to the truth.'

I walked back to my bus with salt licks, love poems, poachers, preachers, fat cops, and scorned lovers on my mind. Somewhere in that thicket of mysteries and motives, I suspected, a murderer was to be found.

I was careful to stay on the grass so as not to fuck up the prints for the state cops. A private investigator is on marginal grounds to begin with, and it was always good policy to show proper respect for John Law.

I got into my microbus and headed for the Wallowa River Inn to have a talk with a lady named Leiat.

The moment she opened the door, Leiat Podebski knew I was on serious business. Lil Peters's murder was all over the news, and Leiat knew I was after the murderer. A few minutes later, we were settled in her tiny living room with a cup of coffee. I said, 'I just got back from Lil Peters's house, where I talked to Bubba Tubig about Lil's murder.'

'Oh?' She took a sip of coffee.

'A complicated business. Hard to figure.' I tried some coffee, too. 'Say, this is good coffee!'

Leiat said, 'I was really fond of Lil Peters, you know. She was good looking, but also smart. Boobs and brains aren't mutually exclusive, despite what some people say. It's too bad Lil wasn't able to go to college and do something with her brains.'

I said, 'You know, I might be able to figure this all out. But I need help to make sense of the hoop,' I said.

'The hoop?'

'We talked about it the other night.

Willie Prettybird's Great Hoop, bequeathed to us, he says, by the animal people.'

Leiat looked me straight on with her pale blue eyes, and said, 'Well, let me have it, John. You're after something specific. I can see it in your face.'

'Figuring out the hoop means knowing the far side as well as the near side. The hoop is connected, and no matter how much we might fervently wish, we're not likely to straighten it out anytime soon. As the saying goes: What goes around comes around.'

Leiat said, 'The way I see it, the Greeks figured out the nature of Willie's hoop way back when, although they didn't call it that. If you think about it, our story-tellers and writers have been repeating the same themes and stories and characters one way or another ever since.'

'There you go,' I said.

'I've got a good memory, and I want to find whoever it was who murdered Lil. What do you want to know?'

I said, 'You know, when Willie and I checked in the other day, you were telling us about Thad Bonnerton the student, how he was a religious nerd in love with a cheerleader and everything. The cheerleader was Lil Peters, I now know that. Then you started to say something else about Thad, but stopped. I've been wondering what it was you were about to say.'

Leiat smiled. 'Everybody knew Thad was a religious nut and had an infatuation for Lil Peters. Those are facts. Nothing malicious there. What I started to tell you was rumor.'

'Rumor tainted by scandal. That is, delicious gossip.'

'That's right.' She took another sip of coffee.

'Gossip, but probably true nevertheless. Will you tell me about it?'

She hesitated. 'Maybe true. Maybe not. I don't have any proof.'

'Gossip's gossip, I understand that. But sometimes gossip helps solve mysteries. It can make sense out of a distant curve of the hoop.'

'Does it bear directly on Monty Hook's problem or on finding Lil Peters's murderer?'

'It might, but I can't guarantee it. I have to hear it first, then match with some other things I've been learning.'

She bit her lip. 'Okay, then, but you have to take it for what it is, unconfirmed gossip, no more. And you have to keep in mind that it happened more than twenty-five years ago.'

'Got it.'

'Thad's father, the Reverend Robert Bonnerton, liked it here. So did his wife. They liked the people in the Baptist church, and the congregation liked them. But a month before Thad graduated from high school, there was a rumor that he had knocked up a neighbor girl. Belinda Nobles, her name was. She was kind of a big girl, quiet, and had complexion problems, as I recall. She didn't have much in the way of friends. She was lonely, I think that was clear.'

'What happened exactly?'

'This was all very hush-hush, of course. Belinda was a sophomore at the time and one of my students, a good one. One day, she announced that she was going to live with her grandparents in Baker because her grandfather had had a stroke, and her grandmother needed help taking care of him. She came back for her senior year as though nothing had happened. Her grandfather had recovered, she said, so she could come home to her family. She graduated with her class, and later went to school at Southern Oregon State College in Ashland. That's the last I saw or heard of her.'

'Is her family still here?'

'No, they moved a couple of years after she finished high school.'

'What about the baby?'

'Delivered in Baker, they say.'

'Boy or girl?'

'Boy.'

'What happened to it?'

'It was adopted by a neighbor of the Bonnertons. This was allegedly arranged by the Reverend Bonnerton and the girl's parents.'

'Was the family who adopted the baby named Childress, by any chance?'

Leiat looked surprised. 'Why, yes, how did you know?'

'Pride of a father.'

'Oh?'

'Remember at the rodeo when Roy Childress won the saddle bronc competition? Bonnerton just about went nuts. The Reverend Bonnerton was married twenty years with only four adopted children. That is, no children other than his son Roy.'

'If the stories are true, Roy Childress is Thad Bonnerton's son, yes.'

'All that lunatic cheering by Bonnerton! It was the natural emotion of a father who was proud of his son. What do you know about Roy's girlfriend, Opal Riggen?'

'She went to high school in Joseph, so I don't know as much about her. She's got a reputation as a . . .'

I grinned. 'In a place like this, you always hear stories.'

'That goes with small-town territory.'

'Like the episode at Milton-Freewater High School?'

She laughed. 'Like that story, yes.'

'I'm less interested in what the hormonal Opal did or didn't do with teenage boys than in what subject she taught?'

'Subject?' Leiat looked puzzled.

'History. Algebra. Physical education. What?'

Leiat furrowed her brows, thinking. 'I believe she taught biology.'

'Biology?'

'Why, yes. Does that help?'

I said, 'Beyond Opal's having an apparent fixation with the ways of the birds and the bees, it just might.'

'If all this helps Monty Hook or contributes to finding Lil's murderer, no problem. But if the story about Thad Bonnerton's teenage mistake shows up in the newspapers, I won't like it a damn bit. I think this business of the smearing of public figures because of youthful indiscretions or their personal lives just plain stinks.'

'I assure you, Leiat, I'm interested in the past arc of the hoop only as it bears on the present curve.'

'Those fundamentalist preachers are not my kind of people, but the Reverend Bonnerton's got a right to his privacy, same as everybody else. These things happen to a preacher's son same as everybody else.'

'I understand completely. Smearing celebrities has become a form of sport that I don't like either, so mum's the word. And thank you very much, Leiat. I do appreciate the help.'

I rose to go, then said, 'Say, Leiat, Bubba Tubig said he'd just got back from the Lariat Room when he got the call from Duane last night. Where is that?'

Leiat laughed. 'In Joseph.' She gestured in the direction of Eagle Cap Mountain, which loomed above Joseph. 'They've got a country and western band there. They say you can find him there every Friday and Saturday night.'

'Oh?'

'Bubba may be a bachelor, but he's never lost his love of dancing. He can't really relax and dance in Enterprise because he's the chief of police here. But that doesn't keep him away from Joseph.'

'I see. Good for him.' I thanked Leiat again and walked back to my unit for a cold beer and a call to Willie Prettybird, to see if he and Bobcat Bill had found anything in their hoofprint chore at the rodeo grounds.

Turned out they had.

The prints belonged to a horse named Pinecone. Its owner was not surprising.

I decided not to return immediately to Lil's house for another talk with Chief Tubig. I had goodies I didn't especially want to share with the Oregon State Police. When Monty Hook and Bubba Tubig were in high school, the stocky guard Tubig had kept pass rushers from flattening quarterback Hook. Cops were blockers, in a way. As professional defenders, they kept the shits from smothering us all.

Now, all these years later, I wanted to give Bubba Tubig a chance to show his stuff in what was surely, by Wallowa County standards, a championship murder case.

22

Whereas the High Country Saloon was a beer-and-wine bar, a tavern according to state law, the Lariat Room in Joseph had a license from the Oregon State Liquor Control Commission, meaning it could serve hard stuff — distilled booze. In places like Joseph, establishments with a hard liquor license ordinarily had a country and western band on Friday and Saturday nights, and that was the case with the Lariat Room.

One went to the High Country Saloon to cool off on a hot day or to kick back and bullshit after work or maybe play blackjack in the back room; one went to the Lariat Room to scope such local action as was available and maybe — oh, sweet God, let it happen — to get laid. In this manner, bolstered by distilled courage, many individual hoops were inadvertently launched.

Joseph was not the kind of place to

have a bar with Italian, Polynesian, or Mexican decor. The folks there didn't give a squat what Alfredo did with his fettucini, and they did not order foo-foo rum drinks mixed with fruit juice, or weird Mexican crap brewed from cactus juice. The men drank their whiskey or vodka straight, thank you; the ladies were more apt to order a screwdriver, a Tom Collins, or Seven-Crown whiskey mixed with Seven-Up — a yucko concoction called a Seven and Seven. When queried by a gentleman as to her desires — in the matter of having a drink — a lady, not wanting to appear inexperienced or classless, knew it was safe to order a Seven and Seven. Sweetish, maybe, but country class nevertheless.

It didn't matter that the High Country had a wall filled with photographs of rodeo action; the Lariat Room was not to be outdone. Here, the photographs were blown-up stills from Western movies and television programs featuring cattle. John Wayne duked it out with Montgomery Clift in the movie *Red River*. A young Clint Eastwood squatted in earnest discussion with his trail boss in the television series *Rawhide*. A cheery Jane Powell, milking a Guernsey cow, looked up at an admiring Howard Keel in a still from *Seven Brides for Seven Brothers*, an improbable musical with a setting not unlike Wallowa County.

In that movie, Howard Keel — from the moment he saw her sitting on a stool milking a cow — had fallen instantly in love with sweet Jane, who was all teeth, freckles, and blue eyes. Wholesome, wholesome, wholesome. Howard told wholesome Jane about how he and his brothers lived on a ranch up in the mountains and the fall snow was coming on, and he might not be able to make it back until spring. He knew immediately that he was in love with Jane. It wouldn't take a month of courting to figure that out. A man knows such things right off. Out there in darkened theaters across America, moviegoers munched on popcorn, presumably sympathetic to Howard's plight.

Later, Howard strode manfully about the brow of a flowered ridge, singing in his rich baritone that within his heart there lived a secret love. He sang that he was prepared to shout this fact from the highest hills and to golden daffodils, although I had wondered, even as a boy, how it was that daffodils were blooming in October or whenever it was supposed to be. After all, the fall snows were coming on, after which the musical brothers were supposed to be snowed in.

In Joseph, where there were presumably plenty of maids who milked cows, the cowboys didn't hang out in the barnyard looking for their Jane Powell. They headed for the Lariat Room, where their quarry sat atop barstools, not milking stools, and not necessarily looking cute or perky. Like Howard, the cowboys knew immediately what it was they wanted, and it wasn't marriage. And they didn't want to wait until the second date, much less springtime.

If the movies were to be believed, times, perhaps owing to the Pill, had changed.

The dance floor of the Lariat was rimmed with small round tables and a clutter and snarl of chairs. The niggardly space reserved for dancing — management could not sell drinks on the space where their customers jumped around — was a square about eight feet by eight feet. It would remain deserted until the gentlemen were properly juiced and so in the proper frame of mind. But this was rodeo time, and getting juiced wouldn't take long.

In the meantime, the Blue Mountain Sh*tkickers, with Bobby Leonard, were taking their places on the tiny bandstand, getting ready to do their Saturday night thing. The musician who looked like he was in charge, who I assumed was Leonard, brandished an electric guitar of crimson plastic, sparkling with what appeared to be glitter. I say he looked like he was in charge; his hair, which was the longest in the musical trio, and his body language said fairly clearly keep-your-eyes-on-me-ladies-I'm-the-chief-stud-of-this-band. Judging from the lumpy bulge in his skintight jeans — it looked more like an untoward growth than genitalia — he went so far as to stuff rags in his crotch, but I bet few women were fooled.

Leonard's bass-playing buddy was a tall, slope-chested, stoop-shouldered young man with squinty eyes, a plowshare nose, a hint of a chin, and an Adam's apple that poked out like an oak burl. He looked like an escapee from a William Faulkner novel, a Snopes maybe, or a Varner. His small, canary-yellow instrument was loaded with fancy knobs to control its electric throbbing.

The drummer, who was wide and stocky, with a full, black lumberjack's beard, whacked on drums of a particularly noxious Day-Glo green.

All three Sh*tkickers, in keeping with the name of their band, wore western shirts and outsized cowboy hats.

The room was quickly filling with people, but I soon spotted Bubba Tubig, who had swapped his police uniform for western garb. He had snaps on his shirt as well as western V-shaped tabs over the pockets, and he wore cowboy boots and a string bow tie. Like the others, Bubba left his wide-brimmed cowboy hat on. Real cowboys in eastern Oregon did not take their hats off inside; they kept them on at all times, a fashion whose purpose eluded me, there being no sun indoors. They couldn't all be bald; the only answer I could figure was that the hats were so big they'd take up all the space on the bar or table, leaving no room for the drinks.

In his cowboy getup Bubba Tubig looked sort of like a cowboy who genuinely loved his beans and biscuits, if not cows. For five nights of the week he was Chief Tubig, the fat cop who patrolled the streets of Enterprise. Now he was duded-up Bubba, nursing a cold bottle of Budweiser and, like the other single men in the Lariat Room, no doubt hoping against hope that this night — what with the town packed with visitors — he would somehow luck out and get his mighty end in.

Seeing me, he waved for me to join him. 'Come on over, Mr. Denson. Plop your behind.'

I plopped it.

He waved his hand to a cocktail waitress wearing net stockings and a butt-hugging outfit that I assumed was supposed to be an imitation of a Playboy bunny costume, but with a difference. Hers was white with black spots, in the manner of a Holstein cow, complete with diminutive tail. Judging by the outsized bodices of the waitresses, which were not artifically stuffed in the manner of Bobby Leonard's crotch, the owner of the Lariat Room was an admirer of large udders.

'What'll you have?' Tubig asked.

'An Olympia,' I said.

'An Oly for my friend, Lydia,' he said. 'And you might as well get another one for me while you're at it.' As Lydia headed for the bar, he said, 'You look like a hound dog on a hot scent. Looking for me?'

'Yes, I am, as a matter of fact. Leiat Podebski said this was part of your Friday and Saturday night drill. Dancing Bubba.'

Bubba laughed. 'A good woman is Leiat. Anthrax. Murders. Life goes on.'

'Leiat also said you were one of the best students she ever had. You had a real flair for writing.'

Bubba, pleased, said, 'Aw, well, that was years ago.'

I said, 'Remember when we first talked,

and I told you that Willie and I are only interested in the truth and seeing to it that our client gets a fair shake?'

'I do indeed.'

'I said we're not interested in credit or having our names in the newspaper, and that if we found anything good, we'd share it with you straight off.' I waited while Lydia served Bubba another bottle of Budweiser and gave me my Oly. When she was gone, I said, 'Much obliged, Chief.'

He raised his beer in acknowledgment. 'Thank the taxpayers.'

'Okay, I'll tell you what. I'll tell you some things Willie and I found out and some possible links. Then we'll see what you have to say.'

Tubig pursed his lips. 'Fair enough.'

'But first, let's get the poetry business out of the way. Did you get all those love poems out of Lil's house last night while Duane took Monty to jail?'

Tubig paled.

I said quickly, 'I say you wrote the poems on your computer at home and ran them off on your home printer. You mailed one poem a year when you were out of town attending the annual convention of the National Association of Chiefs of Police. You printed enough other stuff on that printer that you were afraid the poems could be traced by state forensics people. Maybe there was a telltale glitch in one of the letters or whatever. It wouldn't take much to establish the link.'

On the bandstand, Bobby Leonard went *bra-ang-ang-ang-ang* on his guitar. A little test.

Tubig closed his eyes, then opened them slowly. 'Yes, Mr. Denson, I retrieved the poems from Lil's house. But I certainly didn't kill her. My God! Writing sophomoric poetry to her is one thing. Surely there's no law against that. In fact, I think she may have known it was me all along.'

Bra-ang-ang-ang-ang.

'I'm not saying you killed her. I just had to get the question of the poetry out of the way. You don't want to be publicly accused of being a nut case, I understand that. What I figured out remains between you and me and the fence post. I'm not interested in gossip or having a giggle at somebody else's expense.'

'Thank you.' He looked relieved.

I watched Lydia of the bovine bosom deliver drinks to the musicians, who put them down beside their feet. To Tubig I said, 'Now then, Chief, you were in the same high school class as Thad Bonnerton. I want you to tell me the gossip as you understood it.'

'The gossip?'

Bra-ang-ang-ang-ang.

'About the girl Bonnerton knocked up the spring you graduated. Belinda Nobles. Come on now. You want to get to the bottom of this shit or don't you?'

Tubig sighed. 'Belinda was a big, beefy girl. The story is she had the baby in Baker. She was gone for a year and then came back to Enterprise. The baby, a boy, was said to be the one adopted by the Childress family, one of the neighbors of the Bonnertons.'

'The baby being named Roy.'

'If the story is true, yes.'

Boom-a-ooom-a-ooom-a-ooom. It was the bass player's turn to see if his electronic gadget was in working order.

'So Thad Bonnerton, among other possible motives, might well have made the trip to Enterprise to see his son. It's his only biological offspring, as far as we know. His four children in Oklahoma are adopted. One's own kid is special, whether we like to admit it or not.'

'That appears so.'

'Say Bonnerton's nursed a torch for Lil all these years. Who knows what fantasies he nursed about his triumphant return, all duded up in a three-piece suit and riding in a stretch limousine? Furthermore, he has a bastard son in Enterprise. His son, it turns out, was sent to the slammer for rustling on the testimony of Monty Hook and Bobcat Bill Kemiah. And Monty makes no secret of the fact that he and Bobcat suspect Roy of poaching. They would send him up for poaching again if they could prove it.'

Boom-a-ooom-a-ooom-a-ooom.

Tubig said, 'Everybody knows Monty and Bobcat have been keeping an eye on Childress, true.'

'Under the circumstances,' I said, 'it

374

seems safe to conclude that Childress wishes Monty Hook all the bad luck in the world.'

Boom-a-oooom-a-ooom-a-ooom. The bass player took a sip of his drink, his outsized Adam's apple bouncing like a basketball.

'I think that about covers the territory, yes.'

'Now then, Roy Childress would have heard the story around town about how his father, the famous Reverend Thaddeus Hamm Bonnerton, as a pimple-faced nerd, had a high school crush on the hot-looking cheerleader, Lil Peters. Everybody here knows that, right? Roy even played liar's dice with Lil in the High Country. I saw him.'

Tubig said, 'He probably knows Bonnerton is his father, I agree. And Bonnerton's crush on Lil is a standing joke at the High Country. Every time he has one of his televised revivals, they all yell at her to turn the tube on so she can see what she missed out on.'

'But in high school, as everybody knows, Lil Peters only had eyes for Monty Hook, star quarterback and class president.'

'Right.'

Bobby Leonard adjusted the microphone around his neck and said, 'Welcome to the Lariat Room, folks. Good to see all you cowpokes taking a little break from them poor damn cows. They must all look forward to Friday and Saturday nights. Get a little time off, there.' Leonard grinned broadly, thus indicating that was a joke — cow *pokes*, get it? — and people were supposed to laugh.

To my amazement, they did. I said, 'Now then, if Roy Childress had learned the identity of his real father, he would also know that Bonnerton is constantly in the market for grist for his environmental revivals, wouldn't he? People are always jabbering about this or that environmental outrage, so it would take a really good one to justify a televised revival. The more people who watch, the more money for the Institute for the Restoration of Christ's Bosom, or whatever it's called.'

'That follows.'

'Money for Bonnerton's pocket.'

'He probably prays for oil tankers to run aground.'

Brang-a-rang-a-rang-a-rang. Leonard said,

'Did you hear the one about the guy over by Walla Walla who responded to the employment agency ad for a cook at a sheep camp? He got the job and showed up at the camp with dinnertime coming up, but he couldn't find anything to cook. He saw a sheep tied up out back, so he knocked it in the head and butchered it. The next day he showed up at the employment agency all bruised and beat up. A helluva-looking mess. The employment guy said, 'My God, what happened? Did you fuck up their cookin'?' He said, 'Aw, hell no, I cooked up their fuckin'.''

The bearded drummer gave a roll, and everybody laughed.

I said to Tubig, 'Now suppose Roy Childress gets in touch with his old man and says, 'Look, Dad, for a price your long-lost son can bring this prick Monty Hook down a notch or two and give you a perfect reason to hold an environmental revival on the eve of the all-school reunion.''

Tubig raised his eyebrows and took a swig of beer.

I said, 'By then, Bonnerton would have been contacted by the committee that put the reunion together. Time enough to rekindle the old desire for Lil. See what I'm getting at?'

'I do indeed,' Tubig said.

'You see that fancy Ford pickup Childress has been driving around town?'

'Oh, sure. Loves to drive fast. Duane and I have our hearts set on nailing him before he runs over a pedestrian.'

On the bandstand Bobby Leonard took a hit from his drink, and said, 'Did you hear the one about the kid from Portland who got a job on a ranch just outside of town here? It was his first job, and it seemed like he couldn't get anything right. He asked the foreman what he should do, and the foreman said, 'Boy, what you need are smartnin' pills.' The kid said, 'Smartnin' pills?' The foreman said sure, smartnin' pills, and gave him some rabbit pellets and told him to take three every morning. Well, the kid dutifully ate those rabbit pellets every day for a week, but didn't seem to improve a whole lot. Then one morning, he said to the foreman, 'You know, I think those pills I've been taking every morning are rabbit shit.' And the foreman said, 'Now you're gettin' smart.''

The drummer gave another roll, and everybody laughed.

I said, 'According to what I heard Childress say in the parking lot of the Wallowa River Inn, he paid cash for that fancy Ford. Now where in the hell would he come up with money like that?'

'Good question. You heard him in the parking lot of the Wallowa River Inn?' Tubig looked puzzled.

'He and Opal Riggen were arriving for a little late-night partying with some of Bonnerton's advance crew.'

'Oh?'

'Said it when he was drunk and pissing in Leiat's flowers.'

'Mmmmm.'

'Bonnerton told me Opal's been helping set up the revivals here.'

'Yes, she has been. That's right.'

I said, 'Childress doesn't have a regular job, does he?'

'Not that I know of.'

'Do you know who Pinecone is?'

Tubig furrowed his brow.

I said, 'Pinecone is Roy Childress's horse.'

'Ah, the one he ropes with. Beautiful horse.'

'Whoever delivered the poisoned salt licks on Monty's north spread was riding Pinecone.'

Tubig's eyes widened. 'How do you know that?'

'Willie and Bobcat described the prints to me, and I spotted a matching hoofprint by the Jaycees' hamburger stand at the rodeo yesterday. But there were so many hoofprints that not even Willie and Bobcat could trace them down. So they went to the rodeo this morning and checked out the prints of the horses as they were unloaded from their trailers.'

'Oh, oh.'

On the bandstand, Leonard gave his guitar a couple more warm-up *barannnnnngs*, and said, 'Say, have you folks heard the one about the kid from Joseph who was studying animal husbandry down at Oregon State until they caught him at it?' He looked around, grinning broadly.

The drummer thumped and banged,

and everybody laughed.

Wondering when the Sh*tkickers were going to get on with the music, I said to Tubig, 'Do you suppose Childress loaned Pinecone out to somebody else who delivered the salt?'

'Roy Childress doesn't loan Pinecone out to anybody for any purpose. No way.'

I turned up my palms in a see-there gesture.

Tubig narrowed his eyes. 'What we need now is evidence that Roy Childress contacted the Reverend Bonnerton.'

'Telephone records?' I said.

Tubig nodded. 'I can see to that.'

'Without a court order?'

'No court order needed. Where did he get salt licks spiked with anthrax?'

'Monty Hook tells me anthrax spores are available to anybody with imagination. All you need is a dead animal infected with the disease. One of those bison in Canada, say. That wasn't the first time that disease popped up, only the most recent and dramatic outbreak. Monty's been told a larger culture could be grown by an undergraduate with elementary lab skills. You had any break-ins in the last year or so recorded in, say, a high school science lab?'

'In Joseph last fall.'

The Sh*tkickers swung into action with a rhythmic beat, and Leonard sang:

Oh, ho, lady, you wanna play my song
You just squeeze my fiddle
Directly in the middle
Right there
Directly in the middle
That's got it
Go high diddle, diddle
Squeeze that fiddle
And you can't go wrong.

Several cowboy swains got up to make their move. They did not gyrate separately from the lady as had been the fashion for some years. Wanting to at least touch the female's hands, they danced the swing, best done to country and western music and amenable to dancing in cowboy boots. The attraction of country music, in addition to lyrics that could actually be heard and understood, was that it retained the concept of rhythm, which seemed increasingly foreign to rock and roll.

Deciding that I'd take Irving Berlin over the Sh*tkicker's lead song, I said, 'You know the story about Opal Riggen's short-lived tenure as a schoolteacher over in Milton-Freewater?'

'Everybody knows that story. It was in the newspapers.'

'Do you know what she taught?'

Tubig shrugged.

'She taught biology.'

Tubig's eyes widened. 'Really?

'And she went to high school where? I bet you know that.'

'Joseph,' he said. 'She's a graduate of Joseph High School.'

'After her set-to with Monty Hook in the courts over that paternity suit, she doesn't like him any more than Childress does.'

'You are a thorough man, Mr. Denson.'

I said, 'You want to continue working with me? I repeat what I told you in our first talk: I'm not interested in glory, just the truth and the protection of my client. You can get your picture in the papers if you want.'

'Aw now, I — '

I interrupted him. 'Don't be modest. Your continued reappointment as chief of police depends on your ability to convince the public that you're doing a good job with the taxpayers' money.'

Tubig grinned. 'Well, yes, there is that consideration.'

I said, 'All I want is for my client to walk and Lil's murderer to get his.'

'And for the Reverend Bonnerton to get his — if he had anything to do with bringing an anthrax infection into the county.'

'That, too. It goes without saying.'

'Hell, yes. We start with the phone calls, then we'll need some prints from Opal.'

On the bandstand, Bobby Leonard said, 'Say, did you folks hear the one about . . . '

I got up and left with Leonard telling a story about a guy who rode his horse into a saloon and ordered him a beer.

23

I missed waking up with Lenora Kemiah by my side, but this fact wasn't completely disheartening because I knew, if I pressed my case properly, I could have her there for months if not years to come. It is part of the wiles of a woman to plant such seeds in a man's imagination, and Lenora was no fool. It is the man who is the fool to think that the initial passion will remain at fever pitch, but never mind; there were plenty of hormonal idiots, myself included, who were capable of thinking the hoop would somehow be different for them.

In the end, the present stretch of the hoop was most important. Add each day up, and in the end, there you have the hoop. The Reverend Thaddeus Hamm Bonnerton had allowed himself to become obsessed by the curve out of the past, which was not the most productive strategy for life. As I lay there, thinking alternately of wonderful Lenora and of the Reverend Bonnerton's televised revival at three o'clock, the phone rang.

It was Bubba Tubig, with an edge of urgency to his voice. 'Denson?'

I said, 'Me. What's up, Chief?'

'The shit's hit the fan big, big time, Denson. I mean big time. Turds flying everywhere.'

'Oh? What's happened?'

'Grab your nuts and hold on.'

I laughed. 'I got 'em. Lay it on me.'

'Would you believe Opal Riggen is in the hospital with anthrax splotches all over her hands and arms.'

'I believe.'

'After the cattle came down with the disease the communicable-disease people dropped by the hospital to tell people what they should do if a patient checked in with symptoms of anthrax. So the doctor at the emergency room knew immediately what he had on his hands, thank God. He stabbed Opal in the butt with serum, put her in quarantine, and called me. He said we need to check the blood of everybody who has had personal contact with her.'

'How's she doing?'

'She's hysterical, but she'll be okay, he says.'

'I think I'd probably be hysterical too.'

'This is serious business, Denson. This shit can spread like wildfire.'

I said, 'What about Childress? If anybody's had personal contact with Opal, it has to be him.'

'He's not home, and Opal says she doesn't know where he is. I've got an APB out on him.'

'He's probably got anthrax splotches on his pecker.'

Tubig said, 'The first thing I need to do is find out for sure if there's been any contact between Childress and the Reverend Bonnerton. I got my phone company friend out of bed a few minutes ago. I told him what's happened. I told him I know it's Sunday, but here's a chance for the phone company to be a hero. If he wants to help stop the spread of anthrax in Wallowa County, he'll hustle his ass down to the office and punch up Childress's phone records pronto. It's all on computer, so it's no big deal. He can do it.'

'Ah, good. The wonderful world of the computer. How long will that take?'

Tubig said, 'An hour or two, maybe. He's looking at a half-hour drive to the phone company office.'

'Meanwhile the old second hand goes tick, tick, tick . . . '

'Not funny, Denson.'

'Sorry.'

'Listen, I got a long, long day ahead of me. You want to tag along? I don't mind telling you I need all the help I can get. Duane's okay for traffic offenses and domestic disturbances, but he's not the quickest cop I've ever seen, if you know what I mean. Not that you're any kind of Sherlock Holmes.'

'I'll do anything I can.'

'I'd appreciate it. Also, I like the idea of having an independent witness.'

'So what do you propose we do first?'

'I think our first chore is to go straight to Bonnerton and let him know what happened. He's had contact with Opal in setting up his revivals, so it shouldn't be asking too much that he have his blood tested.'

'A person wouldn't think so. Are you going to tell him any of our ideas about Childress or Lil's murder?'

'I don't figure there's any reason to spook him prematurely. Our first objective should be to prevent him from spreading the disease if he has it. There's nothing illegal or immoral about catching it from Opal. Right?'

'Right. But what if he refuses?'

'Then we go to Judge Ross Millard and ask for a court order. I don't mind telling you, Denson, that if I fuck up, I'll be roasted later on. The public pays me to be cool in the clutch. I have to do everything correctly and in the right order.'

'I already talked to Bonnerton once, pretending to be a writer for *The New York Times* Sunday magazine. You'll have to play along.'

'No problem.'

'Let's do it, then.'

'Hang tight, Denson. I'll be there in ten minutes.'

Chief Bubba Tubig was not impolite in his insistence on talking to the Reverend Thaddeus Hamm Bonnerton on the day of the big show, yet he didn't take shit, either. Tubig strode forth like a corpulent warrior, flashing his badge at whoever was in his path, taking no ifs, ands, or buts. He was the cop in charge, and he had an outbreak of anthrax on his hands; by God he was going to talk to Bonnerton now, not later, and that was that.

After ten minutes of doodle and hoo-hoo from Bonnerton's gophers, yes-men, and Ms. Mannson, media spokesperson, we were ushered into the grandest of the grand tour buses, the opulence of which I thought would have embarrassed anybody who professed to be a minister of the Lord, but never mind.

I clicked on the matchbook recorder in my shirt pocket. I didn't tell Tubig about this. I didn't want Bonnerton to later claim Tubig had set him up.

Bonnerton, wearing cotton chinos and a long-sleeved shirt, received us in a living room whose furniture was upholstered in leather. It was the first time I had seen him out of his three-piece suit, but I couldn't help wondering why, on a warm July day, he was wearing a long-sleeved shirt.

Bonnerton looked puzzled. 'Is there some kind of emergency, Chief?' he asked, extending his hand.

The back of his hand did not look diseased, but it didn't look natural either.

Tubig, pointedly, did not offer his hand in return.

Bonnerton was offended. He cocked his head. Not shake hands! What was this?

Was there makeup on the back of Bonnerton's hands?

Tubig said, 'No offense, Reverend, but under the circumstances it's probably better if we don't shake hands.'

Bonnerton was not pacified. 'Why is that, might I ask?'

Tubig said, 'Opal Riggen has been hospitalized with anthrax.'

I wondered if Tubig too was curious about Bonnerton's long-sleeved shirt.

And those hands?

Bonnerton raised his eyebrows. 'And you think I have it?'

'We have no idea, but if you do, you may be highly infectious. And you need immediate medical treatment. We have to talk.'

Bonnerton, eyeing me, gestured for us to sit on the sofa. We sat. He lowered himself into a squishy easy chair facing us.

Tubig said, 'I believe you've already met Mr. Denson here, from *The New York Times*.'

'Mr. Denson and I have had a chat, yes,' he said.

I said, 'When my editors in New York heard about the outbreak of anthrax, they said to get right on it.'

'I bet they did,' Bonnerton said dryly. 'Just what is it we have to talk about this morning?' He glanced at his watch.

Tubig explained how anthrax is spread and the consequences of infection. 'It can be spread by a simple handshake. Since you and your people have been working with Ms. Riggen, we have to think about elementary precautions for your health. This is for your protection and that of everybody in the community.'

Bonnerton considered that. 'How is it that Opal contracted the disease, Chief Tubig? Have you determined that?'

Tubig said, 'We have no idea, but we have standing instructions from the National Communicable Disease Center in Atlanta to check out all personal contacts of anybody who has come down with the disease. That's why I'm here. If you've caught anthrax from your dealings with Opal, we have a serum to stop it cold. But if it's allowed to spread, we could be in real trouble.'

Bonnerton said, 'Has Opal been given the serum?'

'Of course. She's feeling fine, but she'll have to remain in quarantine for a few days until the chances of her spreading it have passed.'

'Are you charging me with some kind of crime?'

Tubig said, 'No, and you don't have to talk to us if you don't want to. If you do, you have a right to have a lawyer present if that makes you feel better.'

'That makes it sound like I'm suspected of something.'

'I'm only following the instructions of the communicable-disease people. Nobody wants to see an outbreak of anthrax among the residents of Wallowa County. Bad enough that Monty Hook's cattle were infected. It's my job to protect the people of this community. It's as simple as that. If you've caught it, you should get a shot of serum without delay.'

'And the business about the lawyer? What about that?'

'You've watched enough cops on television to know that I have to say that almost every time I fart, begging your pardon.'

'I'm a minister of the Lord.'

Politely, Tubig said, 'Yes, Reverend, I'm aware of that. I'm also aware of my responsibility to the taxpayers who spring for my salary.'

'I feel just fine, thank you. I have no idea how Opal Riggen caught the disease, but she's a Christian woman and a good friend of the Institute for the Restoration of Christ's Bosom. Her catching the disease is a terrible turn of events, and I will pray for her recovery.'

I said, 'The Lord has already provided a serum.'

Bonnerton studied me for a moment, then said to Tubig, 'If you will excuse me, Chief, I have a nationally televised revival to conduct this afternoon that means at least two hundred and fifty thousand dollars that can be used to help clean up the environment. We need every cent we can raise to do a proper job.'

Tubig blinked. 'Truly, Reverend Bonnerton, this is for your own good. It's a precaution only. It can't hurt to make sure.'

'I say again, you're talking to a minister of God, Chief Tubig.'

Tubig clenched his jaw.

Bonnerton looked at me and said, 'You're not really from *The New York Times Magazine*, are you, Mr. Denson?'

I shook my head. 'I'm a private detective.'

'Representing whom, might I ask?'

'My partner and I are working for a

lawyer named Olden Dewlapp, who is representing the rancher whose cattle some miserable, low-down, crackpot son of a bitch infected with anthrax.'

'Monty Hook?'

'He hired me and my redskin pal to run the brainless cock-sucker to ground. We may not be the Royal Canadian Mounted Police, but we do our damnedest to get our man.'

Bonnerton's eyes blazed. 'Judas,' he said. He spat the word at me.

I said, calmly, 'I once had a cat named Judas. Faithful thing, as cats go. Liked to sleep in my lap during the day. At night he prowled around trying to get his end in. But he always shit in the kitty litter.'

'You lied.'

'Like a trooper,' I said cheerfully. 'But not about everything. I did go to Cayuse High School, and I once played right field for Athena when they couldn't field a complete team.'

'Judas!' he snarled again.

I said, 'They found anthrax spores all over Lil Peters's body. Did you know that, Reverend Bonnerton?'

Bonnerton's mouth dropped slightly. 'Why, I thought she was just strangled.'

'Also raped,' I said.

'Raped? They didn't say anything about that in the papers.'

'The cops kept that part out of the papers. She had bruises all over her body. Whoever raped her really did a number on her.'

'I don't believe it,' he said.

Eyeing me, Tubig said, 'I assure you, Mr. Denson's telling the truth, Reverend. Lil was raped.'

'Liars,' Bonnerton said.

I looked incredulous. 'Reverend, Reverend. Do you really think the police are so abjectly stupid as to tell reporters every teensy-weensy thing they know? Their job is to catch assholes, not provide entertaining copy for newspaper reporters.'

'You're lying!'

I shrugged. 'I bet you wouldn't be half bad at liar's dice yourself.'

'Liar! Judas!'

'I'm giving you the straight goods and you know it, don't you, Reverend? Lil Peters was raped.'

'Liar!' Bonnerton was rigid with fury.

I looked him straight in the eyes. 'Lil was a handsome woman, Reverend. Whoever murdered her had himself a good time while he was at it. Why should that surprise you?'

The Reverend Thaddeus Hamm Bonnerton said, 'You will both please go now. I've got work to do.' His voice was tight.

Chief Tubig and I did as we were told.

* * *

We headed for the residence of Judge Ross Millard in Bubba Tubig's squad car, siren squealing. We had work to do and not a minute to waste.

We drove in silence for a moment. Then Tubig said, 'That was quick thinking back there with the rape business. You're a regular snake eyes, Denson. I didn't know you had it in you.'

'That was my bait-the-asshole-and-see-what-happens gambit.'

Tubig grinned. 'It worked. He bit.'

'You think so?'

'He was furious. I think he knows both

about the poisoning of Hook's cattle and the two murders.'

I said, 'Ahh, good. Then Judge Millard will help you out.'

Tubig, holding grimly onto the steering wheel, slid nearly sideways around a corner. 'Maybe, maybe not.'

'No?'

'A judge is a judge, Denson. You gotta remember, this is the good old U.S. of A.'

I said, 'By the way, did you catch the backs of Bonnerton's hands?'

Tubig grimaced.

I said, 'Makeup. I'd make book on it.'

'No way I was going to shake hands.'

I grinned. 'Me neither.' Then I thought of something else. 'His followers at the big show might not be so careful. Remember, at the end of his gig, Bonnerton strides into the crowd giving folks a high five for Jesus. If he's infected with anthrax, that'll be a dandy piece of show business.'

Tubig blinked. 'Oh shit. His high fives. I'd forgotten.'

Tubig's cellular phone rang. It was his friend from the telephone company.

24

Judge Ross Millard's house was surrounded by a board fence, but from where I sat in Chief Tubig's squad car, waiting to be summoned if Millard was home, I could see the front of a modern version of Frank Lloyd Wright's classic prairie house — low and spread out, hugging the land rather than poking up like a giant wart. Copies of Wright's house had dominated American suburbs for years until scarcity of land forced a return to two-story houses situated on the cul-de-sacs and loops named Kensington Road, Canterbury Lane and the other fancy if improbable English names required for streets of dubious dreams.

The house had thick wooden shake shingles and a natural stone facade on the south-facing front. The front door, dominated by a handsome brass knocker, was set to one side of a curtained picture window that faced the handsome Eagle

Cap Mountain, the top of which was still covered with snow. A chimney of cream-colored brick poked up through the shingled roof. If I were to bet, I would have dated the house from the mid-1950s or the early 1960s, and although I couldn't see the rear, which faced the cold winter winds fresh out of British Columbia by way of eastern Washington, I knew it would likely be covered with moss. The patio where the Millard family held its summertime barbecues would be to the rear, a concrete slab.

It was almost noon when Chief Tubig banged the brass knocker. The door was opened by a middle-aged man in Reebok running shoes and a University of Oregon Fighting Ducks T-shirt stretched tightly over a melon belly. He was not fat, like Tubig. He had hairy bird legs. His melon belly poked out from his skinny frame like an embarrassing growth. I had seen pregnant women who looked the same way. His brown hair was close-cropped, suggesting Prussian responsibility, I suppose — more difficult for lice to breed — and he wore stylish eyeglasses with thin, black-wire frames. From Tubig's demeanor, I took this to be Judge Ross Millard, arbiter of justice on this warm Sunday.

Tubig spoke briefly to him, gesturing in my direction with his hand. He looked my way as he talked. Millard asked a question. Tubig answered. Then Millard motioned for me to join them.

I scrambled out of the squad car, flipping on the matchbox recorder in my shirt pocket as I did, and joined them. Tubig introduced us.

'All the way up from Portland,' Millard said, sizing me up.

'Yes, Your Honor. Working for Olden Dewlapp, who is Mr. Hook's lawyer.'

'Mmmmm.' The legal profession was not enamored of lawyers who advertised on television, especially goofy-looking, down-home types like the brothers Boogie and Olden Dewlapp. Private detectives were famous for being marginal types, often frustrated cops or would-be adventurers, better left as characters in fiction.

'With my partner, Willie Prettybird,' I

added quickly, hoping to score points for being politically correct.

'Mmmmm,' he said again. He gave me no points at all for having Willie as a partner. In fact, it was probably a negative. This wasn't good, in my opinion. Millard said, 'Won't you both join me in back? It's a warm day. We can have a cup of coffee while you tell me your story.'

We followed him through a passageway between the side of the house and the garage to the back, where, as I suspected, there was a large concrete patio for barbecues. The patio featured a fancy brick barbecue pit, two picnic tables, and a folding card table around which were folding chairs of plastic webbing stretched between aluminum tubes.

When Judge Millard went inside to fetch the coffee, Tubig looked at me uncertainly. 'What do you think?' he said.

'Like you said, a judge is a judge.'

Tubig grimaced, but said nothing.

'I think it's better to lead gradually to the subject of Bonnerton, him being a celebrity preacher and all.'

'Good thinking.'

A moment later, Judge Millard returned with a tray with an insulated stainless-steel coffeepot, a creamer in the shape of a cow, sugar, and three cups. He put them on the table, and we all helped ourselves. When we were finished, he said, 'Now then, Chief Tubig.'

Tubig cleared his throat and took a sip of coffee. 'A local woman named Opal Riggen is at this moment in the hospital being treated for anthrax, a dangerous and highly infectious disease.'

'I've been reading the papers,' Millard said dryly.

Tubig licked his lips. He told Millard that Opal had been a biology major at Eastern Oregon State College. He told him about the break-in and theft of laboratory equipment at Joseph High School last fall. He told him that radical malcontents had openly advertised the availability of the anthrax bacillus and that minimal lab skills plus a dead animal were all that one needed to grow a culture. He told him about Opal's relationship with Childress and her hatred for Hook, on whom she'd once slapped a paternity suit.

I thought Tubig was off to a good start. He was straightforward and direct, building his case as logically as he could. Get the tough stuff over with first, then compromise with a court order for blood tests. Good strategy.

Watching Tubig over his cup of coffee, Millard said, 'Do you have any direct evidence of a connection between Opal and the break-in?'

'No, we don't.' Tubig glanced at me. 'But when I finish my story, I'll be wanting a warrant to search her house.'

'Of course. Do continue with your story,' Millard said.

Tubig told him that evidence presented by Monty Hook and Bobcat Bill had resulted in Childress's felony conviction for cattle rustling. He said the state police had long suspected Childress was a poacher, and Officer McAllister, Lil Peters's boyfriend, was after poachers when he was killed on Hook's north spread. He told him about the two main tactics of poachers, shining the animals at night and using salt licks.

Millard smiled. 'I've got a fair idea how poachers work, Chief.'

I bet he did. He must have handled dozens of poaching cases in his time.

Undaunted, Tubig told him about the hoofprints of Childress's horse Pinecone that led to the poisoned salt licks. He said we were certain that Roy Childress was the Reverend Bonnerton's son. He told him the story of what he thought happened in 1968. He said he couldn't prove it immediately because the state held adoption records confidential, but if given a chance, he could surely establish Bonnerton's paternity.

After listening to this, Millard raised one eyebrow, but didn't say anything. He looked at me, then back at Tubig, then shook his head like we were the dumbest fucks on the planet. 'So what?' He rested a hand on his outsized stomach.

Tubig cleared his throat. 'I hope to make that clear, Your Honor.'

'Please do, by all means. I'm all ears.'

There was little Tubig could do but

plunge forward. He told Millard about Lil's relationship to Monty, and Bonnerton's feelings for Lil. This fitted into the facts of the case as Tubig had been able to deduce, and it addressed the question of Bonnerton's motive. Neither father nor son was a great fan of Monty Hook.

Millard laughed out loud, his melon belly bouncing up and down with the effort. 'Tell me, Chief, just how is it you know for sure how Thad Bonnerton felt about Lil? Do you even know for an absolute fact that he had an adolescent crush on her?'

Tubig said, 'No, Your Honor, we do not.'

He said, 'Well, then, you're relying on conjecture and hearsay, aren't you? Conjecture and hearsay about a feeling Bonnerton allegedly harbored for a quarter of a century.'

Chastened, Tubig took a sip of coffee.

Millard said, 'Even if Bonnerton did have a teenage crush on Lil, that doesn't prove anything now, does it?'

Tubig said, 'I . . . ' He obviously didn't know what to say next.

Millard said, 'You're an experienced police officer, Chief Tubig. You ought to know better than that.'

Tubig added quickly, 'We also have phone records showing Childress making numerous calls to Bonnerton's cellular phone number over the last eight months.'

'Oh? And what does that prove? Do you have recordings of the conversations that established any kind of criminal intent?'

'No, we don't, Your Honor.'

Judge Millard looked exasperated. 'All you know for a fact is that there has been an outbreak of anthrax on Monty Hook's property, caused by poisoned salt licks. You have circumstantial evidence pointing to Roy Childress. There could be any number of ways Opal Riggen could have caught anthrax. You don't have enough evidence to charge her with the laboratory break-in, and you certainly don't have enough to accuse the Reverend Bonnerton of anything.'

Tubig glanced at me. Time for his trump. He said, 'Judge Millard, if you could set aside for a moment the possibility of criminal action. The federal communicable-disease people told us that a person infected with anthrax could pass it on by merely touching someone. The Reverend Bonnerton will be holding a nationally televised revival this afternoon, and his local contact has come down with it. This is an extraordinary situation. Surely we have enough evidence to establish a clear and present danger to the public health.'

Clear and present danger. I liked the phrase. After all, Tubig wasn't asking for permission to check Bonnerton's blood for HIV. Surely he had carried the day.

'You do?'

Tubig said, 'Yes, Your Honor. I think we do. Clearly.'

Millard blinked. 'And what, exactly, are you asking of me?'

'Is it not possible for you to issue a court order enjoining all people who had recent physical contact with Opal Riggen, including the Reverend Bonnerton, to have their blood checked for anthrax bacillus?'

Millard thought for a moment, then said, 'Why don't you just drive over and ask him? Surely there's no reason to brandish a court order like a Gestapo officer. Appeal to his reason.'

'We already did that, Your Honor. We just came from there.'

'And what did he say?'

'He said no.'

Millard furrowed his brows. 'The Reverend Bonnerton has every right to say no if he wants. What you're proposing violates his right of privacy. He's a minister of the Lord.'

Tubig looked my way.

I was a private investigator, not a chief of police. It was unlikely I'd have to work with this moron again. As politely as I could manage, I said, 'What does his being a minister of the Lord have to do with anything?'

He looked amazed. 'Don't you think we have an obligation to show respect, Mr. Denson?'

'Respect?' Maybe the judge was worried about the Fifth Amendment and self-incrimination. Maybe Bonnerton would have grounds there, but Millard hadn't said so. I wanted to mention the specific separation of church and state written into the Constitution, but thought better of it.

Judge Millard studied me for a moment. No doubt his opinion of private detectives had been confirmed by the temerity of my mild challenge, but what was he going to do, arrest me for contempt of court for mouthing off in his backyard?

He turned to Tubig and said, 'If the Reverend Bonnerton turns out to actually have anthrax, Chief Tubig, you should by all means return and make your pitch again. I'll think about it. In the meantime, you should not get carried away by fantasy based on circumstantial evidence. Get solid evidence, then come back.'

I thought, *Shit oh dear, mister, where are your brains?*

He said, as though to pacify us, 'Based on the circumstantial evidence you've collected, I will sign a warrant for you to search Opal Riggen's house and Roy Childress's residence.'

'They're the same,' Tubig said.

Millard seemed pleased at that news. 'Well, then, easy for you, eh, Chief? I'll fax the warrant to your office within the hour. Will that help?'

Tubig finished off his coffee and rose to leave. 'We'll take anything we can get, Judge. Thank you for your time and the good coffee.'

As I stood, Judge Millard said, 'I'm curious, Mr. Denson. Tell me, do you have something personal against preachers?'

I said, 'No, I don't, Judge, but I think the odds are that priests and preachers travel the same hoop as everybody else.'

'The hoop?'

'They're made of the same flesh and blood and human imagination as you and me and Chief Tubig here.'

Millard considered the question of the hoop, but obviously decided not to pursue it. 'Do you think it was wrong of me not to require the Reverend Bonnerton to take a blood test?'

I looked up at the startling white snow atop beautiful Eagle's Cap, a mountain aptly named. I said, 'Are you familiar with Pascal's gamble, Judge?' Blaise Pascal was the seventeenth-century French philosopher and mathematician who reasoned that if you don't believe in God and are wrong, you wind up in hell. If you do believe in God and are wrong, there is no penalty. Ergo, it's logical to believe in God.

It was my bet that Judge Millard had followed similar logic in deciding not to require a blood check of the Reverend Bonnerton. If he allowed Tubig to arrest or roust a preacher who turned out to be innocent, there would be public hell to pay to anguished Christians, furious that a secular authority with a big belly would dare question a minister of the Lord. If Millard did nothing, there was no penalty. Ergo, better to stand pat.

The trouble was, I didn't think the judge had really listened to what Bubba Tubig had to say about the virulent nature of anthrax.

Millard screwed up his face, thinking. He didn't know about Pascal.

Tubig took my elbow and gave it a gentle squeeze, a signal to keep my stupid mouth shut. He said, 'We truly do have to be going, Judge Millard. What with the Reverend Bonnerton's revival coming up at three o'clock, we've got a lot of work on our hands.'

As Tubig guided me through the passage between the house and garage, he breathed, 'Use your head, Denson. Jesus!'

We restrained ourselves from outright running to Tubig's squad car. We hopped into it and raced away, leaving Judge Ross Millard to look up Blaise Pascal in the encyclopedia.

$$\star \quad \star \quad \star$$

I didn't say anything for a couple of blocks, allowing the furious Tubig to calm down. Then, grinning, I said, 'For whatever it's worth, I thought you did first-rate work, Chief.'

Tubig smiled grimly and clenched his jaw. 'He's the judge.'

I said, 'He seemed quite confident.'

'That's his job. He's paid to know the law. He's supposed to be confident.'

I said, 'What do we do now?'

Biting his lip, Tubig squealed around a

corner. 'We follow the drill. We do the best we can with the time we have.'

I said, 'Lucky us to have judges to protect the public from storm troopers like you. What an evil bastard you are, picking on preachers like that.'

Tubig rolled his eyes. 'Right.'

'What you need, Chief, is a videotape of a smoking anthrax spore. Nail this case down.'

Bubba Tubig gave me a look. 'A smoking anthrax spore. Sure. Sure.'

I pulled my matchbox recorder out of my shirt pocket and turned it on.

Tubig grinned. 'All right!'

'I got our conversation with Bonnerton, too.'

'Good man.'

'Willie calls me Dumsht.'

'Dumsht?'

'For dumb shit. I didn't tell you about the recorder so Bonnerton or Millard can't later accuse you of setting them up. I'm a private dick. People expect me to be devious.'

25

One hour . . .

One hour before the Reverend Thaddeus Hamm Bonnerton's televised big show . . .

One hour and counting . . .

Chief Bubba Tubig, checking the Timex on his fat wrist, made a sour face.

I knew what he was thinking. I said, 'Judge Millard said he'd have the warrant ready within the hour.' The warrant, unfortunately, had not yet arrived.

Tubig said, 'Fuck the warrant. I'm going to drive out to Open Hole's little shack and goddamnit kick in the fucking door if necessary and find out what's there. If Opal wants to sue me or the City Council wants to fire me, fine. I don't give a squat.' He geared down for a corner, and we slid sideways, tires squealing.

I said, 'I think I'd probably do the same under the circumstances.'

'Can you believe I have to work with assholes like Millard? Can you believe?'

'I read the newspapers,' I said.

'Respect. I'm supposed to show respect to a preacher who may have deliberately caused a man's cattle to be infected with anthrax. Jesus H. Christ!'

A stop sign was coming up. Looking both ways for traffic, Tubig flipped on his siren and ran it cold at high speed.

'You're a regular Nigel Mansell. They oughta put you on the Indy circuit.'

Tubig smiled grimly. 'I'm glad I brought you along for a witness, Denson. If this shit turns out for the worst, I want somebody who was there and heard and saw what happened.'

Another stop sign coming up . . .

I double-checked my shoulder harness.

Tubig slowed to make sure the way was clear, and we sailed serenely across the intersection.

'Opal's little house is just down the street here, another couple of hundred yards.'

Suddenly, coming the opposite way . . .

A red Ford pickup.

Childress's.

With two men in it.

The Ford was going so fast I didn't have a chance to see who was in it.

Without a word Bubba Tubig pulled a U-turn in the middle of the street, and set off in hot pursuit.

'Did you see who was in it?' I said.

Tubig, concentrating on the road, clenched his jaws. 'No. But it's Childress's pickup.'

Tubig's squad car was souped-up, but the Ford was packing a lot of engine. Within a minute we were out of Enterprise, heading west on Wallowa Lake Highway with the Wallowa River on our left. We passed the Wallowa River Inn on our right and kept flying, blue light flashing on our roof, siren going *Ooop-eep! Ooop-eep! Ooop-eep!*

Tubig, with the pedal to the metal, couldn't stay with the Ford, but it looked like the city's squad car had enough poop to stay within eyeshot.

Down the road, the Ford swerved, but kept going.

Then whoa.

In front of us.

A deer . . .

Tubig swerved too, and went into a slide.

He said, 'Hold on.'

'I'm holding,' I said.

We hit the side of the road with a *whack!* and sailed serenely off, turning once before *sploosh!* we landed wheels down in the Wallowa River.

As we floated downstream, sinking slowly in the frigid water, Tubig said, 'Aw, shit. You okay, Denson?'

'I'm fine.' I began unbuckling myself.

'Water's colder than a well-digger's ass,' he said.

'A perfect four-point landing. One complete spin, and we're both still alive. I'd give it a nine-point-nine.'

'Wonderful,' he said. The car had sunk to the bottom.

We rolled the windows down and struggled out into the water. We waded ashore and climbed up the bank. We were soaking wet but otherwise no worse for our misadventure.

A minute later, we saw a Chevrolet sedan coming from the direction of

Enterprise, and Tubig stepped into the middle of the highway with his hand up, gesturing for the car to stop.

The driver, a middle-aged woman, pulled to a stop, looking concerned at the sight of the dripping chief of police.

'What happened?' she said.

Tubig gestured to the top of the squad car sticking up from the water. 'Oh, my friend and I had a little accident. Do you suppose we could use your car for a few minutes, Alice?'

Alice seemed uncertain. 'If it's important, I suppose . . . '

'It's extremely important, I assure you, Alice.'

'Of course, Chief.' Alice slid over to the passenger's side. I got into the back seat and buckled up.

As he spun gravel heading west, Tubig said, 'Alice McCready, this is John Denson. Alice owns the local beauty salon, Denson.'

I said, 'Pleased to meet you, Alice.'

Alice said, 'What is this all about, Chief?'

Tubig said, 'It's a long, long story, Alice. But I guarantee you're doing a

420

public service. The city doesn't give out medals, but we'll owe you one.'

'No problem. As long as the two of you aren't hurt,' she said.

'Sorry about getting your seats all wet,' he said.

'They'll dry out,' Alice said.

We found Roy Childress's Ford pickup about five miles down the road. It was abandoned, and there was blood on the front seat.

There was no sign of the passengers.

★　★　★

We drove back past the squad car, still resting in the Wallowa River, and continued on to Enterprise. We'd no sooner got ourselves the city's second squad car and let Alice McCready go about her business than Tubig received a call from a state cop named Rob Harper.

Harper said three teenage boys fishing a stretch of the Wallowa had fished the bodies of two adult males out of the water. They had been murdered. 'Somebody cut their throats,' he said.

Tubig sighed. 'ID?'

'They still had their wallets, complete with credit cards and money. They're both from Enterprise. Figured you might know them, Bubba.'

'I bet I know who one of them is. Shoot,' Tubig said.

'The first is one William Coney, forty-six, of an Enterprise address.'

'Bill Coney owns the Texaco station here in Enterprise. And the second?'

'One Roy Childress, age twenty-six.'

'I win my bet. Does Childress have red marks or splotches on his skin?'

'He's got something on his hands and arms, yes. Boils of some kind.'

Tubig bit his lip. 'Did you handle the body?'

'I turned him over.'

'Listen carefully, Rob. Drive the boys to the hospital immediately, and tell the people there you've all had physical contact with a corpse that's infected with anthrax.'

'What?'

'You can send somebody else back for the corpses who can handle them properly. Do it now, please. They've got a serum that'll stop it in its tracks, so don't worry. But you have to get it taken care of.'

'Shit!'

Tubig glanced at his watch.

I checked mine too. 'Eight minutes until showtime,' I said.

Tubig said, 'Bill Coney drives a dark blue 1992 Chevrolet Caprice, a four-door model. You'll find it parked somewhere near the tent on Ant Flat Road where the Reverend Bonnerton's holding his revival at three o'clock.'

'That's just a few minutes from now,' Harper said.

'Unfortunately. The tent's outside the Enterprise city limits, so it belongs to you and the county. Make sure Bill's Chev is locked. Tell whoever locks it to wear gloves and to post a guard to make sure nobody fucks with it or touches the door handles.'

'Will do, Bubba.'

'You take those kids to the hospital right now, Rob. You'll all be okay, but you need to see a doctor. Tell the doctor that you handled a corpse infected with anthrax. They've already got one patient down with anthrax, and they know what to do down there.'

'Got it. Tell me who you think did this, Bubba?'

'The Reverend Thaddeus Hamm Bonnerton.'

'The preacher? What?'

Tubig sighed. 'But I suspect we'll have to deal with it after the revival. Right now, you need to see a doctor.' Tubig signed off and slumped behind the wheel of the squad car.

Sitting on the passenger side, all buckled up for action, I looked at my watch again. Five minutes and counting. 'I say Bonnerton got into a fight with his kid over my snake-eyed story about Childress's raping Lil. Bonnerton was so furious he murdered him.'

'Looks that way,' Tubig said. 'He was in love with Lil, just like me and half the customers in the High Country. It was one thing for his bastard kid to murder her to protect them all from the anthrax investigation, but raping her while he was at it was another thing entirely.'

'That hit directly at Bonnerton's nuts. She was his turf, not his kid's.'

Tubig said, 'Last I heard, preachers've got bothersome nuts same as everybody else.'

'Bonnerton didn't want to drive Childress's pickup back to town because we were on their tail. So he flagged a car down, murdered the driver for safety's sake, and threw both bodies into the river.'

'And drove back to town in Bill Coney's Chev,' Tubig said. 'I think that's it.'

'What do we do now?' I said.

Tubig clenched his jaw. 'If I call Judge Millard again, he'll only tell us to come back with more evidence. He's, uh, not driven to rash action, is one way to put it.'

'He's afraid of a backlash if he screws up.'

'Millard doesn't mind if I stick my dick in the grinder, but he's determined to stay well clear of pissed-off Christians. You have to ask yourself what happens if we stop the revival at the last second and it turns out we can't find any physical evidence linking Bonnerton to the murders. See how that works?'

26

Bubba Tubig was the cop; he was in charge, not me. I did what I was told and did it in triple time. When he wheeled up to Food City and told me to go inside and buy rubber gloves, I did just that, running through the store, looking wild-eyed for the section where they sold household cleansers.

I grabbed two pairs of green rubber gloves and headed for the exit, throwing a twenty-dollar bill at the woman at the checkout.

'I'll get the change later,' I shouted, pointing at the squad car in front of the door where Tubig waited, blue lights flashing.

When I slid onto the seat, Tubig handed me a small revolver. I opened my mouth to protest, but he shut it quickly.

'Save the bullshit for later. You're now Deputy Denson, and we've got work to do.'

'Deputy Denson?'

'That's right. I've called the state police. They should be ten or fifteen minutes behind us.'

I shut my mouth and held on as Tubig burned rubber and shot through Enterprise at a dangerous speed, headed for Ant Flat Road. With his free hand he retrieved a badge from the glove compartment and gave it to me. 'Pin this on your pathetic chest.'

'Oh, come on,' I said.

'Do it.' He braked for a corner.

I did.

He accelerated out of the turn. He said, 'Okay now, Deputy Denson, I want you to listen up. We've got Plan A and Plan B. If we get there before the show starts, we go immediately into Plan A; we go backstage and haul the son of a bitch out of there pronto, screw warrants and legal consequences. The first duty of a cop is to protect the public.'

'Right. And plan B?'

'If we get there after the show has started, we let him do his thing. He has to physically touch people to infect anybody.

When he gets ready to give his high fives for Jesus, we rush the stage like Clint Eastwood and John Wayne and cut him off at the pass.'

'More like Bud Abbott and Lou Costello.'

Tubig gave me a look. 'We do our best to stop innocent people from being infected.'

'What happens if Plan B doesn't work?'

'Well, then, we add Plan C. By that time the state cops will be there to help, and we'll set up roadblocks at the entrance so we can sort out people who had contact with Bonnerton. If he has anthrax, we have to contain it. We cannot and will not allow it to be spread to the rest of the community.'

The tent was coming up. Tubig wheeled the squad car to a halt. We flung the doors open and began sprinting for the tent. In this emergency, I thought Tubig managed truly surprising speed.

We were too late for Plan A. The show had already begun. The only thing we could do was watch from the rear of the main aisle, armed to the teeth and with rubber gloves poking out of our hip pockets.

The Reverend Thaddeus Hamm Bonnerton's opening was more dramatic than the warm-up revival that I had seen; this time, he strode onto the stage in his banker's getup with the smoke from Monty Hook's cattle rolling up in the background, which I agreed was a more effective tactic.

If he was distraught at having murdered his son and an innocent motorist less than an hour earlier, he didn't show it. The faithful had gathered in the big top and were tuned in across America, so the show would go on no matter what. In that respect, he was nothing if not a gallant trouper. He launched immediately into his Old Testament stories about Moses and Aaron and the awful pharaoh and the soot and boils on the cattle and the rest of it.

Television monitors in the corners of the big top let the faithful see what the show looked like to the folks back home. The cameras moved in for a tight shot of Bonnerton's sincere, sweaty face, working his marks on behalf of all the beautiful and indispensable flora and fauna that graced the bosom of Christ.

If Bonnerton had worked up to the soot and boils and the indifferent pharaoh in his warm-up revival, what in heaven's name was he saving for the big show? Surely the best tactic was to save the most dramatic stuff for the last.

He paused to mop his sweaty forehead with his handkerchief, a tic he had apparently lifted from Jimmy Swaggart in his prime. If Bonnerton did not sweat as much as the earnest Swaggart, it was a close call.

The cameras suddenly closed in . . .

As Bonnerton stripped off his jacket.

The faithful, spurred to action by obvious shills among them, began to clap rhythmically.

Bonnerton loosened his tie.

The applause, encouraged by the shills, grew in volume, *clap-clap-clap*. This was punctuated by spontaneous shouting and encouragement.

He rolled up the sleeves of his shirt.

A man shouted, 'Go for it, Reverend!'

Another hollered, 'Do it!'

The faithful rose, cheering.

Bonnerton threw his arms skyward in triumph.

Those faithful in the front rows stared transfixed at the figure before them. Those farther back, including Bubba Tubig and me, watched the close-up action on the monitors. In an NFL football stadium, the best action was ordinarily repeated on monitors; the same was apparently true of a modern religious revival.

What we saw on the monitors was ugly. Bonnerton's forearms were covered with evil, pussy red splotches. If the festering pustules itched or caused Bonnerton other misery, he didn't show it.

'We were right. Sweet Jesus help us,' Tubig said.

The Reverend Thaddeus Hamm Bonnerton had obviously been infected with anthrax.

That was why he had been wearing a long-sleeved shirt on a warm July day. The backs of his hands — all that Bubba Tubig and I had seen — still looked as if they had been spared the vile infection. We'd been right. He'd been wearing makeup on the backs of his hands.

Bubba Tubig, looking pale, bit his lip.

We could see the disease clearly on the monitors, but we knew what we were looking for. The people in the tent did not. And for all they knew, he had a severe heat rash or sunburn. Also, could the faithful in front see it clearly? I didn't think so. And even if they knew what it might be, did that make a difference in their frame of mind? After all, the Protestant fundamentalist Jim Jones had conned over nine hundred people into committing mass suicide in Guyana. Nutball followers of the Baghwan Sri Rajneesh put poison in a salad bar in The Dalles, Oregon. And David Koresh had caused scores of people to go up in smoke in a horseshit Armageddon in Waco, Texas.

With the Reverend Thaddeus Hamm Bonnerton's skilled encouragement, these people had plunged themselves into the great emotional release of an evangelical revival, an intellectual warp and womb. In this state of mind they were convinced that no matter what trials lay before them, the ecstacies of faith would surely prevail and their dear, sweet Jesus would intervene on their behalf.

It was foolish to believe that Bubba Tubig and I could somehow prevent the pending tragedy, but we had to try.

★   ★   ★

I know there are those Christian faithful who hold that the Prince of Darkness is never far from us, and through the centuries unfortunate souls, in the name of Christendom, have been whipped and flogged and torn apart upon the rack and burned at the stake in an attempt to exorcise the devil from them.

Saint Joan of Arc was lashed to the stake and torched to rid her of Satan's breath. Arthur Miller's justly famous play *The Crucible* was based upon charges of possession and witchcraft in Salem, Massachusetts, and millions of readers had been gripped by William Peter Blatty's best-selling novel *The Exorcist* and the inspired performance by Linda Blair in the movie.

I do not believe in demonic possession, but if ever I had set eyes upon Lucifer, I know it was at that moment.

Tubig and I watched, dry-mouthed, as Bonnerton strode to and fro on the stage, apparently oblivious to the hideous, telltale splotches on his arms. For me, he was no longer Thad Bonnerton, vengeful nerd, or the Reverend Thaddeus Hamm Bonnerton, greedy fuck and unimaginable hypocrite. Ham Bone stood revealed in all his consummate snake-eyed evil: he was Lucifer incarnate. Satan. The Prince of Darkness.

No faithful Christian should recoil at the notion that the evil Prince should choose to appear in the guise of a man of the cloth. History was filled with examples for believers, for which there was no other explanation.

Could we forget the wretched excesses of the fifteenth-century Spanish priest Tomás de Torquemada? Torquemada, the Grand Inquisitor, adviser and confessor to Queen Isabella I and King Ferdinand

V, of Jewish descent himself, forced nearly two hundred thousand thousand Jews to leave Spain because they refused to be baptized. Torquemada authorized and supervised the torture of thousands of Spaniards accused of heresy, witchcraft, or blasphemy. The screams of those who were mercilessly skinned alive or stretched until their spines popped yet echoed through the pages of history.

Did we not have the sublime example of Rodrigo Borgia, Pope Alexander VI? Pope Alexander was a splendid host of Vatican parties. This included the famous Ballet of Chestnuts: after Alexander and his guests had copulated until they were limp, they enjoyed the spectacle of fifty naked courtesans retrieving chestnuts from the floor with their nether parts. Another charming get-together featured the frenzied mating of horses in a Vatican courtyard. But this, it was said, was not as good as the grand party in which Alexander's son Cesare entertained the Pope and his guests by shooting criminals who had been driven like animals into the same courtyard.

And did we not have the example of Reverend Jim Jones?

Were these figures possessed of Satan? For many Christians, it was obvious they were, and who was I to argue with matters of faith? But I thought it more likely they were simply anomalous if predictable assholes who appeared from time to time on Willie Prettybird's Great Hoop — evil jacks-in-the-box, popping up to spread their manure in the common camp. There was nothing to be done but whack them upside the head, each in turn, and brace ourselves for the next.

* * *

On the stage, the Reverend Thaddeus Hamm Bonnerton was getting down to the nitty-gritty. 'By now you've all heard the news that the anthrax that afflicted Mr. Monty Hook's cattle here in Wallowa County, Oregon, came from infected salt.' He paused, sweat returning to his face, then continued: 'Yes, salt. Well, now, salt is no stranger to the Bible, is it? The Bible tells us that salt is used as a seasoning and as an antiseptic and as an offering. And in the Old Testament, we are told how Abimelech destroyed the city of the people of Shechem and covered it with salt.' He waited, then shouted, 'Covered it with salt!'

The camera followed Bonnerton as he strode back and forth with furrowed brows in what, presumably, was furious, important thinking. Then he stopped and leaned forward, and whispered hoarsely, 'Would you all please turn your Bibles to the Old Testament, to Leviticus two, three.' He waited, then quoted from the passage. 'The Lord said, Season all your grain *And every oblation of thy meat offering shalt thou season with salt; neither shalt thou suffer the salt of the Covenant of thy God to be lacking from thy meat offering; with all thine offerings thou shalt offer salt.*'

Mopping more sweat from his face, he looked up, as though to address the heavens. 'Add salt to your offerings. Yes! In Ezekiel forty-three: twenty-four, the Lord admonished the priests to offer a male goat without defect for a sin offering. The priests were to sprinkle salt on the goats and burn them as an offering to the Lord. Let me repeat that.'

I wondered if Monty Hook, no doubt watching this on television in the High Country Saloon, had been moved to throw a beer bottle through the tube.

Bonnerton said, 'Let me repeat that, and I want you to listen carefully: to atone for their sins, priests were to offer a perfect male goat. Well, if the priests had had an opportunity, over the generations, to breed domestic cattle, as we have today, the Lord would have asked for a perfect Angus, wouldn't He? Or a perfect Hereford? I want you to think about that for a moment. The Lord said the sinners were to sprinkle salt on these perfect animals and burn them as an offering to the Lord.'

Bonnerton stared at his feet, then to the heavens again. 'Now we can begin to understand what has happened here in Wallowa County. In fact, the Lord has chosen this place, at this time, to remind us, hasn't he? We have the salt, poisoned by anthrax, we are told. We have the animals. The animals have been burned. They have been burned to atone for our sins. They have been set ablaze, and we watched the dreadful smoke on our television sets. Is this not necessary sacrifice?'

He paused, apparently waiting for the necessary-sacrifice business to sink in. 'Is this not a reminder for us to care for the Lord's gift, for the earth that nourishes us, or we shall all perish? Little imagination is required. We have all the facts we need: the salt, the sacrificial animals, the burning.'

Bonnerton grimaced dramatically. 'You know, I was wondering why the Lord summoned me here from my travels. The Lord is speaking through me, I am aware of that, and I assure you I do not take the responsibility lightly. He has given me the mission of reminding Christians of the birthright which is this wonderful land of ours. He has chosen me to travel about the land and remind Christians to clean up after themselves. And as my guide, He has given me the Bible, His word. Now, why, I ask, should He choose this place of all spots? It's a good question, is it not?'

Bonnerton again strode in silence so that his questions might be considered. Never mind that he really didn't expect an answer. The rhetorical questions followed by silent striding were part of the drama.

Now he held both arms out, punctuating every word with a gesture. 'The answer to those questions, of course, is in the Bible, as we knew they would be. The Lord does not purposefully leave us in ignorance, my brothers and sisters. He causes us to ask questions that need to be asked. He has already given us the answers, but we are sometimes too blind or arrogant or even, let me say it, too stupid to recognize them. Will you please turn to Numbers eighteen, nineteen, and we will hear the rest of the reason why cattle in Wallowa County have been poisoned by salt.'

He waited for the people under the big top, and presumably people watching on television, to open their Bibles to the correct spot.

Bonnerton said, 'Now, I know the

complete reason why the cattle were poisoned. And I will be honest with you; until this morning I did not know for sure. I studied the Bible, and I prayed. I knew the death of cattle was a sacrifice to the Lord, but the full meaning of it escaped me. Brothers and sisters, those cattle were poisoned by salt as an offering to atone for our sins against the bosom of Christ. In Numbers eighteen, nineteen, it says that whatever offerings the Israelites present to the Lord, they and their sons and daughters will receive as their regular share. *'As their regular share.'* As they give, so shall they receive. The Lord says it is an everlasting covenant of salt before the Lord for the Israelites and your offspring.'

I was not a biblical scholar, but it seemed to me that Bonnerton did not mention that Christ called his disciples the salt of the earth. Never mind, Lucifer was no doubt a selective, if not indifferent, biblical scholar. For him rhetoric and delivery were just about everything.

Bonnerton shouted, 'Let us now, in the name of our sweet Lord, Jesus Christ, demonstrate to the world our undying determination to respect and care for the mother earth that nurtures us all, no matter what the cost!'

I said, 'Almost time for Plan B, don't you think?'

Tubig glanced back, looking for the state cops, who had not yet arrived. 'We're getting close,' he said. He yanked his gloves from his hip pocket and started putting them on, and I did the same.

Bonnerton shot his arms dramatically in the presumed direction of the heavens as his shills ignited the amen chorus to action.

Tubig said, 'Now, Denson!'

Tubig and I sprinted down the center aisle, firing our pistols into the ceiling. Tubig shouted, 'You're under arrest, Reverend Bonnerton! Halt! Stay where you are. Do not leave the stage! I say again, you are under arrest!'

From above us, the Prince of Darkness glared imperiously down, face a sheen of sweat. On his arms and hands, bloody pustules dripped. Why didn't these people react? Why didn't anybody recoil with

443

horror? There was clearly something wrong with this earnest specter.

I suppose the shrinks would say this was a form of mass hysteria; Bonnerton had disempowered the faithful by the passionate intensity of his will, and so they saw nothing.

'You're under arrest!' Tubig shouted again as the faithful, infuriated by these outrageous pistol-bearing pagans, began spilling into the aisle, blocking our way. Tubig, refusing to yield, shouted, 'The Reverend Bonnerton is infected with anthrax! He is highly contagious. Please stand clear of him. Stand clear!'

But nobody heard, or certainly nobody listened. And Bonnerton, flashing a triumphant, conquering grin, plunged into the crowd, his arms — encrusted with vile, pussy boils and oozing pustules — spread high above his head in victory.

Tubig and I were surrounded and consumed by the maddened crowd, a form of emotional wildfire. We were barbarians, soldiers of evil in their midst. We kept firing our pistols, partly to jar people to their senses and partly to defend ourselves lest we be torn limb from limb, but ours was a pathetic, useless attempt to stop the madness.

There was a commotion behind us. The state police had arrived at the back of the tent like a troop of cavalry in a John Ford western. Tubig and I, back to back, mouths dry and sphincters tight, began our retreat to the safety of the uniformed officers. We would have to make do with Tubig's Plan C.

Ignoring the ruckus and confusion of cops and enraged revivalists, the arrogant Prince of Darkness did his demonic thing among the assembled believers, spreading the horror of anthrax with every comforting hug and congratulatory handshake.

★ ★ ★

Closing in on midnight — with the awful business of the Reverend Thaddeus Hamm Bonnerton's ill-fated revival behind us and Bonnerton in the hospital under police guard — we all went out to dinner at the Pheasant Café: Monty Hook, Bobcat Bill Kemiah, Willie Prettybird, Bubba Tubig,

Leiat Podebski, Lenora Kemiah, and me.

Although Hook had suffered terrible losses in the last five days, he was not broken, and he was in a celebratory mood. Lil Peters's murderer had been found, and the man who had poisoned his cattle had been brought to justice. Justice denied eats and grinds at the victims, and although justice delivered can never erase the past, there is something about it that soothes the soul. Hook had suffered setbacks in the past, and he would recover from this one as well.

While we waited for our T-bones, rib eyes, and prime ribs — compliments of Hook — Lenora Kemiah gripped my hand.

Leiat Podebski said, 'Judging from that scene on television, Edgar Allen Poe should be with us tonight.'

Leiat was right; the sight of the diseased Bonnerton plunging into the crowd of faithful was a scene straight out of Poe.

'Hubris,' I said.

Leiat said, 'Thad Bonnerton had it when he was seventeen years old. He refused to read Shirley Jackson's short story, 'The Lottery,' because he said it was evil. In fact, his church had announced that it was evil, and probably nobody there had actually read it. He has that arrogance now. It is the hubris also of Prince Prospero, who was convinced he was above catching the disease.'

This was a reference to the doomed host of Poe's macabre party — held in the face of advancing plague — in *The Masque of the Red Death*.

I said, 'It was Bonnerton's undoing.'

'I think so,' she said.

'It was Bonnerton's hoop, come full circle,' Willie said.

Grinning, Bobcat Bill said, 'You know, Chief, we all thought you and Denson were had dads when you went charging down that aisle with your pistols blazing. A couple of nutballs. If the state cops hadn't shown up like the cavalry, you'd have been in real trouble.'

Tubig laughed. 'Aw hell, where's your faith, man? Deputy Denson and I had matters firmly in hand.'

Willie said, 'Sure you did. Knowing Denson like I do, I bet he had to change his shorts after it was all over. It made

447

exciting television, though, I have to admit.'

We all had a good laugh at that. I remembered Bonnerton's casual squashing of the old lady's tomatoes in Food City the day Willie and I had arrived from Portland. Because she was indifferent to Bonnerton's much-coveted celebrity, he had destroyed her tomatoes. A sick kind of satisfaction, in my opinion.

Lenora leaned against me and murmured, 'Forevermore.'

I said, 'Did you read Poe in the reservation school?'

She nodded yes.

Leiat Podebski grinned. She approved.

Of the lady named Lenore, Poe's black raven, perched above the chamber door, had quoted, 'Nevermore.'

'Forevermore,' Lenora whispered again.

Forevermore. It was sweet to think so. From such sentiments new hoops were often launched.

THE END